MIXING BUSINESS WITH PLEASURE

"Tell me you aren't going to sift through that pile tonight?" Noel's jutted jaw indicated the packages Eden had deposited. When she didn't answer right off, he added, "Why not wait until tomorrow when I can help you? We'll establish a schedule where I work on my furniture in the morning, and come over to help you in the afternoon. That way we'll blow through this stuff in record time."

It sounded like a good idea. Alone it would be a tedious process. "Deal," Eden said, extending her hand.

Noel took the hand she proffered, but instead of shaking, squeezed it. "Told you we'd make a good team." He pulled her toward him and lowered his voice. "Personally and professionally."

He left little doubt as to what he meant. When he released her hand and linked an arm around her waist, she tilted her head to receive his kiss. She wasn't disappointed. The kiss started off slow then built in intensity. His tongue probed her mouth, demanding that she give him all: body, soul, and something more. Despite the fact it was all happening too fast, with a man she didn't trust, Eden held nothing back.

BOOK YOUR PLACE ON OUR WEBSITE AND MAKE THE ARABESQUE ROMANCE CONNECTION!

We've created a customized website just for our very special Arabesque readers, where you can get the inside scoop on everything that's going on with Arabesque romance novels.

When you come online, you'll have the exciting opportunity to:

- View covers of upcoming books
- Read sample chapters
- Learn about our future publishing schedule (listed by publication month *and author*)
- Find out when your favorite authors will be visiting a city near you
- Search for and order backlist books from our online catalog
- Check out author bios and background information
- Send e-mail to your favorite authors
- Meet the Kensington staff online
- Join us in weekly chats with authors, readers and other guests
- Get writing guidelines
- AND MUCH MORE!

**Visit our website at
http://www.arabesquebooks.com**

EDEN'S DREAM

Marcia King-Gamble

Pinnacle Books
Kensington Publishing Corp.
http://www.arabesquebooks.com

Acknowledgments

I could not have finished this book without the help of some very special people. My thanks and deep appreciation to the members of my Broward County critique group: three talented writers, Linda, Debbie and Marilyn. To Chuck, who was forced to fend for himself during those long hours of writing, and who still helped me with action scenes when a man's perspective was required. Thank you all. I couldn't have done this without you.

PINNACLE BOOKS are published by

Kensington Publishing Corp.
850 Third Avenue
New York, NY 10022

Pinnacle, the P logo and Arabesque, the Arabesque logo are Reg. U.S. Pat. & TM Off.

First Printing: November, 1998
10 9 8 7 6 5 4 3 2 1

Printed in the United States of America

One

Eden Sommers' hands caressed smooth flesh. Slim pickings, but better than nothing.

She sighed, then mumbled, "Hardly the cream of the crop, but certainly edible." With that, she dropped a half dozen sickly looking yellow tomatoes into her shopping cart and headed up the aisle.

At such a weird hour, who would have thought there'd be so many people out. She consulted her list and tried desperately to ignore the tightness in her chest, the sound of her own hollow breathing. Hands clasped around the handles of her cart, she squeezed her eyes closed, willing the dizziness to go away.

The first time she'd had these peculiar feelings was the day she'd learned of Rod's death. That time she'd thought it was a heart attack. But six months and several sessions in therapy had given them a name. Panic attacks.

Eden felt herself losing touch with reality. The roaring in her ears was almost deafening, and though the temperature in the grocery store was close to arctic, she felt a fine layer of sweat beading her upper lip.

Determined not to give into the weird sensations, Eden plowed down the aisle.

Reality slowly came into focus when a man yelled, "Hey, watch out." The sound of metal against metal reached her. She'd rammed into the man's shopping cart.

A warm hand covered Eden's. She looked up into eyes that could only be described as the bedroom variety. Emerald green with long lashes. Cats'-eyes her mother would call them. Eden preferred to term them greener than green and built for seduction. Eden's free hand reached to cover her mouth. She'd been confronted by a ghost. One word escaped. "Rod?"

"I beg your pardon."

The voice wasn't Rod's. Still staring, Eden realized she'd made a mistake. The man's complexion was a shade darker, his hair a touch curlier. And Rod didn't have laugh lines around the edges of his eyes.

A gravelly voice penetrated, worried and a little anxious. "Are you all right? Can I get you something? Water?"

Eden shook her head, willing the vision to disappear. At a third glance, he didn't look much like Rod, though he sure reminded her of him. She was sure she'd seen him someplace before. Where? She would have remembered the height, the regal bearing. She would have remembered those eyes.

To cover her confusion, Eden focused on his shopping cart. A half dozen cans of tuna fish, a package of low-fat muffins, a carton of skim milk, magazines—the kind that told you how to take care of your body—toilet paper, and stacks and stacks of TV dinners.

She jolted back to the present when a hand waved inches from her face and a puzzled voice said, "Are you on some kind of medication?"

Refusing to meet his gaze, Eden flushed. It would be a logical conclusion to come to, given her sweaty appearance and disoriented state. She couldn't blame him for thinking she was on drugs. The average person didn't shop after midnight, nor did they ram a shopping cart full of contradictions into someone else. Already she'd acquired lettuce, a half dozen tomatoes, potato chips, dip, yogurt, milk—the fattening kind—assorted candy bars, canned goods—the kind that needed heating up—cat food, and cigarettes.

"I think I know you from somewhere," Eden began hesitantly.

A flicker of something sparked those emerald eyes. An actual smile surfaced. Flashes of white against ebony. "That's what they all say."

Oh, God. He thought she was trying to pick him up.

He came to her rescue before she could crawl into her cart and wheel herself away. A hand, the nails meticulously trimmed squares, clasped hers. "Noel Robinson. I'm your next-door neighbor."

So that's where she'd seen him, next door, though not very often. He, too, seemed to come out only at night. Eden gulped a huge mouthful of air. "Eden Sommers. Nice to meet you, Noel. Sorry about running into your cart. I'm usually not this scatterbrained."

He smiled another gut-wrenching smile, one that went directly to her heart. "No harm done. Are you all settled in?"

"Getting there."

"Gardening must be taking priority then." His smile took the sting from his words. Maybe he was spying on her, or how else would he know that she was up early, before even the first jogger, hacking away at the soil. Gardening had replaced therapy, though she wasn't about to tell him that.

Instead she said, "The weather's been so beautiful. When the sun's out in Seattle, it's hard to stay indoors."

Noel Robinson nodded. Laugh lines around those magnificent orbs fanned out. For the first time she noticed the cleft in his chin and squelched the urge to trace it with her fingers. "I know what you mean. This is truly God's country."

"Are you a native?"

Noel's smile disappeared. His eyes no longer sparkled. A beat later, he grudgingly said, "No. I guess I'm somewhat of a gypsy. I'm from here, there, and everywhere."

Translation: mind your own business. She'd been firmly put in place. Eden sensed he'd shut down. What she couldn't fathom was why. Had she been too forward? She pressed on, for some unknown reason prolonging the conversation. "Gee, I'd pegged you for a Northeasterner."

Noel remained silent as if waiting for her to go on. His eyes held hers for a second too long. Eden felt the heat in her cheeks, a flutter at the base of her gut. Something about the man made the insides of her mouth go dry. Could be the regal bearing, those long, long legs, stuffed into tight Levi's. The wide chest, muscles rippling under plaid. Or was it simply that he reminded her of Rod? For something to do, she bent over, ripped open the package of potato chips and offered him one.

With another flash of white, he declined the chip she proffered. "Sorry, never touch the stuff. It's a cholesterol nightmare. See you around." He moved off, leaving her staring at his tight, denim-clad behind.

Eden expelled the breath she'd been holding and made an attempt to get it together. What had possessed her? She hadn't been interested in men since Rod, her fiancé, had been pronounced missing, then dead. She'd felt that a large piece of her heart died with him. Her faith in men too. Still, she'd focused her energy on finding out everything she could about that plane crash. Now here she was acting like a love-starved teenager, drooling over some stranger.

Eden wheeled her cart down the aisle, following Noel

Robinson's rolling gait. Even from the back he made an attractive figure. To still the thoughts that rotating butt set loose, she buried her head in the grocery list. When she looked up he'd disappeared.

Panic attack totally under control, Eden paid for the groceries then loaded her bags into her gray Cherokee. Minutes later, she pulled up in front of the tiny house on Mercer Island inherited from Grandma Nell. As a child she remembered it being little more than a cottage, but as she grew older, and real estate prices shot sky-high, it had undergone a metamorphosis. Necessary renovations had been completed and the cottage slowly evolved into a dream home. Today, every imaginable modern amenity filled the redwood interior.

Designed to bring the outdoors in, floor-to-ceiling windows ran the length of the house, and perfectly positioned skylights gave a feeling of spacious airiness. The moon's rays illuminated the open-floor plan, making the house appear larger than its fifteen-hundred-square feet. Both kitchen and bath had been updated, and outside, a secluded terrace held a redwood hot tub and comfortable chairs.

Whistling softly, Eden balanced a couple of recycled paper sacks on one hip and turned the key in the lock. She headed for the L-shaped kitchen and unloaded her bags. No sooner had she set down her packages than a hairy bundle of fur shot across her ankles meowing pitifully. Eden bent over and scooped up the cat. "Hungry, Kahlua?"

The feline, knowing she could easily con her mistress, played it to the hilt. The meow became a heart-stopping wail, forcing her to set the cat down on the counter and pop open a can of sardines. Eden swigged an open bottle of spring water as the animal gobbled up her food.

Outside, a car pulled up. Eden heard the door slam

and the sound of muffled voices. Immediately she guessed it to be the same men who visited next door, usually once a week, and at a late hour. Still, curiosity drove her onto the poorly lit terrace to watch two men climb Noel Robinson's winding front steps.

Like detectives in B movies, both were huddled in dark trench coats. One wore a fedora low on his brow, the other a cap. They darted furtive looks around before stealthily climbing the stairs.

Noel's front door cracked an inch, then wider. His head poked out. He threw the door open. Not for the first time, Eden wondered what type of business would be conducted at such an ungodly hour. It seemed odd for men to arrive late at night, spend an hour or less, then leave. She had a sneaking suspicion they weren't there to play chess.

Eden glanced at her watch. The illuminated face put the time at a little after one. Her gaze returned to the house as she rested her rear end against the covered Jacuzzi, sipped her water, and waited for the scene to unfurl. Noel Robinson's silhouette was still outlined in the doorway. She could swear he looked directly at her.

Inside, the phone rang. Eden cocked an ear in the direction of the sound. Torn, she turned back to the neighboring house in time to see Noel's mocking salute. Too embarrassed to acknowledge his greeting, she raced for the phone.

Just as the answering machine clicked on, she grabbed the receiver and shouted over the message, "Hello."

"Eden?"

"Hi, Mom." At the sound of her mother's voice, the tension she'd carried up to that moment dissipated.

"Eden, honey, I couldn't sleep. Tell me how are things going?"

Eden twirled a lock of straightened hair around one

finger. Things had been going fine until she'd run into Noel Robinson. Only recently she'd been the grieving fiancée, the woman whose heart had been ripped out. Only sheer willpower had pulled her out of the dark funk she'd languished in and made her stop taking the pills the doctor prescribed. She'd finally come to terms with losing Rod, come to terms with his betrayal, and put her guilt to rest. Though the hurt was still there, at least it was manageable, and the panic attacks now came less frequently.

"Eden?" Her mother sounded worried. "Are you all right? I mean you're in Seattle all alone. No family. No means of support."

"I said I was fine, Mom," Eden snapped, instantly regretting her outburst. Though her mother tended to be a worrywart, she'd remained the one constant in Eden's life, standing by her through the entire gruesome ordeal: Rod's memorial service, her periodic lapses of sanity when grief clouded her judgment, her indefinite leave of absence. Reaching for the pack of cigarettes she'd tossed on the counter earlier, Eden struck a match.

"You're still seeing Rod's ghost?" Cassie Sommers probed.

Eden inhaled and counted to ten. She'd live to regret the day she'd admitted to having seen Rod's ghost. It had been right after he'd died when his face loomed at her from every corner. Eden's therapist had attributed the hallucinations to shock, the mind's savvy way of coping with trauma.

Mrs. Sommers' voice pulled her daughter back to the present. "Eden, please tell me you're not?"

Eden took a long drag on the smoldering cigarette, giving in to the habit she'd worked so hard to kick five years ago. She exhaled her words. "No, Mom, I'm not."

"Are you sure you don't want me to fly out? I worry

so about you being alone. Isn't Mama Nell's house sort of isolated? If memory serves me well that house became her refuge after Pappy died. It became her place to hide from the world. Now you're doing the same . . ."

"Please Mom, don't . . ." Eden softened her tone. "Mom, you know I appreciate your offer, but I am thirty years old and I like being alone. It helps me focus." What Eden didn't add was that she now had time to investigate Rod's murder.

Her mother's frustrated sigh came through loud and clear. A gregarious woman like Cassie Sommers would hardly understand why anyone would enjoy being alone. "Okay, don't take my head off, but if you change your mind . . ."

"Have you heard from Bill, Helga, or the kids lately?" Eden asked, changing the subject. Her brother, Bill, had chosen an Air Force career. He'd been stationed in Germany for the past decade or so, married a local girl, and started a family. Eden adored her little niece and nephew.

Fifteen minutes and three cigarettes later, Eden hung up, pleading exhaustion. Needing air, she practically ran back to the terrace.

The black sedan remained in Noel's driveway. A dim light came from the interior of his house. Again, Eden wondered what the men did at such weird hours. Though Noel Robinson didn't exactly fit the drug-lord stereotype, a likely conclusion would be drug dealing. Still, in the brief moment she'd met him, he'd seemed much too clean-cut for that. She'd picked up on a definite sense of integrity. But Noel's lifestyle required money; a beautiful house with a full water view didn't come cheap. Judging by square footage alone, utilities had to cost a fortune. Eden had never once seen him go off to work, nor did he leave the house except to go jogging. How he earned his money was definitely open to speculation.

A stream of light illuminated the doorway of Noel's house. The men were leaving. Eden lit another cigarette and watched them take the stairs two at a time. Bits and pieces of their conversation drifted her way.

"You need to be more careful. . . ."

"I think they might be on to you. . . ."

Eden didn't hear one word of Noel's reply but she'd heard enough to confirm her suspicions. She felt strangely let down, disappointed actually. There'd been something about Noel Robinson she'd liked. He was the kind of man you wanted to get to know better.

The next morning, Eden woke early, threw on bright red sweats and an oversized shirt, and raced outside, coffee mug in hand.

A cool spring breeze greeted her as she ran down the winding stairway leading to rolling green lawns. Overgrown wildflowers created borders separating the neighbors' property. To her right lived Noel Robinson, and to her left was an elderly couple, seldom seen. She galloped across carefully tended garden beds, determined to finish her herb garden today.

Trowel in hand, Eden dug into the moist soil. She breathed in the clean spring air, cleared her mind, and concentrated only on the row of holes she mechanically dug. After a while, she leaned back, fumbled for her cooled coffee, tossed it down, then lit a cigarette. Then flexing cramped limbs, she gingerly eased upright and began a series of stretches and bends, compensating for the exercise classes she sorely missed.

The pounding of sneakers against concrete broke her concentration. Eden moved to the side of the house, hoping to get a better view of the jogger. She sucked in her breath, as high-topped Nike sneakers; skimpy white gym shorts; and a huffing, puffing, Noel Robinson headed her way. Noel's bare chest slowly filled her vision. His curly hair stretched flat against his head and beads of perspiration trickled down his face, settling in the thick patch of hair around his solar plexus. In a futile attempt to stop the sweat, he dabbed at his chest with the towel draped around his neck. Eden dragged on her cigarette as if dependent on it for life-giving air. She exhaled a huge smoke ring and waited for her stomach to settle. Noel Robinson was one fine man even at this early hour.

As if sensing he was being watched, Noel back-pedaled. "Morning," he grunted. His voice sounded even more gravelly than the night before.

"Morning," Eden answered, openly gaping.

Jogging in place, he pointed at her dangling cigarette. "Nasty habit."

For some reason his comment irked her. Who was he to judge her when he didn't have a clue what she'd been through? She wondered how he'd cope if he'd lost his lover only six weeks before their planned wedding.

"That's a matter of opinion, and I didn't ask for yours," Eden snapped. "Just be thankful it's not a cigar."

"Touché." Noel seemed amused that he'd pushed her buttons. Using the towel, he dabbed at his forehead then patted his taut middle. "What are you doing up at this hour, anyway?"

Painfully conscious of each trickling rivulet of sweat on the man facing her, Eden waved the trowel at him. "Gardening."

"You do that a lot."

Eden changed the topic. "Aren't you going to be late

for work?" She already knew the answer. She'd never ever seen him dressed for business.

Noel's affability disappeared. He muttered something she didn't hear, then said, "See you around," and jogged off.

Pushing Noel Robinson firmly out of mind, Eden returned to the abandoned garden. She placed mint, thyme, basil, and sage into the holes she'd dug, then smoothed dirt around the roots. As she sat back to admire her handiwork, a movement on the second floor of Noel's house captured her attention. Outlined in the window was a very pleasing view of the man himself.

A burgundy towel rode Noel's hips and he used a striped towel to dry his hair. Fascinated, Eden gaped as sepia muscle rippled with each circular motion. She followed the fluidity of each movement, the insides of her mouth dry, her breathing labored. The towel inched downward and Noel made no attempt to hike it up. Eden's eyes popped as the perfectly proportioned butt of Noel Robinson came into view. Heat flooded her cheeks and her stomach did an ominous flip-flop. A feeling she refused to acknowledge surfaced. On the double, she jogged back to her house.

She scooted through the back door at the same time Kahlua chose to escape. The cat bounded over her insteps and Eden raced after her. Kahlua, a citified cat with no claws, would not fare well outdoors.

"Kahlua!" Eden cried. "Kahlua!"

She bounded across rolling green lawns, the Maine Coon Cat several yards ahead of her. Exasperated, she watched Kahlua leap over the hedge and disappear into Noel's front yard.

"Darn cat. I'll get you for this." Eden muttered, already knowing that no amount of threats would bring Kahlua back.

On the other side of the bushes, the cat's meows

taunted her. Taking a deep breath, Eden straddled the hedge.

Just her luck Kahlua would choose to hide on Noel Robinson's property.

treated inside to wait. Tail at full mas...
bounded up the stairs on three...
her like a magnet. Eden...
going on, now...
shro...

Noel Robinson peeked through the _____ d just
lowered. A shapely red derriere filled his v___ incredible, but he'd just been thinking about his nosy neighbor, and presto she'd appeared.

Through a stroke of good fortune he'd managed to
rent the house next door, bringing him one step closer
to his goal of getting to know Eden Sommers. Truth be
known he'd enjoyed spying on her these last few weeks.
She was an incredibly good-looking woman, with skin
the color of honey, and legs guaranteed to stop you in
your tracks. Huge brown eyes with long, long lashes
dominated a heart-shaped face that needed no cosmetics to render it stunning. High cheekbones, nostrils that
flared slightly, and a full pair of lips completed the package. *Easy, boy. You've been suckered by a pretty face before.*

Noel smiled as the object of Eden's search sauntered
across his front lawn directly behind her. Thinking
quickly, he raced down the stairs, entered the kitchen,
poured a bowl of milk, and returned to the terrace.
"Psssst," he ventured, "Psssst." Keeping his voice low,
he added, "Here, kitty," and set the bowl down.

He watched Eden crouch on her knees, head partially
submerged in the bush. Noel saw the corpulent cat sniff
the air suspiciously. He picked up the bowl, jiggled it
in the direction of the cat, set it back down and re-

..st, the animal
..legs, the milk drawing
..., obviously unaware of what was
..lay chest down, her head and shoulders
..ded in greenery.

While the cat quickly lapped up the milk, Noel crept
up behind her. Sensing his presence, the kitty threw a
suspicious look over one shoulder but showed no signs
of leaving. Noel bent over, scooped the animal into his
arms, and stroked the feline's fur. "Did you run away
from Mama?" he crooned.

The cat purred. A tiny pink tongue flicked. She made
short work of the milk on her whiskers.

Noel decided it was time to have fun with his reclusive
next-door neighbor.

"Can I help you find something?" he shouted.

Eden's body jerked. As she backed out of the hedge,
Noel suppressed the desire to laugh. Every hair on his
neighbor's head pointed in a different direction. A collection of leaves and buds nested as if waiting to bear
fruit; her sweatshirt was covered with burrs and sticks.
Even from this distance he sensed her embarrassment.

Feeling contrite, Noel held out the mischievous cat.
"This creature wouldn't be what you're missing?"

"Kahlua, you bad girl," Eden said, waggling a finger
at her pet. Seeing Noel's amused expression, she
smoothed her hair.

The cat's lids remained tightly closed. She ignored
Eden, purred loudly and settled more comfortably in
Noel's arms.

Impulsively, Noel gestured to Eden with his free
hand. "Come on up?"

Eden hesitated. She threw him a look that he could
only interpret as fear. Why was she so skittish, he wondered?

"Hey, I don't bite. And I'm not known to kick animals

or old people. See." He held the cat out. "Even your cat knows I'm trustworthy."

Eden started up the stairs slowly. Noel watched her climb those stairs as if heading for the gallows. Did he have body odor or something? True he'd been short with her last evening, but he didn't think he'd been rude. Besides, in his business, you had to be cautious. Telling a virtual stranger his life history could be suicide.

Eden stood on the landing now. Smiling, Noel hurried to greet her. He held out her cat. "Hi, Kahlua's mother."

For a beat too long, his gaze met startled brown eyes. Noel felt the electricity in the air. His fingers brushed the back of Eden's hand as he placed the cat in her arms. At last he broke the stare and flicked a spot of imaginary lint off his jeans. Romance was definitely not part of the plan, especially with a fickle airline type. He'd been there, done that. Never again. Even so, he heard himself say, "How about a cup of coffee? I just made a fresh pot of decaffeinated."

A tinge of pink colored the honey of Eden's skin. Noel held his breath. "Come on, you can spare a moment," he cajoled.

"Thanks, that's very kind of you."

He crossed the wraparound deck and headed indoors. Eden followed with Kahlua. Inside smelled like cedar. Vaulted wooden ceilings, awesome glass walls, and masses of greenery hung from the rafters. Noel led her to a chocolate-leather sectional positioned in front of a fieldstone fireplace. An oak parsons table held an assortment of books and magazines and rested on a plush goat-skin rug. Eden took the seat he indicated, sinking into the comfortable upholstery.

"Set Kahlua down right there." Noel ordered, patting

the spot next to her. "Now, what do you take in your coffee?"

"Black's fine," Eden said, settling Kahlua.

When Noel turned away, the cat followed him.

Eden's tense voice caused Noel to look back. "There's something wrong with Kahlua's back leg."

Sure enough, the cat hobbled.

"What's wrong, kitty?" Noel asked, bending over to examine Kahlua's limb and gently probing the animal's paw. Eden held her breath, thinking of the vet bill. Noel ran a thumb over Kahlua's footpad. He touched the sleeve of her sweatshirt and said, "I think I found the problem. See." He beckoned her closer. "Somewhere in her roamings, your cat picked up a thorn. If you hold her, I'll get some tweezers." He deposited the cat on Eden's lap, then disappeared.

Eden expelled the breath she'd been holding. Her leave of absence status meant living on a strict budget and already her meager savings had dwindled. Thankfully, there'd be no vet bill. After twisting her hair into a single braid, she reached for a magazine on the coffee table and flipped through it, quickly turning each page. A puzzled frown surfaced as she stopped to read a few paragraphs of an article entitled, "What went wrong with Pelican's Flight 757?" Rod's plane.

Why would Noel Robinson have a copy of *Flight International* magazine? she wondered. What interest would he have in planes or crashes? Eden glanced at the cover of the periodical, her eyes focusing on the tiny white label. Noel subscribed to *Flight International*? No, not exactly. The label was addressed to a Noah Robbins of Germantown, Maryland. Though the names were awfully similar, Noel could have borrowed the magazine, she supposed.

He returned with tweezers and two steaming mugs of coffee. He set the cups down and took the seat next to her. For some inexplicable reason his closeness made her uneasy. Could it be the heat from his skin radiating a warmth that the coffee couldn't rival; the clean, fresh fragrance of the soap he'd used to shower. God, she needed her space. Noel Robinson threatened the walls she'd built around her heart, made her want to examine her feelings for Rod. She needed a cigarette badly.

Kahlua made purring sounds and fickle creature that she was, climbed onto Noel's lap. He maneuvered the animal's body until he could see the hurt paw and with tweezers held between slender brown fingers, plucked out the thorn.

"See, that didn't hurt," he said, nuzzling the animal's head with his chin. Setting Kahlua back on Eden's lap, he pointed to the untouched cup. "Your coffee's getting cold."

With stiff fingers, Eden brought the mug to her lips. She took a deep swallow, savoring the rich liquid. "Hmm, heaven. I'd hazard a guess it's not the grocery-store variety."

Noel didn't answer right off. He lifted his cup, sipped and confirmed, "Actually, it's a special blend I picked up—" then abruptly changed the topic. "So tell me what made you move from—"

"New York City."

"I should have guessed."

Eden bristled. "What's that supposed to mean?"

Noel patted her forearm. Where he touched tingled. In a protective gesture, Eden tightened her arms around Kahlua.

Sounding contrite, he said. "Hey, I didn't mean to offend you. It's just the accent's usually a giveaway."

"Oh." The word whooshed out. Now she planned on giving him as good as he'd given her. "All right Mr. Smart Alec, it's your turn. Where are you from? And don't give me this business about here, there, and everywhere."

The seconds ticked by. At first she thought he wasn't going to answer, then finally, "You were close last evening." He scooped Kahlua off her lap and abruptly stood. "Now that you've seen the living room, want to see the rest of the house?"

She was too busy processing information to answer right off. Close? Did that mean Maryland? Eventually she focused on his question, nodding. She'd always loved houses, the more unique, the better. What seemed like a lifetime ago, she'd had aspirations of becoming an architect. Over the years she'd modified that dream, deciding that interior design might be more realistic. Now Rod's untimely death had put an end to those hopes. With no one to help her, school would hardly be an option. A hectic work schedule didn't allow for both.

"I'd love to," Eden said at last, realizing this might be her only opportunity. Most likely she'd never see the inside of Noel's house again. She didn't plan on getting tight with him.

"So what do you do?" Noel's question penetrated.

Eden shot him a quizzical look. He discouraged inquiries of a personal nature but was interested in her life? "Right now nothing," she answered.

"Oh?"

They'd entered a sterile looking kitchen. Noel made a sweeping gesture. "My kitchen. A place that hardly gets used."

Eden bit the insides of her cheek so as not to smile. She took in the pristine white tile, and remembered the stacks of TV dinners piled into his shopping cart last evening. Graciously she said, "You do make good coffee, though."

A flash of white acknowledged the compliment. The

cleft at his chin was even more pronounced. She'd seen his handsome face someplace before. Where? And she'd heard the name Noah Robbins.

Quickly, Noel guided her across wooden floors and down a long hallway. Every inch of wall space was covered by ornately framed works of art. Originals she'd guess, judging by the signatures. Recognizing the work of Lee White, America's foremost black artist, Eden stopped to admire several pieces.

Noticing Eden's interest in White's rendition of mother and child, Noel said, "You must like art."

"Only if it speaks to me."

He quirked an eyebrow. "Does that piece speak to you?"

"Very much."

They'd come to a closed door. Noel threw the door wide. "I think of this as my library." His gesture included an austere room where a burgundy-leather couch dominated. A bookcase held what easily had to be hundreds of books. Against one wall were unfinished pieces of furniture.

Spotting a handsome armoire, Eden headed over to it. "Is that your work?" She moved in closer, running a hand over the rough wood. "Nice."

Noel beamed his thanks and quickly changed the topic. "What did you do when you worked?"

Why was he so interested? Having nothing to hide, she answered him honestly. "I'm a quality assurance supervisor for Pelican Air. I'm on a leave of absence, taking stock of my life."

Noel perched on the sofa, his arms folded across his chest. "How come?"

"How come, what?"

"How come you're taking stock of your life?"

His directness surprised her, and though several months had passed, she found it difficult to put her feelings into words. Still, maybe telling her story to a virtual stranger with no preconceived notions would be therapeutic. It certainly wouldn't hurt. She chose her words carefully.

"I lost the man I loved several months ago, just weeks before we were—supposed to be married. Since then, I've taken time off to regroup, reevaluate my life so to speak."

"I'm sorry."

Eden heard compassion in his voice; he seemed to sense her pain. A muscle in his jaw worked overtime and his green eyes were hooded.

Noel's voice invaded her thoughts. "How did you lose him? Something tells me he didn't just walk out on a beautiful woman like you. He'd have to be crazy."

Eden attempted to ignore the compliment. Noel Robinson had a silver tongue, she'd have to remember that. "He didn't walk away." *But in a sense he had.* "He was killed." There, she'd said it.

Something in Noel's eyes sparked. He covered the space between them. "Killed?" He repeated, taking her hand. "Killed, as in intentionally done away with? I'm so sorry, Eden."

"I think he was murdered," Eden said quietly.

"Come." Noel had tucked her hand in his. He tugged her along. "Let's go sit on the sunporch where it's more comfortable."

The room ran the length of the house and was aptly named. Floor-to-ceiling glass walls permitted the morning sun to shine in, and at the same time gave an unobstructed view of Lake Washington. Eden sat on an elaborately carved wooden bench next to Noel. He'd replenished their coffee and both held mugs. "So tell me," he began, "how was your fiancé murdered?"

Eden mumbled her words, refusing to look at him. "Rod was killed in a plane crash."

"I'd hardly call that murder."

"I do." The words rushed out, toppling over each other. "What if that plane wasn't serviced properly? What if it had a history of mechanical problems that never quite got fixed? What if senior management knew that it should be sitting in a hangar somewhere being repaired, yet they made him take that plane out with eighty innocent people on it?" She began to cry.

"That's a pretty serious accusation." Noel said softly. One hand began a slow massage of her back and neck. His other hand tucked wisps of hair from her face. She sobbed uncontrollably now, and Noel pulled her into his arms, offering his wide chest for comfort.

Eden found a haven in his strong arms. Her face pressed against a T-shirt smelling like Tide. Underneath her cheek was pure, sinewy muscle, and with every heave, she felt those muscles ripple. "You have no idea how I hate to cry," she murmured. "What you must think of me."

Noel tilted her chin up till she looked at him. His eyes were equally misty, though no tears fell. "Know what I think?" he paused, waiting for Eden to ask, then continued. "You're a beautiful woman who just happens to be vulnerable right now. That's what I think." Impulsively he brushed her lips with his.

Oh God, she wasn't ready for this. She had to get her composure back. She hardly knew the man. Even worse, she didn't trust him. She inhaled a mouthful of air and rested her head against his chest. "Sorry. Now I've ruined your shirt."

"No, I'm the one who's sorry. I shouldn't have done that."

His apology surprised her. Drug dealer or not, he was Mr. Gallant.

Eden shifted safely away from Noel. "Thanks for the

coffee and comfort, but I've got to get going. I've taken too much of your time already."

Noel just nodded. "I'll see you home," he offered.

Panic built in Eden. The tightening in her chest heralded the arrival of another attack. She couldn't let him see her in that state. Not again. "Oh that's not necessary," she jabbered, racing from the room before Noel could protest. She almost tripped over her feet getting away from him.

"You forgot something," Noel called from the terrace.

Eden turned in time to see him hold up Kahlua. His biceps bulged under the tight-fitting T-shirt as he brought Kahlua to her.

"Okay girl," he joked, turning the cat over. "Next time it's my turn to visit."

"Wh-what," Eden stuttered, knowing there wasn't a remote possibility of that happening. Not in this lifetime anyway. He would be an unwelcome visitor at best. She couldn't risk him getting too close.

The imp inside made Noel press the issue. "I take it your mom doesn't plan on issuing an invitation, Kahlua." He scratched the cat behind the ears. "See you sometime old girl."

Eden thanked him for his help and ran.

Three

Eden sat hunched over the kitchen table, scanning a collection of newspaper clippings she'd meticulously arranged. She exhaled a perfect smoke ring and flicked her ash in the vicinity of an overflowing ashtray. Rotating her neck to ease the cramp at her nape, she picked through the pile to find the most recent article.

Ever since Rod's death she'd read voraciously, perusing every newspaper that covered the tragedy of Flight 757. What boggled the mind was that the Federal Aviation Authority and the National Transportation Safety Board could not agree on what had caused the crash. Even so, the rag sheets had labeled it pilot error. Their assumption galled her. Rod had been Pelican Air's best pilot, and though they'd had a falling out, she hated to see his reputation tarnished.

Eden forced herself to concentrate on the *New York Times* clipping in front of her. The headline, "Captain's Competency In Question," was a rude reminder that even the best succumbed to sensationalism. How dare they besmirch Rod's name, especially when he was no longer around to defend himself. The print blurred as Eden focused on the picture accompanying the caption. Rod stared back unflinchingly, the epitome of cool. His cap sat at a rakish angle, just like the first day she'd laid eyes on him. As the memories surfaced and the floodgates sprang open, Eden stubbed out her cigarette.

She cried not so much because she missed Rod, but because of guilt. When her tears threatened to ruin the print on the paper, she pushed the articles a safe distance away. Eventually her sniffles turned to full-fledged sobs, and a pounding noise finally filtered through.

"Eden?"

Eden looked up to acknowledge Noel's presence. He hovered at the open glass door, uncertain of his welcome. It had been at least a week since she'd seen him. "Wh-what do you want?"

He didn't answer immediately but crossed the room, Kahlua cradled in his arms. After setting down her cat, he crouched at Eden's side and pulled her into his arms. "Go ahead and cry. Let it all out. I won't say a word, I promise," Noel crooned.

Sniffling, Eden sought the haven of his arms once again. She leaned her head against his chest and let the tears soak his freshly laundered T-shirt. When she was finally able to speak, she croaked, "Where did you find Kahlua?"

"Asleep on my terrace. Didn't you miss her?"

She'd been so engrossed in her newspaper articles she hadn't even missed her cat. She wasn't about to tell him that.

Noel continued. "I checked on her off and on. When I realized she'd been asleep for more than two hours, I thought that was long enough, so I decided to bring her home." He stroked Eden's hair, making soothing noises.

Rather than her sobs subsiding, his touch provoked a reaction she was determined to ignore. Hiccupping her words, she said, "I—should—be thanking—you, not—sobbing—my brains out."

"Nothing to thank me for. This was the perfect excuse to visit. And a good thing too. I haven't seen Kahlua's mother in . . . what is it?" he paused. "Ten days."

So he'd been counting the days too. So had she, although she'd not made an effort to seek him out. There was something about him that still made her wary. Most likely it was those strange men paying nocturnal visits to his home.

Noel's calloused fingertips traced the edge of Eden's jaw. Kahlua's soft purr intruded on the silence.

Eventually, Noel whispered, "Look at me, Eden." He tilted her chin back until her eyes held his. "Hiding in here and perusing newspaper articles isn't going to bring your fiancé back."

She knew that, but finding Rod's murderer might help assuage her guilt. It had made her more determined than ever to find those responsible for his death. And she wasn't really hiding, just taking a little sabbatical. She'd never been a coward.

A little voice inside reminded her that her mother had voiced similar concerns. "I'm not hiding," she said in a shaky voice.

"You're not? What do you call this then?" Noel made a sweeping motion to include the newspaper articles on the table.

"Research," she justified. "My need to piece together why Flight 757 went down. If I can do that, I can finally put closure to this whole ordeal." Her voice sounded almost normal now.

"And what have you found so far?"

He seemed more than casually interested. Why should he care? Still, it would be good to talk to someone outside the travel industry. Someone to whom she could explain that Rod had not been the incompetent pilot the newspapers made him out to be. Eden handed Noel the article clutched in her hand.

"Right here, it says that Rod had been flying for ten-plus years. That he'd flown that route at least once a week." She jabbed at the words with her finger. "That he was a vocal union rep, and constantly at odds with management. Why then would a rabble-rouser take a plane with even minor mechanical problems up? Stranger than that, how could a plane just fall from the sky?"

Noel's face remained inscrutable as he scanned the article. At last he looked up. "Could he have grown too confident? Or was he playing hotshot pilot with an insatiable need to defy the odds?"

His response ignited Eden's anger. She pushed out of his arms, and stood, arms splayed. The chair went toppling. "How dare you say that!"

A look of surprise flashed across Noel's features. He scrambled upright. "Eden, I didn't mean . . ."

"Not another word!" She crossed one arm over the other and glared at him.

"Eden. Be realistic. The best of us make mistakes. When we do something over and over again, it becomes routine. Rod could have grown careless."

It wasn't something she hadn't thought of herself, but to hear someone else say it . . . well, that was too much. "Rod was the consummate perfectionist. He cared too much about his passengers to risk their lives." She turned her back on him.

"Perhaps whether he flew or not wasn't exactly in his control," Noel speculated, "But couldn't he have just said no and waited for a maintenance crew to fix the problems? His decision to leave those blocks cost lives."

"He would have said no," Eden insisted. "Rod would never have taken that plane up even if there were minor mechanical issues. I knew him that well. He wouldn't have left the jetway until the last No-Go item was repaired."

"No Go?" Noel frowned, clearly puzzled. "What does that mean?" He squinted at her.

She'd forgotten he wouldn't know the jargon. But he did seem to know a great deal more than the average person with macabre interest. Come to think of it, he'd referred to the chocks under the airplane's wheels, as blocks, not normal for a lay person. Who was this man? she wondered. Still, he was easy to talk to and had managed to worm so much out of her already. She'd told him things she'd never voiced to another soul.

Eden plucked a tissue from a box on the counter. She blew her nose, sniffed, and turned around. "No Go is airline lingo for mechanical problems needing repair before takeoff. Why are you so interested?"

Noel's voice sounded incredulous, though he ignored her question. "I thought every mechanical item had to be repaired before a flight was airborne?"

Eden shook her head. "No, not necessarily. Only those affecting the operation of the aircraft. Minor items, for example a seat that failed to stay in an upright position, isn't a No-Go item. You'd just make sure a passenger didn't sit in it."

"Hmmph."

"Hmmph, yourself," Eden snorted, her mood lightening. Impulsively she asked, "Would you like a cup of coffee?"

Noel smiled his magnificent smile, emerald eyes twinkling. "Now you're talking."

"I've got a great brew from Kenya," she jabbered, digging through the cupboard to find the box.

"Sounds delicious. Any chance it's decaf?"

"You're in luck."

She looked back to see that he'd taken the seat she'd vacated and was already absorbed in the newspaper clippings. Grabbing the coffeepot, she scooped coffee into the filter, added water, and flicked the switch to the On position.

"So what do you think?" Eden asked, leaning over Noel's shoulder. "Isn't it interesting how each newspaper seems to have a different perspective on the crash? Did you read this one?" She tapped the column with the tip of her finger.

"Umm hmm. That's the one where the reporter thinks it was a missile."

"It's not that far-fetched. Several people swore they saw a ball of fire in the sky right before the plane lost control."

Noel tossed over his shoulder, "And if I remember, one of them was flying high on heroin. I'd hardly call him a reliable witness."

"What about the others?"

Noel turned, his face now inches from hers, so close she could smell the mint on his breath, see herself reflected in his pupils. "Wasn't one of them recently released from a looney bin? I'd be more inclined to go with the cockpit's failure to adequately monitor flight instruments, than any of this other stuff."

He flashed that dazzling smile presumably to let her know he was teasing, and though angry with him, his smile totally unnerved her. She took a step back, placing safe distance between them. "So how do you know so much about the Pelican crash?" she asked from her new safe position.

Noel's smile faltered, though he made a quick recovery. "I read a lot. Smells like that coffee might be ready."

And so it was.

She poured them both cups and took the seat across from him, determined not to let him off the hook. "But seriously. How come you're so well-informed?"

He blinked once, twice, then carefully put on his

poker face. "No more well-informed than the next guy. The Pelican Air disaster has made every newspaper. It's been front-page news for weeks."

Somehow she didn't believe that was all there was to it. He was hiding something, she was sure of it. She quirked an eyebrow. "So it's only morbid interest? Sheer curiosity on your part?"

The glint in his eyes told her she was treading on sensitive territory. Noel seemed to scramble for words. At last he said, "Actually it's a little bit more than curiosity, or a penchant for gossip, that has me interested. I lost my best friend on that flight."

"Oh God, I'm sorry." The words tumbled over each other. She reached for his hand across the table. "I feel terrible prodding you, asking why you were interested. I should have backed off. I sensed you didn't want to talk about it."

Noel's hand curled around her fingertips. Their gazes locked and held. As ridiculous as it might seem, she knew with certainty that their connection was both mental and physical. But even that thought did nothing to assuage her doubts about him, her suspicions that he wasn't telling the whole truth.

Eden opted for safer ground. "How long have you lived on Mercer Island?"

Noel took a sip of coffee and set his mug down. "Actually I'm new to the area. I only moved here a couple of weeks before you did."

She was dying to find out why he'd chosen Mercer Island and how he'd managed to acquire such a terrific house. Instead she asked, "Where from?"

Noel's hold on her hand tightened. Eden's body flooded with warmth. Covertly, she studied his features. He had cheekbones sculptured in pure granite, a pair of lips that most women would die for; the bottom one pouting slightly, and beautiful, beautiful hands. Artist's hands, fingernails squared to perfection. What would it be like to have those hands explore her body? she wondered. *Stop it!* A little voice inside screamed. *You've lost your mind. You just met this man.*

Noel's response pulled her back to the present. "My, you're certainly full of questions." He released her hand, pushed back his chair, and stood. "Some time we'll have to share life stories, but not today. I've got work to do."

"Work?" Eden blurted, her hormones in overdrive. "I didn't think you worked."

"I create pieces." She must have looked puzzled, because he contributed, "I'm a furniture designer actually, and if I don't finish the piece I'm commissioned to do, I'll be an unemployed one. Thanks for the coffee." He headed for the door, hesitated for a moment, then retraced his steps. "Hey, would you consider jogging with me tomorrow?"

When she didn't answer right away, he looked pointedly at the overflowing ashtray, adding, "That's if you're up to it."

It had been a long time since she'd pushed her body to its limit. Truth be known, she missed the exhilaration of a good sweat. And he had issued a dare. "What time did you have in mind?"

Noel's eyebrows flew skyward. He seemed startled that she'd actually agreed. "Is six too early? It's pretty cool then and the roads are usually deserted."

Eden nodded her agreement. "Six it is then." She waited until he'd left before lighting up a cigarette. The whole time he'd been there she hadn't felt the urge to smoke.

The rumbling noise of a failing engine penetrated Eden's subconscious. She watched helplessly as the plane plunged out of control. The staccato sound grew in intensity as the jet exploded, spewing metallic parts and huge balls of fire. Eden's eyes popped open. She groped her way out from under the covers, her heart beating wildly. God, her mouth tasted gritty and her head felt as if a wild war dance had been performed on her skull. Wide awake now, when the noise repeated itself, she recognized it for what it was, someone pounding on her back door.

Eden gazed at the digital clock on the night table. Oh God, she'd overslept. Already she was ten minutes late for her jogging appointment with Noel. It had to be him banging on the door.

"I'm coming. Give me a minute," she shouted over the racket, scrambling to gather clothes.

"Better make it soon," Noel shouted back. "That's if you want to go jogging before the sun's up."

Eden stumbled toward the bathroom. She splashed cold water on her face, quickly brushed her teeth, ran a comb through her hair, swept it into a knot on the top of her head, and slipped on T-shirt and boxers. She raced back to the bedroom, fumbled through drawers to find socks, and shoved her feet into sneakers.

Noel's nose was pressed against the sliding glass door when Eden entered the kitchen. He backed off quickly when she released the safety latch and slid the door open.

"Well, good morning," he greeted, in a voice decibels too loud. "By chance I wouldn't have woken you?" He tapped the face of his watch pointedly. "It's fifteen past six."

Eden blushed. "Sorry," she mumbled, focusing on his athletic legs and crisp white shorts hugging muscular thighs. Even at this outrageous hour, he looked the picture of cool. His togetherness irked her. Refusing to look him in the eye, she hissed, "All right. You made your point. The alarm didn't go off. Why didn't you just leave without me?"

Noel's voice softened. "I wouldn't do that. We had a date and you're not that late anyway. Shall we?"

Eden ignored the arm he offered. Date? Was that what this was supposed to be? She'd never have agreed to a date. Hoping he wouldn't notice her inflamed cheeks she hurriedly said, "Ready if you are."

Together they jogged down a winding road bordered by honeysuckle and overgrown shrubbery. Red and yellow poppies peeked from the foliage. A soft breeze cooled the heat in her cheeks, and she took small puffing breaths of the crisp morning air. When they rounded the bend, the briny smell of the lake filled Eden's nostrils. As a child she'd adored the salty smell. As an adult she loved it for the memories it evoked.

Noel's voice invaded her thoughts. "So how's the investigation coming? Were you able to fit any more pieces of the puzzle together?"

Eden shook her head. In an attempt to keep up with him, she concentrated on placing one foot in front of the other, before answering. "Not really. But I'm planning on calling a coworker today. Lori Goldmuntz's husband is a supervisor on the ramp and he's got access to maintenance logs. If my hunch proves right, I'll be a lot closer to clearing Rod's name."

"How do you figure that?"

She debated not telling him, then decided it wouldn't matter. He didn't know the people she worked with. "You see, each plane has an identifying number on its tail. Industry people refer to it as the tail number. It's a registration number, really. I'm going to ask Lori to fax me the maintenance logs for aircraft number N3332F. That's the tail number of the plane Rod was flying. Guaranteed, Lori will get that information to me today."

Noel shot her a quizzical look. "And you plan on doing what with this information?"

She was starting to tire, but Eden flashed a smile of undisguised superiority his way. Her chest was on fire and they'd only gone a quarter of a mile, but she wasn't about to tell him that. She would keep up with him if it killed her. "I'm going to count—the number of times that plane's been in the hangar for repair," she panted, "see—what types of mechanical problems—the aircraft's had in the past."

Noel's breath came easily, nothing like hers. He was in much better shape, she conceded. And he didn't smoke. His coolness really did irritate her.

"What if the plane does have a history?" he challenged.

Eden's rib cage hurt. She had developed a stitch in her side. "I'll let you know—later. Till then—I'm pleading—the fifth."

A couple in matching bright red windbreakers jogged past them. Noel acknowledged their salute. Once the twosome was out of sight, he stopped and jogged in place. "You okay? Or should we turn back?" he asked.

Eden's head bobbed back and forth. She couldn't form the words to answer. Her chest felt as if a cannon had exploded in it. "I've—got—ta sit—down," she rasped.

Noel grabbed her arm before she could follow through on her words. "No, you don't. Take deep breaths. Keep your legs moving. You've got to cool down."

Her brain had a hard time following his instructions. She looked longingly at the rolling terrain on either side, wishing he would let go so that she could sink onto the springy grass, lie down, and die. But she followed his advice anyway, closed her eyes, took deep breaths, and willed away the pain. Even so, she was conscious of Noel's hands under her armpits, keeping her upright. Gulping for air, she leaned into him.

"Eden? Eden?" Noel's voice penetrated. "Open your eyes and look at me. Keep those legs moving now, girl. Slowly. You can do it. Yes, that's better. Good girl."

Opening her eyes, she found Noel's concerned green ones scrutinizing her. His hands caressed her hot cheeks, the thumbs massaging her jawline. "Feeling better?" he whispered.

Mesmerized by the connection, she nodded, her breathlessness this time having nothing to do with her inability to answer him.

"Baby, I shouldn't have pushed you so hard. I should have been more thoughtful."

Baby? Where did that come from?

Noel's hands on the nape of her neck forced her head back. Their gazes held. There was that crazy feeling of déjà vu all over again. Eden forgot that they were on the side of the road, in full view of the neighborhood. She wrapped her arms around his waist and pulled him closer. When his mouth covered hers, she parted her lips and accepted his tongue. As the kiss deepened, time and place ceased to exist. The sound of pounding feet broke the lip-lock. Heart racing, Eden stepped out of his embrace and put a respectable distance between them.

"May I have some water?" she asked, hoping that such a mundane question would bring with it normalcy.

For a fleeting moment, Noel's warm fingers stroked her cheek. He reached for the bottle at his hip and turned it over. "Of course. Don't gulp though, take tiny sips."

The pounding came closer. A female jogger, a striped towel draped around her neck, whizzed by. She threw them a curious look and waved.

Noel's white smile caressed Eden's face. "Ready to head back?" He held out his hand.

"Yup. Now that I've got my breath back." She took his hand as if it were the most natural thing in the world.

Making irrelevant small talk, they walked back. In front of her house, Noel asked, "Eden, would you mind if I helped with your investigation?"

His question threw her. Why, after weeks of maintaining his distance, did he suddenly feel the need to get close? Obviously something more lay behind the question. Today, he'd been so sweet, so utterly charming, she'd let her guard down. She'd almost forgotten she didn't trust him. "Why would you want to?" she quizzed.

Noel took seconds to answer, then said, "Ty MacMillan was the brother I never had. I still haven't gotten over his death. He was my age, thirty-five. Like you, I guess I seek closure."

"You know, this may not be the best partnership," Eden warned. "We'd actually be working at cross purposes. I'm bound and determined to prove Rod's innocence, and you're bound and determined to crucify him."

Noel held her wrists while her treacherous heart thudded in her chest. She couldn't have said no to him if she wanted to.

"No, Eden," Noel answered, "Crucifying's too strong a word. I just want to uncover the truth."

Four

Noel cradled the phone between ear and shoulder. "What time are you planning on getting here?" he asked.

While awaiting a response, he stabbed his fork into a coagulating mess of chicken française and made a face. Despite following the microwave instructions to the letter, dinner had turned out disastrously.

"Eleven's good," Noel confirmed, chewing slowly. "Just make sure to bring a full wallet. You guys owe me big time."

He took another stab at the chicken, then gave up. Microwave tray in one hand, cordless phone in the other, he pushed back from the table. Dinner was disposed of in a nearby trash can.

Noel turned his attention back to the phone. "Now what kinda question is that? Didn't I tell you I'd find some way to meet her, and I did. Even better, I may have convinced her to let me help with her investigation." He chuckled, acknowledging the barb on the other end. "I'm a fast worker! You should talk. Now, don't even go there. All right, enough already," he said, "Gotta go, see you later." Abruptly, he hung up the phone.

Noel's stomach gurgled as he searched the cupboards for something to replace the dinner he'd dumped.

He'd never quite mastered the art of cooking, never needed to. Where he'd come from, sustenance could be purchased on any city block. If he didn't feel like eating in a restaurant, takeout was a mere phone call away. Amazing how drastically life had changed for Noel Robinson.

Eventually, he found tuna fish and a can opener. He plopped a couple of slices of whole wheat in the toaster and swore when someone knocked on his front door. *Visitors? The boys weren't expected until eleven.*

A second knock came before he'd figured out how best to handle his unwanted company. A female voice threatened, "If you know what's good for you, Noel Robinson, you'll open up or I'll feed your dessert to Kahlua."

Noel chuckled at the thought of Eden on the other side, bringing him dessert. Must mean he hadn't scared her off. Taking the can of tuna with him, he hurried to answer.

As he flung the door wide, his words tumbled over each other. "Eden, how nice to see you. Come on in."

The object of his most recent fantasies held out a covered dish and smiled sweetly. "Brought you something," she chirped. "It's not exactly cherries jubilee, since all I had was bread, and a gallon of milk about to spoil. But bread pudding it is."

Noel snapped his mouth closed. His gaze remained riveted on Eden's face. He'd never seen her with makeup before and words failed him. Eden Sommers wasn't just incredibly good-looking, as he'd originally thought, she was one stunning woman. Those cognac eyes with lashes lengthened by mascara, issued a definite challenge. She'd curled her hair, and a layered mane swirled loosely about her heart-shaped face. Just the right touch of sienna had been added to cheeks and lips, and her trademark sweats had been exchanged for a denim micro-mini. Noel's gaze shifted to take in a pair of dynamite legs that even Tina Turner would envy.

"Earth to Noel." Eden called, snapping her fingers under his nose.

"Uh . . . yes . . . where are my manners." He caught himself and stepped aside to let her in.

A tangy smell of something utterly bewitching preceded her. Noel followed the slight swish of her hips, praying that by the time they faced each other he would have his emotions under control.

Seemingly oblivious to his interest, Eden tossed over her shoulder, "Where shall I set this down?"

"Here, I'll take it." He relieved her of the dish, his fingers accidentally brushing hers. Her touch triggered a chain reaction, starting at the tips of his fingers and traveling downward to settle in his groin. The hunger he felt had nothing to do with his empty stomach. "Want to join me for a tuna sandwich?" he growled.

Eden scrunched her nose. "No thanks, I hate tuna. Is that all you're having for dinner?"

"It was, until this." Noel lifted the covered dish and stuck a finger inside. He scooped out a generous portion of bread pudding and plopped it into his mouth. "Do you like pizza?"

Eden thought about the peanut butter sandwich she'd devoured before coming over. She was still ravenous.

"Love it. What did you have in mind?"

"There's a little Italian place a couple of blocks away, makes great pizza, almost as good as . . . New York. Why don't you grab a seat. I'll put this away, change clothes, and we're off."

Eden sat on the leather sofa, wondering why she was even there. All her life she'd never acted impulsively. But today she'd done a lot of soul-searching, and concluded, that although Noel had said some pretty harsh things about Rod, he'd only voiced what the majority of the world thought: Flight 757's crash had resulted from pilot error.

Her initial anger over with, she looked at things far more rationally now. What did it really matter that Noel blamed Rod? He had a right to his beliefs and so did she. She could put aside their differences to gain his help if more would be accomplished with two people investigating. Besides, time and facts would prove her right, and time was something she didn't have much of.

Eden grabbed a magazine from the coffee table. She glanced at the cover, registering that it was another copy of *Flight International*. This time the address label had been removed. Why? she wondered as she flipped through pages of articles circled in bright red magic marker. She'd just begun to read gruesome speculation about the Trans World Airways tragedy when the phone rang.

On the third jingle, Eden yelled, "Should I get that?"

Either Noel didn't hear, or didn't care to answer, so Eden went off in search of the phone. As she approached the kitchen, the answering machine clicked on. A man's southern twang queried, "Hey, Rob . . . Robinson, where are you, big guy? You forgot to tell me how much stuff you need me to bring."

Eden froze. Stuff? Were her suspicions confirmed? Was Noel really a drug dealer masquerading as a furniture designer?

She reached for the receiver as a hand clamped her shoulder, turning her around. Eden pressed her hand to a pounding heart. "You startled me, Noel . . ." she said, her words trailing off. In his collarless denim shirt and skintight jeans Noel Robinson gave new meaning to the word *fine*.

"Didn't intend to. I'll get it." Noel pushed the button on the remote and mumbled into the phone, "Robinson, here." He listened for what seemed an eternity, then began to laugh. Eden heard him say. "Thanks, but I'm going out to eat." Then before ringing off, "None of your business, boy. Didn't your mama teach you good manners?"

Eden was certain she'd been the topic. The moment he hung up she asked, "What was that about?"

Noel seemed amused. Amused and preoccupied. "Just a friend checking up on me. He wanted to know if I needed something from the store."

Eden knew he was lying. That prompted a sarcastic comment. "A very caring friend. Wish there were more of those around."

Noel's hand at the small of her back moved her along. He bent over to whisper, "You're too young to be this cynical."

Eden shot him a withering look.

The short drive to the restaurant was completed in silence.

"We're here." Noel announced, pulling into a crowded parking lot. "Think we can manage to have a good time?" His raised eyebrows indicated he had doubts. After executing a series of maneuvers, he successfully squeezed his Camry into the only vacant spot. Before Eden could set one foot on the ground, he was at the passenger door, holding it open.

Eden hastily straightened her skirt feeling Noel's gaze sear her legs. She ignored the desire in his eyes, took the arm he offered, and walked with him toward an A-frame building.

"This looks interesting," she said, dismissing the jittery sensations his closeness evoked. Even so, Noel's masculine scent invaded her senses. Dope peddler or not, the man had definite sex appeal.

"It is. The restaurant's been in the Di Murio family for years, or so I've been told." Noel answered her unspoken question. "Not in this building though. The original burned to the ground and they've since rebuilt."

"Gee, for someone who's not been around here long, you sure know a lot."

Noel chuckled. "I make it my business to ask a lot of questions."

"Amen."

Inside, the entire population of Mercer Island gathered, or so it seemed. Eden noted their attire. The lumberjack look was definitely in. Levi's and plaid shirts were about as fashionable as it got, and she felt positively overdressed.

Again, reading her thoughts, Noel confirmed, "You look terrific, and we fit right in. We are wearing denim."

A perky, dark-haired beauty approached, jiggling size thirty-eight bosoms and plastic menus simultaneously. "Welcome to Di Murio's," she greeted. "The wait's about twenty minutes. May I have your name?"

Noel gave his name, collected a beeper, and led Eden to an outdoor bar.

When they were seated, he asked, "What would you like to drink?"

Eden inhaled the crisp spring air, tempted to answer, "Single-malt Scotch," knowing that would shake him up. Instead, she said, "We're having pizza, so Chianti should go nicely." Already she'd gotten the feeling that he viewed her as both entrée and dessert. That made her self-conscious.

"Chianti it is then." Noel signaled to the waiter.

After the waiter had taken their order and departed, Noel teased, "No cigarettes tonight. Not feeling well?"

Now that he'd mentioned it, she wanted a cigarette

badly. And there were smokers at the bar, so it wasn't exactly frowned upon. Eden reached for her purse.

"Please don't." She caught the look in his eyes and hastily dropped her hand.

"You don't like smoke?" she challenged.

"I despise the smell and hate the habit. You would, too, if you watched your father die of lung cancer."

"Oh, Noel." Eden reached for his hand across the table.

"Excuse me." The waiter returned carrying the Chianti and two glasses on a tray. To give the server space, Noel released her hand. He steered the conversation to less emotional ground. "Were you able to get in touch with your friend?"

Somehow she'd known he'd come back to that. Eden sipped her wine, debating how much to tell him. She finally said, "Yup. Lori's already faxed me over a bunch of stuff."

There was a distinct glimmer in Noel's eyes when he responded. "Have you given any thought to my proposal, then? I still think we'd make a helluva team."

Eden opened her mouth to tell him she'd given it a lot of thought, and team wasn't exactly what came to mind, but the scraping of his chair against polished wooden floors stilled her words. "The beeper just went off," he said. "I think we've been summoned. I'll have the Chianti sent to our table."

He approached Eden's side of the table and offered his hand. Folding her hand into his seemed the most natural thing in the world.

The same over-endowed hostess escorted them to a table covered in red-plaid. Flickering candles dripped wax over empty Mateus bottles, creating patterns against a cream-colored wall. Noel held out a chair and waited for Eden to sit.

Once their hostess was out of sight, Noel said, "I'll

be happy to top off your wine." He wore an amused look.

Eden decided it wouldn't hurt to have another glass. It might even relax her. "Sure."

Conversation ebbed and flowed. Over pizza and the last of the Chianti, Eden asked, "Noel, did you always want to be a furniture designer?"

Noel's hand covered his mouth, suppressing a cough. Quickly he dabbed the corners of his mouth with a napkin.

"You okay?" Eden eased his water glass closer.

"I'm fine. Crust went down the wrong way." Noel lifted the glass and gulped the water. "Now to answer your question, I did want to be a commercial pilot at one point. Sadly that didn't work out."

"Why didn't it?" *Why did he fascinate her?* Eden traced the patterns on the tablecloth while awaiting his answer.

"Because my folks didn't have money. When my father became ill we existed on welfare checks and what little money I made from my paper route. After high school, I was lucky to apprentice with a furniture designer. I did the night-school thing and graduated college by the skin of my teeth. By then, the dream had died."

"I'm sorry." She seemed to say that a lot around him.

"Don't be. I'm happy doing what I do."

Whatever that is, Eden thought.

Across the table, he reached for her hand. His eyes burned a slow path across her face, leaving a warm tingle in its wake. His next question grounded her. "So tell me, when can we go through the maintenance sheets your friend sent you?"

"We?"

"You are going to let me in on your investigation?" It was a direct challenge.

Eden decided to keep him guessing, though she'd

already decided she needed him. "Any particular reason I should?"

Noel finished off the last of the Chianti before extending the bait. "Because two heads are better than one. And because I just might have some information you need."

She remembered the copies of *Flight International* magazine and the articles circled in red. She was sure Noel knew a whole lot more about Flight 757 than he was letting on. Come to think of it, his interest in the crash seemed almost an obsession. The thought crossed her mind that there might be more to the story than just losing his best friend. Still, with his information and her Pelican Air connections, they might make a formidable team.

"Okay."

"Okay?" Noel's delight was evident. In the candlelight, the cleft in his chin was even more pronounced. He flashed his Colgate smile and squeezed her hand. "Let's shake on a successful partnership and an interesting friendship."

He surprised her by turning her hand over and slowly bringing the palm to his lips. The kiss was so fleeting she barely registered that it happened, and just as quickly, he released her hand and signaled for the check. "Let's skip dessert. We'll have your bread pudding tomorrow." He stood and made a point of glancing at his watch. "I'm running late for an appointment and would really appreciate you accepting a rain check."

Unable to believe the tactless manner in which he'd ended the evening, Eden's eyebrows arched. She responded in saccharine tones. "You're conducting business at this late hour?" Rising, she gathered her purse, and focused her attention on the crisp twenties he'd dropped on the table, anything to avoid looking at him. "Do you need change?"

"No, tip's included." Noel draped an arm around her shoulder and pecked her cheek. Sounding contrite, he added, "Eden, I'd give anything to spend the rest of the evening with you, but I can't. I'm already committed, and you must admit our dinner was rather impromptu. I'll make it up to you another time."

What colossal gall he had. What she really wanted to say was "Not in this lifetime, baby." Instead she forced herself to smile, the combination of Chianti and his masculine scent making her senses whirl. Boy she would do anything for a cigarette. Noel Robinson was smooth. Too smooth.

She kept quiet throughout the short drive. At last, Noel pulled the Camry up to the curb in front of her house. "Home, sweet home," he announced, coming around to the passenger side to open the door and offer his hand. Eden took the hand he offered, but shrugged free once she was out of the car.

Not disconcerted in the least, Noel followed her up the poorly lit pathway. On the landing of her front steps he turned her around to face him.

"Thanks for agreeing to have dinner," he said, touching the tip of her nose like a little boy. "I really enjoy your company."

"The feeling is mutual." She laughed nervously, forgetting that only moments ago she'd been peeved.

"Eden," Noel said, cupping her face between his palms, "You do know there's strong chemistry between us."

Before she could say another word, he pulled her close until their bodies touched. His lips trailed the sensitive place behind her ear, the edges of her jaw, and dipped to claim her mouth. His probing tongue found a welcoming home inside.

Eden closed her eyes and let the kiss sweep her away. This man whom she distrusted, but liked more than she should, evoked wild feelings. Feelings that were too new to explore. Something about him drew her, making her forget she'd come to associate love with betrayal, loss and a great deal of pain. And she couldn't even begin to explain why, from the moment she'd set eyes on Noel, she'd felt an unexplainable connection. A feeling she'd come home.

The hum of a car's engine broke the mood. Eden stepped out of Noel's arms. His reluctant, "I've got to go, baby. Will I see you tomorrow?" was lost as a car door slammed. She forced herself to look at the black Mercury Sable parked in front of his house and not at his tight buns as he walked away. The automobile was the same one she'd seen before, carrying the same men. She watched Noel return the men's bear hugs, then lead them up the winding front steps. He threw her one last look before disappearing inside.

Eden unlocked her door and stepped in. She stumbled as a ball of fur streaked past, forcing her to clutch the doorjamb for support. "Kahlua," she cried, already knowing it was useless. Her cat would be back when she was good and ready.

Even more frustrated, Eden slammed the door hard. The miserable beast could stay out all night if that's what she wanted; maybe she'd even move in with Noel. Let's see how he'd enjoy chasing her or changing litter. Eden flung her pocketbook on the antique dining table, then rummaged through it. She needed a cigarette now. To hell with Noel Robinson and his gruesome stories of lung cancer; he'd already done enough damage, penetrating the tight cocoon she'd woven around her heart, making her feel again. To top that off, she had a runaway cat to contend with. She could strangle the animal. Strangle Noel Robinson, too, for that matter. Where were those damn cigarettes?

At last, Eden located an almost full pack of Merits. She jammed a butt into her mouth, struck a match, and inhaled deeply. And though the cigarette tasted metallic, she repeated the action. Nicotine would eventually steady her nerves, she hoped. That failing, she might even resort to Scotch. Anything to keep her hands busy and not listen to the little voice in her head, and its insane whispers. She couldn't be attracted to Noel Robinson. Not her. She wouldn't let that happen.

What was she thinking? She'd allowed lust to get in the way of reason. Holding the lit cigarette, Eden slid the back door open. She flopped down on the patio chair and swung her feet onto the covered Jacuzzi. Dragging on the cigarette, she exhaled loudly. It tasted awful. She ground the butt under her heel. Chianti and cigarettes obviously didn't go down well.

Noel's blinds were partially closed, still, she could see the silhouettes of three men. Oh, to be a fly on the wall and hear the discussion around that table. What could be a plausible explanation for these late-night visits? Poker? She didn't think so. Could Noel be an undercover cop or was he just an unsavory character? Eden's imagination ran the gamut. What if he was a participant in the Witness Protection Program? It was an outlandish thought that had possibilities. That would certainly explain his secretiveness, his house, his supposed occupation.

She grasped at straws, looking for reasonable explanations to justify his existence. It made her even more determined to find out what he was hiding.

Five

"Eden," Noel called, his nose pressed against the sliding glass door.

She appeared not to hear him and sat hunched over the kitchen table, absorbed in a mess of papers.

"Eden!" Noel shouted, rapping once, twice, then waiting for her to look up.

At last she glanced over, quickly removed red-rimmed glasses and, spectacles in hand, headed in his direction.

The moment the door slid open, Kahlua raced in. The cat rubbed herself against Eden's ankles, meowing loudly. Noel proffered the bouquet of yellow tulips hidden behind his back and spoke quickly, "I've brought you a peace offering to make up for no dessert last evening. May I come in?"

A wide smile replaced Eden's serious expression. She greeted him like a long-lost friend. It was a good thing he'd thought of the flowers.

"Of course, but Noel, you shouldn't have," she said with genuine delight.

"Yes, I should, and I have. It's the least I could do, given the abrupt end to our evening. I really am sorry, Eden."

Her smile indicated she'd already forgiven him. "Your flowers are beautiful, absolutely gorgeous, and my favorite," she said, accepting the arrangement. She sniffed at his gift, and in a melancholy voice added, "Tulips always remind me of spring in Central Park."

"That's right, you're a New Yorker." He'd checked out Eden Sommers' background thoroughly, knew that she spent many of her free days in the park, even knew the hospital where she was born.

"Born and bred. The park's one of the few places you go to escape the concrete jungle."

"Am I forgiven then?" He touched her cheek.

She looked at him with those huge brown eyes, waiting for him to go on. What could he tell her without jeopardizing his cover? "I'd made plans with friends," he finally admitted. "I couldn't exactly cancel at the last minute. I'm sorry."

"Apology accepted." Again she buried her nose in the bouquet.

"So, what are you doing?" Noel glanced at the cluttered table.

Eden perched her oversize glasses on her forehead. "Why don't you sit and I'll tell you." She gestured to the one chair that wasn't cluttered. "Have you had lunch?"

Noel nodded. The abandoned tuna from last evening could qualify as lunch, he supposed.

"Coffee then?"

"No thanks. I'll take water if you have it." He sat on the chair she indicated, Kahlua at his feet.

Eden returned with a tray holding his tulips, two glasses, and a bottle of Pellegrino. She set the vase, drink, and glasses down, brushed a stack of papers aside, then took the seat across from him.

"I've been going through some of the maintenance logs," she said, gesturing to the haphazard pile. "They've given me a headache."

"Find anything?"

"Nothing unusual so far. Though I haven't had a real opportunity to read each log entry in detail." She massaged her temples, shifted her glasses to a safer position at the top of her head, and continued. "Frankly, this has gotten overwhelming, and Lori's supposed to send me more."

Noel fanned out the papers in front of him. His strong point was organization and this lady could definitely use his help. "Why don't we start by putting these in order?" he said, "Have you figured out how far back they go?"

"I've got six months of stuff all dated 1995. The rest, Lori's having delivered by courier."

Noel drummed his fingers on the table as he planned his mode of attack. "Okay. Here's what we'll do. We'll go month by month, starting from January. Anything that says January you hand to me. I'll put it in date order."

They worked through the better part of the afternoon, putting order to the mess. Noel insisted they set up folders and Eden generated labels from her computer.

After a while, Noel came to stand behind her, "Quitting time," he whispered. His hands massaged her aching shoulders. Kahlua remained fast asleep under the table.

Eden trembled under his touch.

"You okay?" He shot her a puzzled look.

"I'm fine. Just suffering from withdrawal." Eden laughed nervously. She turned, stretched out her hands, and pretended to shake. "I haven't had a nicotine fix all afternoon. I'm dying."

Noel's eyes twinkled, making his laugh lines even more pronounced around the edges. "I wondered if you'd quit."

Eden stuck out her tongue. She stood and shook out her limbs. All that sitting made her feel like a pretzel. "If you must know, I've decided to cut back." She omitted mentioning that she'd considered giving up cigarettes altogether. They no longer tasted right, but she wouldn't give him that satisfaction.

"Wonder of wonders."

Eden shot him a look that could freeze water, her tart response cut off by the doorbell. Immediately she sensed Noel's unease and hastened to reassure him. "Probably someone delivering the maintenance logs. You stay put. I'll check it out."

She returned with two huge envelopes, waving them in his direction. "Ta daaa! Lori came through. Our packages have arrived."

Noel tried his best to tamp down his own excitement. "How did your friend manage to accomplish so much in so little time?"

"You don't know Lori." Eden gushed, "My guess is that she roped Michael into bringing home the logs. . . ."

"Michael?"

"Her husband is a supervisor on the ramp, remember? Lori also has several able and willing children." Eden tossed the envelopes on the table.

"We should be thankful for all those eyes and hands then. Now tell me you aren't going to sift through that pile tonight?" Noel's jutted jaw indicated the packages Eden had deposited. When she didn't answer right off, he added. "Why not wait until tomorrow when I can help you? We'll establish a schedule where I work on my furniture in the morning, and come over to help you in the afternoon. That way we'll blow through this stuff in record time."

It sounded like a good idea. Alone it would be a tedious process. "Deal," Eden said, extending her hand.

Noel took the hand she proffered, but instead of shaking, squeezed it. "Told you we'd make a good team." He pulled her toward him and lowered his voice.

"In fact I think we'd make a helluva team, both personally and professionally."

He left little doubt as to what he meant. When he released her hand and linked an arm around her waist, she tilted her head to receive his kiss. She wasn't disappointed. The kiss started off slow then built in intensity. His tongue probed her mouth, demanding that she give him all: body, soul, and something more. Despite the fact it was all happening too fast with a man she didn't trust, Eden held nothing back.

"Noel," she eventually panted, her shortness of breath having little to do with the kiss. "Noel . . . we've got to stop."

"Why?"

His hands played with the sides of her breasts releasing an ache that needed soothing. What had happened to the wall she'd built around her heart?

As the first beads of sweat dotted her brow, she remembered her doctor's advice. *"Take deep breaths, Eden. Visualize you're in a safe place with someone you trust . . . your mother, maybe."*

But Noel Robinson wasn't her mother; he was the catalyst for what promised to be a full-blown panic attack, unless she took control.

"Noel," Eden gasped, pushing him away. "Aren't you hungry? We've worked like dogs all day. Perhaps I can cook you dinner, that is, if you're willing to go to the store with me."

As the kiss and his ministrations ceased, Eden counted to ten and concentrated on her breathing.

Noel seemed equally shaken. He smoothed his hair with an unsteady hand and managed to get out, "Sure I'm hungry, Eden, starving as a matter of fact, but not for food."

It wasn't what she wanted to hear. *Concentrate, don't give in to those feelings of disorientation. Focus on your breath-*

ing. It worked. The tightness in her chest eased and the dizziness dissipated. She was even able to joke, "And I thought it was your stomach talking."

"You're actually offering me a home-cooked meal?" Noel repeated, sounding incredulous.

"Yes I am. I'm a good cook," Eden added defensively. "At least I used to be."

Noel pushed a strand of hair from her eyes. "Can you make real fried chicken and a dozen or so plump biscuits?" His breath warmed her cheeks.

Eden laughed in his face. *Wasn't this the man who thought potato chips were a cholesterol nightmare?* She couldn't hide the amusement in her voice. "I think I can handle that." *The fried chicken and biscuits, not him.*

She found her car keys and waved them at him. "Shall we go then?"

"I'm right behind you."

An hour later they returned from the grocery store, Noel balancing two recycled paper sacks on his hip.

"Where shall I set these down?" he asked.

Eden gestured to the kitchen counter. "How about right here? Thanks for the help. Your mama certainly raised you right." She smiled, meaning every word. Noel had been the perfect gentleman, opening doors, and insisting on carrying the groceries.

Though he returned her smile, he seemed taken aback by the compliment. "You're welcome, and, yes, my mother was a stickler for good manners. Believe me, if we acted up, we got knocked upside the head."

Images of Mrs. Robinson floated through Eden's mind as she dug through the grocery bags removing chicken parts, flour, and buttermilk. To hear Noel talk, you'd assume his mother was one tough cookie. How then could she have raised a son who most likely was involved in something illegal? "Do you have brothers and sisters?" Eden asked, squelching unsavory thoughts.

"One of each. How about you?"

Eden removed another bottle of Pellegrino from the refrigerator, set it down, then said, "A brother. Want water or the sweet tea we bought?"

"Sweet tea."

The shrill ringing of the phone ended the exchange. Eden frowned. No one knew she was at Grandma Nell's house except for her mother and Lori. Lori, she'd already spoken to twice today. Her mother normally didn't call until phone rates were lower.

Had she been alone, she would have ignored the persistent ringing and waited for the machine to pick up. Noel's quizzical look thrust her into action. Eden set down the carton of tea and reached for the receiver. "Hello."

Silence on the other end. "Hello?" she repeated.

Crackling static greeted her, followed by a man's muffled warning. "Keep your nose out of business that don't concern you."

"What?" She was conscious of Noel hovering, invading her space.

The spooky voice continued, "You heard me. I'm warning you, lady, leave well enough alone. Flight 757's crash ain't none of your concern." A click and the conversation ended.

Eden's hand shook as she replaced the receiver. Sweat beaded her upper lip. She felt as if she would throw up.

"You okay?" Noel's warm hands massaged her shoulders. He swung her around to face him.

Refusing to give in to panic, Eden gulped mouthfuls of air. "That was the strangest call."

"Oh?" Noel arched an eyebrow waiting for her to continue.

"The person never identified himself. Just threatened me."

"What did he say?" Noel poured two glasses of iced tea. He handed her one.

"Told me to stop snooping. That Flight 757 was off limits."

"Is this the first call you've gotten like this?" Noel asked cautiously.

Eden nodded. She took a seat at the kitchen table, gulped her tea and said, "No one knows I'm here, except for Lori, my mother and you. . . ." She looked at him horrified, realizing that he could easily have arranged that call.

"Eden," Noel said, reading her mind. He sat in the chair next to her and took her hands. "Think about it. Why would I have someone call you? What would be my motive? I'm equally interested in finding out what caused the crash."

Why indeed? She looked into Noel's troubled green eyes, for some crazy reason believing him.

"Eden, didn't you call Rod's death murder? Didn't you imply that there were problems with that aircraft?"

She acknowledged his comment with a bob of her head and waited for him to go on.

"You even suspected that a high-ranking person at Pelican was the reason that plane stayed in service."

"Yes, I know. . . ."

Noel's finger touched her lips, silencing her. "Eden, I've never made it a secret I suspected pilot error. Why would I threaten you? What difference would it make to me whether you continued your investigation or not?"

What he said made sense. *Unless it was sabotage and he was the mechanic who'd worked on that plane.*

"I'm a furniture designer, for Christ's sake," Noel continued, sensing her skepticism. "I'm in no way connected with your airline. But let's say that someone had knowledge of an improperly serviced plane, an aircraft that shouldn't be in the sky, then got wind that some woman was investigating the death of her fiancé, they'd feel compelled to stop her."

"You're right," Eden acknowledged warily. Rising, her thoughts scattered in a thousand directions, she searched the cupboards for a big mixing bowl to prepare the biscuits.

Noel came up behind her, linked his arms around her waist and drew her against his body. He smelled of Irish Spring. His warm breath tickled her ear. Eden leaned into him, liking the way his body fit against hers. He felt solid as an oak and just as hard. She squeezed her eyes closed, refusing to believe he'd have reason to hurt her.

"Now that I've scared you to death," Noel said, planting a kiss on her earlobe. "Let me buy you dinner."

"No way." Eden gently detached herself from the circle of his arms and handed him the package of chicken. "I promised you chicken and biscuits and I aim to please. Rinse these, please."

They worked together to prepare the meal and soon the aroma of frying chicken filled the kitchen. Noel, who'd been assigned to set the table, sniffed the air appreciatively. "How much longer?"

"Another few minutes. I just have to put more dough into the pan so that there will be plenty of biscuits. Why don't you grab the honey and butter, then start on the salad if you'd like."

"But of course, Madam." He removed the salad from the refrigerator, grabbed the honey and butter, and set them on the table.

Eden placed a basket of crisp, golden chicken next to Noel's tulips. She set down a dish of plump, honey-colored biscuits and went in search of the carton of iced tea.

"I've got wine as well," she offered.

"Nope. Tea's just fine. Goes well with chicken and biscuits."

Eden took the seat across from him, glad that the tulips provided a barrier behind which she could hide. His closeness made the air around her evaporate.

Her safe spot quickly disappeared when Noel got up, moved the vase to the counter and flashed a cocky smile. "Now isn't the view much better?"

Though her stomach fluttered, Eden refused to acknowledge his loaded comment. For something to do she passed him the biscuits. "Here, have one."

Fascinated, she watched him load his plate and pour on honey, before slowly following suit. When she looked up again, a tiny golden glob dribbled from Noel's lips. She longed to reach over and kiss the spot where amber colored the ocher. Better yet, she wanted to lick the honey away.

Noel, oblivious to her scrutiny, said between mouthfuls, "I've been thinking, Eden, didn't your friend Lori have help from her husband getting those logs?"

Eden slowly pulled herself back to earth. She nodded, dreamy-eyed.

Noel took another bite of biscuit. "Wouldn't Lori's husband have relied on someone else to get him the information he needed? You did ask for a couple of years worth of records."

This time remnants of flaky biscuit and delicious butter lingered on his lips. Eden chewed carefully before swallowing hard. "There's always the possibility Michael needed help."

"Let's say I'm one of the rank and file," Noel speculated. "My boss asks me to dig up two years of mechanical records on a plane that crashed, I'd be real curious.

During my break, I might even tell the other guys about my assignment."

"True. But how do you explain why someone called me here? How would they have gotten my number?"

Noel waved the chicken leg he was holding. He smacked his lips. "Umm, umm, umm. You can cook."

Eden rewarded the compliment with a smile. Unable to resist touching him she reached across the table to dab his lips with her napkin.

Warm fingers wrapped around her wrist, holding her captive. Noel's eyes, flecks of green-gold, mesmerized. His voice, pure gravel against pitch, said, "Can you be sure that only your mother and Lori have your number? And is it possible that your mom could have given that information to other relatives? Could Lori have given that information to Michael?" Noel's emerald gaze kindled a spark deep within her loins. This was sheer madness. She'd been without a man far too long.

"If your fax and phone number are the same, and the Goldmuntz children helped their parents . . ." Noel continued, seemingly oblivious to her reaction.

His words hit home. Eden finished his train of thought easily. "That means that all three Goldmuntz children had that number. . . ."

"—And whoever else they told about their project. And let's not forget the person who dropped those logs off. Isn't he a Pelican employee?"

Eden didn't want to think about it. Up until that eerie phone call, she'd considered the six square miles or so of Mercer Island her haven. Refusing to voice her fear, she said, "I've got ice cream for dessert."

Noel made a face.

Eden decided to call him on it. "Now don't get sanctimonious on me," she jabbed, slipping from his reach, and pointing her finger at him. "You've just devoured two pounds of chicken and an equivalent amount of fattening biscuits, so another bowl of cholesterol won't hurt."

Noel picked up his plate and stood. "How about if I help with the dishes?"

"No dessert, then?"

"No, thanks. I'm stuffed."

As they cleaned up the kitchen, Eden again had the uncanny feeling she'd seen him before. She wondered if he'd tell her the truth if she asked. "Noel," she began, "why is it I get the feeling that I've met you before?"

Noel stacked the last plate in the dishwasher and latched the door. He wiped his hands on the towel she gave him. His voice grew serious when he said, "I would have remembered if we'd met, Eden." He dropped the damp towel on the counter and pulled her closer to him. "I'd have a hard time forgetting."

She was lost in his eyes, lost in the moment. When he dipped his head to claim her lips, she wound her arms around his neck and brought him closer. As their bodies melded and the kiss deepened, her defenses weakened.

Against her hair, Noel whispered, "Eden, I want to make love to you."

His hands cupped her bottom, pressing her closer. She felt his arousal and knew he meant business. If she said yes, he would take her right there, on the hard kitchen floor, if that was what she wanted. She wasn't ready yet.

"Noel," she said, "I want—" *What did she want? Assurance, that he was who he said he was?*

"Anything, baby, anything."

"I want us to—stop."

Noel's arms fell to his sides. Eden stumbled.

"If that's what you want. Fine by me."

"Noel," Eden pleaded, "I hardly know you."

He was already at the door, his voice cool. "No big thing. I understand. Would you mind if I took some of those files with me? I'd like to review them before we meet again."

"Sure." Eden thrust a stack of folders at him. "Noel, I'm really sorry."

"No problem."

Silent messages arced across the space as their eyes held and locked. For a moment she imagined she saw regret there and something more. A ringing phone reminded them of the outside world.

Six

The rude intrusion brought the present sharply into focus. Eden's heart thudded as she glanced in the direction of the sound, then back at Noel.

"Would you like me to get that?" Noel asked.

"Please." Her voice sounded strained, as if all oxygen had been cut off from her lungs.

Noel quickly retraced his steps, grabbed the ringing phone, and shouted into the receiver. "Listen you bast . . ." Embarrassment flashed across his features as he caught himself, and in more amenable tones added, "Yes, Eden's right here." He handed over the receiver, and with an exaggerated grimace, mouthed, "Sorry. It's your mother."

Eden's lips twitched as she pictured her mother's shocked expression on the other end. No doubt her cheeks were puffed in outrage. Making an effort to squelch the laughter bubbling below her diaphragm, she braced herself for the inevitable slew of questions to follow. "Hi, Mom. Isn't this somewhat early for you?"

"Eden, who was that man?"

Eden tried her best not to giggle. "What was that?"

"You heard me. That man, Eden. Who is he?"

Noel raised his hand, wiggling his fingers. Having the grace to at least look sheepish, he edged his way toward the door. He paused on the threshold, winked, and stage-whispered, "Call me later. My number's on the table."

She could kill him, just kill him. He'd abandoned her, leaving her to handle the maternal inquisition.

Her mother's voice penetrated. "Eden, answer me, child."

"Sorry, Mom, I was saying good-bye to someone."

"Funny, you never mentioned *someone* before. Are you seeing this man, Eden?" This time her mother sounded leery.

Now where had she gotten such a crazy idea? Eden chuckled nervously, her mouth refusing to formulate words. Seconds later she said, "Noel's my next-door neighbor, Mom. He comes by to help me every now and then." She quickly shifted gears. "So how are things at home?"

An interminable number of seconds passed before her mother answered. Eden exhaled when the talk turned to family. Then out of the blue her mother said, "Eden, I went to the post office to pick up your mail like you asked me to. It was mostly junk except for one yellow slip. I signed for the registered letter, thought you'd want me to."

The idea of certified mail immediately put Eden on edge. "Who's it from?"

"Your job, I think. The envelope's got Pelican's address. Want me to open it?"

"Sure."

Eden wrapped the cord of the receiver tightly around her fists and eased into a nearby chair. What now?

Through the earphone she heard the rustle of paper and a harrumphing sound as her mother cleared her throat.

"Pelican wants to know when you're coming back to work."

Eden had expected something like that, except not

this soon. The last note from her doctor had granted her an indefinite leave of absence, but she'd known that at some point Pelican would pin her down to a definite date. Sinclair Morgan, her boss, had been extremely accommodating so far. That goodwill obviously couldn't go on forever.

"What exactly does the note say and who signed it?" Eden asked.

Her mother read it to her, summarizing with, "You need to call to arrange a physical. It's signed by the Director of Human Resources and your boss is copied."

Eden expelled the breath she'd been holding. The requisite form letter. She'd call her doctor before contacting Sinclair. That should buy her at least another month.

"I'll handle it, Mom," she hastened to reassure.

After more chitchat, the conversation ended. Eden picked up one of the huge envelopes Lori had sent her and headed for the bedroom.

Noel snapped his laptop closed and wearily wiped his eyes. He'd had difficulty concentrating ever since Eden had received that bizarre phone call. No stranger to threats himself, the call bothered him. Was Eden a target now?

He massaged his aching temples, playing back what he'd been through over the past few months. He'd been forced into hiding after the last attempt on his life. The threats had begun when he'd started asking questions about the Pelican Air crash. Then when he'd appeared on the news and done the talk-show circuit, they'd escalated to more than warnings. He'd actually begun to fear for his life.

At one point a letter bomb had been sent to his home. Thank God he'd been smart enough not to open an envelope with no return address. He'd been shot at, narrowly escaped being run over by a car, and the plane he owned with a couple of buddies had been sabotaged. Hell, they'd even killed his cat. More and more this house on Mercer Island had become a welcome refuge. As an added bonus, he'd been able to rent the house right next door to the woman who might help put those elusive pieces of the Pelican crash together.

He'd moved to Washington State by design, betting that Eden Sommers would soon follow. She'd been described as the gorgeous fiancée of the pilot who'd crashed that plane and he'd hoped to worm his way into her confidence.

Noel's interest had piqued after reading a newspaper article in which Eden was purported to be the last person Rodney Joyner had spoken to before he died. The pilot's last words could easily reveal his state of mind. Noel had convinced his friends to do a background check on her, and learned about the house she'd inherited. When she'd dropped out of sight, he'd known she would eventually show up like a homing pigeon. The bonus was his ability to rent the property next door. What he hadn't counted on was his irrational attraction to the woman. Now that attraction was sidetracking him from doing his job. He needed to concentrate, get the information he needed, and hightail it out of there before he did something stupid, like fall in love.

Forcing Eden Sommers from his mind, Noel returned to the folders on his desk. The ticktocking grandfather clock in the corner reminded him of the hour. He'd just e-mailed a coded message to his boss, and any minute Gary should be calling.

Even so, when the phone rang, Noel jumped. He'd never been this edgy. As images of Eden's lovely, honey-colored face clouded his vision, he reached to answer. He smiled, picturing sparks of outrage flashing from those huge brown eyes as her mother grilled her. Instinctively he knew there would be hell to pay when he heard from her again.

Noel ignored the tug in his groin. His voice was more gravelly than ever when he answered. "Hello."

A man's voice bubbled over with excitement. "Robby, my man, got your message, figured I'd touch base. Your plans seem to be moving along nicely."

Noel squelched his disappointment and forced himself to say, "Hi Gary, how are things on your end?"

"Promising. We got a great lead today. We were able to speak to the second officer's ex-wife. She claims he had a drinking problem. Could be she has an ax to grind but you never know. It's worth a shot. Claims the guy had been a functional alcoholic for more than twenty years. According to her, he'd been known to hit the bottle before reporting for duty."

"Not good. Don't airlines have specific rules about alcohol consumption before flights? Like no drinking nine-and-a-half hours before a flight?"

"I don't know the exact number of hours, just know they do. Each airline might have a different policy." Gary paused for a moment. "Doesn't it make you wonder if Captain Rodney Joyner was that engineer's drinking buddy? I mean this accident hasn't made a whole lot of sense so far. The only plausible explanation for experienced pilots to have a plane practically fall out of the sky is impaired judgment."

Grasping where this was heading, Noel drummed his fingers on the desk in front of him. His voice grew pensive. "That's an interesting theory, Joyner having a drinking problem. Let me see what I can find out."

Gary chuckled derisively. Noel heard the underlying skepticism. "You're planning on asking the Sommers woman if her man had a drinking problem?"

"Hardly."

"Then exactly how are you going to obtain that information?"

"I have my ways."

This time Gary snickered outright. "So it's like that, Rob, you sly dog."

"Like what?"

"Joyner's body's not even cold and you're screwing his fiancée."

His boss' crude remark angered Noel. Gary made it sound like he was a callous dog, like he was using Eden. That he would do anything to get information, even sleep with her if that's what it took. Not that making love to Eden wasn't something he'd obsessed about lately. What bothered him was that Gary made her sound cheap. Obviously he didn't know the woman. Bedding Eden Sommers would be a definite challenge.

"Not that it's any of your business, but I'm not sleeping with the woman," Noel snapped. Then in modulated tones, he quickly added, "I'll keep you informed if anything further develops." He hung up.

Too agitated now to concentrate and too upset to sleep, he went in search of a drink. He grabbed a beer from the refrigerator and deciding he needed air, wandered onto the terrace. He leaned against the railing, looking in the direction of Eden's place. Her house was shrouded in darkness, though a flickering flame, followed by a tell-tale glow caught his attention. He knew she was out there. Knew she was smoking those cigarettes. Tempted to fly across space and rip the disgusting thing from her hand, he shouted across the distance, "Hey, I thought you'd quit."

Silence. Then a smoldering butt flew in his direction and Eden's defiant tones rang out. "I never said I quit, just that I'd cut back."

Her petulance actually made him smile. He'd always

liked women with gumption. "Touché," he called, raising his bottle to salute her.

"Clasp your ankles. Keep your heads down." Eden heard the emergency commands clear as day. She said a quick prayer before hastening to comply. Around her, the cacophony increased. Venturing to look up, she saw the young mother seated beside her scream and clutch a whimpering baby to her bosom. Eden tried desperately to tell the woman she held the child in the wrong position, that on impact she would smother it. She should be bent over with her arms linked around the infant. Words failed her as her tongue refused to cooperate. She darted a glance down the aisle to see what the flight attendants were doing and noticed Rod heading her way. She exhaled a sigh of relief. He would save her.

"Rod," she said, sitting up straight, her arms reaching out toward him. "Do something. Make the plane level off."

Apparently he hadn't heard her since he just kept walking.

The sputtering engines made the passengers scream even louder. Eden yelled at Rod's retreating back. "Help us, Rod! For God's sake, help us!"

Her words were lost in the loud explosion that followed. Billowing balls of fire filled the cabin, obliterating him from her vision. Eden's chest tightened as the lump in her throat rose to choke her and the acrid smell of smoke filled her nostrils.

She jolted awake.

It took several seconds before reality returned. Sweat poured off her body, soaking the sheets beneath her. The ache at her temples exploded into a thundering headache; the typical reaction after one of those dreams. Squinting into the darkness, she focused on the illuminated face of the clock on the nightstand. Five-thirty A.M. Might as well get up. There would be no more sleep now.

Too wound up to lie in bed and stare at the ceiling, Eden headed for the bathroom, splashed cold water on her face, and waited for the pounding in her head to ease. She searched the medicine cabinet for the aspirin bottle, shook out two pills, and downed them with a glass of tap water. After changing into sweats, she headed for the kitchen to make coffee.

While waiting for her pot to brew, Eden roamed the terrace. A brisk morning breeze cooled her cheeks and provided a soothing balm to her aching head. Vibrant shades of green greeted her in every direction. Emerald lawns, lush olive shrubbery, and jade woodlands reminded her of Noel's eyes when his mood changed. Above, a cloudless sky promised a beautiful day.

As if she'd willed him to appear, the object of her imagination materialized on the deck across from her. Even from the distance she could tell he wore skimpy black jogging shorts and a white Nike T-shirt, the bill of a red cap pulled low over one eye. Awed by the sight of his raw male presence, Eden's mouth hung open. When his arms reached overhead in an exaggerated stretch, and his powerful biceps flexed, she thought she would lose it. Nibbling on her lower lip, she continued to gape.

As if conscious of being stared at, Noel glanced her way. A smile so warm, Eden could practically feel it, transformed what little of his face she could see. He acknowledged her presence with a raised hand and a challenge. "Want to come jogging with me? I promise to take it easy this time."

Eden forgot the headache plaguing her. She returned his smile. "I might take you up on your invitation later

this week. Right now I'm contemplating going into Seattle."

"Oh? Anyplace special?"

Actually the thought had just entered her mind. "The
public library," she called.

Noel pushed his cap to the back of his head and
leaned over the railing. "When are you planning on
leaving?"

"Mid-morning, after the traffic dies down."

"I'll come with you."

"What about your wor . . ."

The sentence dangled as he saluted her and disappeared inside.

Eden had just slipped on black leggings and an oversized cotton shirt when Noel rapped on her door. She
tied a red bandanna around her neck, patted her hair
in place, and hurried to answer.

Through the glass door she spotted him, denim
jacket hanging from his index finger, Kahlua held in
the crook of his arm. Lately, the fickle beast spent more
time at his place than hers. Eden slid the door open
and beckoned them both inside. She did her best to
keep a blank face, though her pulse raced. She focused
her attention on Kahlua, scratching the tip of the cat's
ear. "Hello, Judas. Am I to assume you've already been
fed?"

"Two cans of Nine Lives, plus dry food," Noel
proudly supplied.

"Tell me you didn't." Eden sighed, accepting Kahlua
and Noel's fleeting kiss.

"Did I do something wrong? She seemed really hungry, ate every bit."

Over Kahlua's body, their eyes caught. Noel's held a
flicker of an emotion she didn't dare acknowledge. The

butterflies in her stomach beat a wild tattoo. She lowered her gaze to the open collar of the Tommy Hilfiger shirt where a suggestion of chest hairs were visible, and caught her breath. She wanted to rest her head against his chest, tangle her fingers in those hairs, and let her tongue explore the hollow of his neck.

Noel broke the hypnotic spell. "Who's driving?" he asked.

"Me. The jeep's more comfortable."

"Good point. But the Camry's faster."

Eden jiggled her car keys at him. "Humor me. I'm the one who wanted to go."

On the way into Seattle, Eden hugged the left lane of Interstate 90. A white Buick Riviera followed.

"Do you always drive this fast?" Noel's hands splayed across the dashboard as bits of gorgeous scenery literally whizzed by.

Eden switched lanes, settling for a more central position. So did the Buick. "Is that better?"

"You're good," he acknowledged, patting her knee. "The proverbial truck driver and certainly much better than I am." Even as he begrudgingly paid her the backhanded compliment, his head moved from side to side, checking the traffic.

Eden accelerated. The speedometer shot past seventy. "You sound surprised."

"I am. Aren't most New Yorkers weekend drivers? Don't they depend on the subway to get back and forth?"

How did he know so much about New Yorkers? He'd once admitted to being from the other coast. Could he possibly be from New York? Eden kept her voice neutral. "I'm hardly a weekend driver. I keep erratic hours, live in Manhattan and work in Queens. Waiting on some isolated corner or in a smelly subway is the last thing I want to do."

"Can't say I blame you." Noel stretched denim-clad

legs. He laid an arm across the back of her seat, his fingers expertly kneading the nape of her neck. It took everything she had to concentrate on the road ahead.

Eden flashed him one of her more dazzling smiles and plunged on. "You never quite said exactly where you were from?"

Noel's fingers tangled her hair, massaging her scalp. "I thought I'd told you."

"No, you didn't."

A beat too long. "I was born in Baltimore."

"Ah," she said. "Then I take it you've been to New York at least once."

"Why would you say that?" He pointed in the direction of a green sign. "You're about to miss your exit."

Eden cut off the driver to her right and exited the highway. The Riviera trailed her. At a more sedate pace she made her way down Fourth Avenue. "That car's been on my tail the whole way here," she commented.

Noel turned to look out the rear window as the white car changed lanes, zooming by them. It had tinted windows. His face was impassive when he said, "Probably just another tourist." Gazing at budding trees framing buildings with unique architecture, he switched the conversation, "This is some city."

"Beautiful isn't it. Course I'm partial, I spent a lot of summers here. There's something about lush greenery and water that makes me feel—Did you see *Sleepless in Seattle?*" she darted him a look, blushing fiercely when he winked at her.

"Of course I saw the movie. Didn't every die-hard romantic?"

His voice warmed her, sending a tingly feeling to the tip of her toes. He'd just admitted he was romantic.

On the opposite side of the road an Infiniti pulled away from the curb. Eden quickly claimed the spot. It began to drizzle when they crossed the street. Eden

breathed in the smells of spring as they picked their
way through a crowded bus stop, and around vagrants
who'd made the front of the library home.

She led the way through a worn first floor and up
the escalator. She decided the downtown library could
definitely use a face-lift. On the second level, she edged
her way toward the rear, Noel on her heels. Spotting
the sign for magazines and newspapers, she headed for
a clerk manning a white Formica desk.

"Can I help you with something, miss?" a deep male
voice asked. A middle-aged hippie, stuck in an obvious
time warp, peered at her through granny glasses.

Noel quickly inserted, "We're interested in looking
at some of your old papers. I assume you have them on
microfilm?"

The clerk scratched his ear with a much used pencil.
"Depends what you're looking for."

Eden's spirits plummeted. Behind her back she
crossed her fingers. "You must have the *New York Times.*"

The clerk fingered a graying curl, then tucked the
escaping lock behind one ear. "Most certainly. Our copies go as far back as 1851. Can I help you find something?"

Eden's shoulders sagged with relief. Noel took control of the conversation. "You can show us where the
microfilm's kept." He clasped cool fingers loosely
around Eden's elbow.

The clerk's nicotine-stained finger pointed the way
as they followed his direction.

Two hours later, Noel decided enough was enough.
He finished reading an article speculating on why the
flight had been delayed, and turned his machine off.
The delay had not been a well-publicized fact. Initial
reports had indicated air traffic, now he wasn't so sure.
He'd have to pursue this new angle. He looked over at
Eden busily scribbling notes.

"I'm famished," he said, coming up behind her, resting his hands on her shoulders and squeezing gently. "Let's take a lunch break."

Eden rubbed weary eyes and leaned into him. Noel could tell she was wiped out and probably ravenous. Most likely she'd skipped breakfast for a gulped cup of coffee. A break was definitely overdue.

"Lunch sounds delightful, Noel. Did you have someplace in mind?" she asked.

"The man at the information desk says Pike Place Market is right up the street. So is the waterfront. Game?"

"Game."

They returned the microfilm and Eden, taking the hand Noel offered, followed him out.

Seven

"Did you uncover anything new?" Eden asked, pushing her almost empty plate of fried oysters away.

"I'm not sure."

Eden shot a quizzical glance Noel's way and waited for him to go on. They were seated on the terrace of a tiny restaurant on Alaskan Way, boasting a huge sign, Best Seafood On The Waterfront. Noel had decided they should try it to see if it lived up to its name.

Across the table, he raised a crinkled paper napkin to swipe at his mouth and offered her a forkful of salmon. "Want to try some?"

"No thanks. I'm stuffed."

Noel's next question came out of left field. "How come you never talk about Rod?"

"Wh—at?"

"Rod, your fiancé. Is he still a painful topic? I'd think there would be some good memories to share."

Inwardly bristling, Eden wondered why he'd evaded her original question. Did he think she would discuss Rod with him, of all people. And what exactly did he mean by, "I'd think there would be some good memories to share." Did he know that she and Rod had fallen out? Was he baiting her?

Avoiding his gaze, Eden looked in the direction of the harbor where old fishing vessels, passenger ferries, and pleasure boats jockeyed for berths. She inhaled the tangy scent of salt and tilted her face toward the sun. "I'm usually not big on discussing my personal life with anyone. But since you asked, what is it you'd like to know?"

Noel seemed nonplussed by her curtness. He flashed her another devastating smile and claimed her hand across the table. "I'm not anyone, Eden. You should know that by now."

"No?"

His lips brushed her fingers. "I'd like to think I'm your partner . . . and friend. For God's sake, we're working as a team to uncover who knows what. I'd think that signifies trust on at least some basic level." His thumb made circular patterns across her balled fist.

Trust. Such a misleading word. She'd never trust another man again. Their relationship, tentative as it was, was more that of forced dependency, created by a mutual need to understand why a terrible tragedy had occurred. She wasn't about to put those thoughts into words. "Umm hmm. I suppose."

"Can I get you folks anything else?" their waiter interrupted.

Noel dismissed the query with a wave of his hand. "Eden," he said, after the man was out of earshot. "I'm only asking about Rod so as to have some sense of what he was like. You must admit the press vilified him and made him sound like a daredevil both on the job and off. They alleged he was a big partier. I'm having a real hard time envisioning you two together. I mean, you seem to have a good head on your shoulders. Rod, according to the press, was a wild man, someone so totally self-centered he'd willingly risk people's lives for the sake of cheap thrills."

Eden managed a weak smile. "That wasn't Rod. You must have read the article in *People.*"

"I did. That's why I'm curious to hear what the real Rodney Joyner was like."

Eden swallowed the lump at the back of her throat. She was over Rod finally, but bittersweet memories still mingled with guilt. She'd never admitted to another soul that hours before that fateful flight, she'd broached the subject of breaking their engagement. For months after, she'd chastised herself, wondering if she had in some way caused that crash.

"Earth to Eden?" Noel waved long, brown fingers in front of her eyes. "You're a million miles away."

"Sorry." She picked up her glass and gulped the remaining liquid. "Rod was a complicated man," she began hesitantly. "He had passionate beliefs and an undaunted need to ensure right prevailed over wrong. That's why he was such a good union rep." She paused, letting the memories take over, then caught herself. "His pilot buddies referred to him as 'the great orator.' He had a way with words, you could say. Actually, that's one of the reasons I was attracted to him, he wasn't exactly the strong, silent type. Like most opinionated people he could be hotheaded, but he was never one to take unjustified risks."

"Was he a big drinker as the papers implied?"

Eden blinked at the bluntness of the question. Given Noel's opinion of Rod, she knew her answer might be taken the wrong way. Still, something compelled her to go on. "Rod liked his booze, if that's what you're asking. But he was ex-military and extremely disciplined. He would never drink on the job. I'd have a hard time getting him to have a glass of wine the day before a flight."

"Really? That's certainly contrary to what the papers said. Wasn't he involved in a drunken brawl in a Miami bar just weeks before the crash?"

Eden shrugged her shoulders. That incident had

shaken her to the core, though she'd never admit it to the man seated across from her. She went with the abridged version.

"Rod was on a two-day layover. From what I gathered, the entire crew was soused. They'd been on a South American trip for the past ten days and were letting off steam. Rod claimed that things got a bit rowdy and he tried his best to move the party out, but then the second officer made an off-color remark to a female patron, and everything ignited. The woman's boyfriend came at him with both barrels. When Rod came to the officer's defense the whole thing turned into a free-for-all. The rest you read in the paper."

"Was Rod so friendly with the second officer that he felt obliged to come to his rescue?" Noel's brows were skeptical commas.

"Hardly." Eden remembered the pilot, a ruddy-faced man with a penchant for drink; she'd disliked him. She plunged on, "There's an unspoken bond that exists between crew members, an ingrained loyalty, so to speak. You don't walk away when one of your own's in trouble." She omitted mentioning that Rod had once referred to the second officer as a horse's ass. The pilot was already dead, so why sully his memory? Out of allegiance to Rod, and because she was a little embarrassed, she didn't share the other version of the story, either.

The way she'd heard it, there'd been a woman involved. Rod had supposedly left the bar with that woman. The fight had been instigated by the jealous boyfriend on their return, and the second officer was the one who'd come to Rod's rescue. That was the real reason she'd asked to postpone their wedding. She'd been mad as hell and decided she couldn't forgive him.

Noel changed the conversation. "Did you want coffee or dessert?"

"Neither, thanks. We really should be leaving."

Noel squeezed Eden's hand and gestured for the check.

A week later, on an unusually humid day, Eden raced down the cobblestoned path of her front yard to check the mail. She swiped beads of sweat from her face, reached into the mailbox and withdrew a fistful of papers.

She wore cutoffs, a T-shirt knotted at the waist, and her hair looped into a messy topknot. She'd spent the greater part of the afternoon gardening. With temperatures well into the eighties, she was long overdue for a break.

As Eden flipped through flyers and junk mail, she barely acknowledged the white car whipping by, though something about its tinted windows seemed vaguely familiar. Searching her memory, she wondered where she'd seen the automobile before. The encounter hadn't been exactly pleasant, of that much she was sure. She dismissed her nagging unease, and focused on the letters in hand.

"Hey, good-looking."

Noel's voice, though initially startling, drew a reluctant smile. Every sense heightened as he loped across the lawn, black folder in hand, covering the short distance between them. Time had gotten away from her. There would be no opportunity for the shower and quick change of clothing she'd planned.

"Hi," Eden mumbled, surreptitiously gazing at him, then focusing again on the letters she held. Warmth flushed her cheeks as she sensed him closing in. She could feel the goosebumps on her arms rise; the butterflies in her belly begin to flutter. God she'd lose it if he touched her.

"Cute," Noel said, tapping the haphazard knot at the top of her head.

Eden's hair fell under pressure. She shuffled a manila envelope with her name and address typewritten, pushed back an eyeful of hair, and glared at him. "Now look what you've done."

Noel feigned innocence. "What?"

Though somewhat irritated, her lips twitched. No way could she resist that smile, the sparkle in those killer green eyes. "You're incorrigible," she grumbled.

"Thank you. I've been called a lot worse. Can't blame a man for liking loose hair and short shorts." He ran a finger across her cheek.

Eden's stomach flip-flopped. "Is that your way of complimenting me?" she looked at him openly for the first time. He was drop-dead gorgeous in those navy gym shorts. Much too fine for his own good. And hers. The yellow polo shirt he wore rippled with every muscle. Quickly, she hooded her eyes, moistened dry lips, and tried to ignore the feeling of his hand in hers. It was a losing battle. Noel slipped his arm around her waist and walked with her to the open front door where Kahlua hovered. The cat purred a greeting.

"Hey, buddy." Relinquishing his hold on her, Noel bent over to pet Kahlua. The cat immediately wrapped her fuzzy body around his bare legs and began to croon in earnest. "Okay, I hear you." He set down his folder, picked up the feline and followed Eden.

Inside, Eden tossed the mail on the kitchen table. The manila envelope, bearing Pelican's return address, could wait until after Noel left. This afternoon, they had more pressing things on the agenda. She opened the refrigerator, removed bottled water and a pitcher of iced tea, and set them next to the mail. Marveling at how easily they'd fallen into a comfortable routine, she located a couple of glasses.

With Kahlua still in his arms, Noel leaned against pristine beige counters, openly admiring her. In his free hand he accepted the tea Eden offered, then raised his glass in toast. "We did it, girl. We got through this mess. Seems like we should be going out dancing to celebrate." His arched brow issued a challenge.

Eden clinked her glass against his. "No, we shouldn't. We've accomplished quite a bit but we still have a lot more work to do. You know I'll need you to help."

"Well thank you for the kind acknowledgment." He sipped his tea, eyeing her over the rim of his glass.

What she said was true, over the past week they'd practically accomplished miracles. While much of it had been tedious, at times requiring a magnifying glass to decipher, they'd persevered. The end result had been Noel designing a spreadsheet denoting the types and frequencies of mechanical problems the aircraft experienced. He'd also tracked the plane's service history.

"I meant it. Thanks for the help."

Accepting her graciousness with another enigmatic smile, Noel added, "Let's not forget I had a dedicated partner to keep me motivated." He set his glass on the counter, put Kahlua down, and pulled Eden against him. Tea flew over the rim of her glass, dousing them.

"Now look what you've done." Eden ignored her own wet bosom and dabbed at the widening stain on his shirt.

The hardness of Noel's pectorals reminded her that she couldn't let him get too close. She was only human after all. Her hands pressed against a chest as solid as granite, she stared into mesmerizing eyes.

Noel took advantage of her momentary confusion. He placed butterfly kisses against her neck, and made growling sounds. "Humor me," he said in his gravelly voice, "Let's forget this tedious business and go out and have some real fun. I'll spring for dinner if I can persuade you to slip into a little black dress and three-inch heels." He nibbled the sides of her neck, adding, "We might even find a good jazz club and go dancing."

Though Noel's offer was tempting, his kisses unbelievably sweet, she somehow found the strength to say no. "I think we should stick to our schedule. What if I get called back to work next week? Where would we be?" she pushed another handful of hair from her eyes, adding, "Now go get your spreadsheet. I'll order takeout if we get hungry."

Noel sighed his exasperation. "Okay, you win." He released her, raised both arms in surrender and backed off. "What did I do with that folder?"

Eden felt a tinge of disappointment that he'd given up that easily. It had been ages since she'd been out. Really out. She'd always loved jazz. Dancing had been something she and Rod enjoyed. She slapped the folder on his chest and forced her voice not to sound maudlin. "Right here. Now sit."

Two hours later, they were still trying to determine if other aircraft in Pelican's aging fleet had had an equivalent amount of problems.

"With nothing to compare it to," Noel said, "How fair is it to assume these mechanicals were excessive."

"But look at how many times the number two engine's been worked on," Eden argued.

Noel rubbed his eyes wearily. "No one's debating that. Still, there's no hard evidence to attribute the crash to engine failure."

"And there's no hard evidence to support pilot error," Eden countered.

"All right. I concede. We're both tired. Let's give this a rest for today." He snapped his folder shut. "We'll review the spreadsheet and our collective newspaper articles tomorrow and . . ." he paused, seemingly choosing words carefully, "talk about why the flight was delayed. Did you know about that?"

Nodding, Eden spoke over the lump in her throat. "Rod called me from the airport."

"How come you never mentioned it before?"

"What? The call or the delay?"

"Both."

"It didn't seem that important."

It had been important to her. Their last conversation was still crystal-clear in her memory. Rod had called during that delay to plead with her not to postpone their wedding. When she'd remained resolute, they'd argued.

"I'd like to discuss your phone call tomorrow, and the delay." Noel said, his eyes burning with intensity. "Now, what are we doing about dinner?"

Dinner? She'd been so caught up she'd forgotten all about eating. Again, she'd let the time get away. Wasn't it she who'd promised him take-out food. She pulled out the nearest drawer in search of menus and fanned them out on the counter. "Chinese, Mexican, Thai, Indian? You pick. I have to go to the bathroom," she said.

The phone rang just as she returned.

"Can you get that?" she asked.

"Sure thing."

Seconds later, Noel set the receiver down, a strange expression on his face.

"Who was it?" she asked, keeping a respectable distance between them.

"Haven't a clue. The person hung up."

Eden shrugged. "It's good that you answered then. Saved me from being rude to an obnoxious salesperson."

It was a safe assumption that it was just another nuisance call. People selling everything from time-shares to vacuum cleaners were always calling around dinnertime.

"Have you had more of those phone calls?" Noel asked, deliberately switching the conversation. His eyes remained fixed on the menus.

She knew exactly what he was asking. Truth was, in the last week she'd had a number of hang ups and quite a bit of deep breathing, but no more threats. She refused to give voice to her fear. "No. I would have told you."

"Would you?"

Across the room their eyes caught and held. She knew he knew she hadn't told him the whole truth.

"So did you decide what you're ordering?" Eden asked, changing the tenor of the conversation.

"Yup." Noel folded his arms, slanted a look designed to melt the coldest of hearts, and said, "A beautiful woman in a little black dress and three-inch heels."

"But Noel I don't . . ." The back door slid closed on her words. "Have a black dress."

The hypnotic music of George Benson filled the smoky room, weaving its unique magic. For the first time in a long while, Noel felt totally relaxed. Tonight he would go with the flow, let his defenses down and see what happened. He'd perused the phone book, found this tiny rhythm-and-blues club in nearby Tacoma, where he would be just another face in the weekend crowd.

Surreptitiously, he glanced at the tiny dance floor where a handful of couples swayed. His fingers drummed a beat against the table while his feet tapped out a melody. Soon George's tune faded, and Natalie Cole's sultry voice warmed him. He was in seventh heaven. "Unforgettable" was an all-time favorite.

"Let's dance," he said, pushing his chair back and taking Eden's hand.

Eden's eyes sparkled as she silently acquiesced. He could tell by the subtle dip and sway of her shoulders she would be a good dancer. Placing his hand on the small of her back, he maneuvered her through the crowd.

While Eden hadn't exactly accommodated his request for a little black dress, the red mini she'd chosen made his pulse quicken. The slinky number had a generous scoop neck and was almost backless. It sent a provocative message. Somehow he had the distinct feeling she'd chosen it deliberately, knowing it would drive him crazy.

On the dance floor, she fit comfortably into his arms. Her tiny pout acknowledged her discomfort when he wrapped his arms around her waist, forcing her to link her hands around his neck. This felt better than heaven.

A bewitching odor of wildflowers mingled with vanilla tickled his nostrils. The scent was familiar and dangerous. Gayle, his ex-wife, a flight attendant, used to wear that same perfume. He wouldn't think about Gayle now. Couldn't. She was ancient history. He hoped she was happy with her pilot.

The tempo picked up and Noel loosened his hold on Eden. As he twirled her around, he got an eyeful of shapely legs. He inhaled audibly when her dress hiked up even further giving him a glimpse of golden thighs. What he wouldn't give to have those legs wrapped around his waist. The thought made him miss a step and caused her to stumble.

"Something wrong?"

Pulling himself together, Noel twirled her again. "Nope, everything's perfect except for my two left feet. I like this song, don't you?"

"Hmm."

He closed his eyes and tightened his hold on her waist. A mistake. He could feel the smooth skin of her back and every lean inch of her body molded against his. Her ample breasts grazed his chest, producing an ache in his loins. His slacks suddenly felt too tight. To hell with reason, he wanted to possess her body and soul. But common sense kicked in. Business and pleasure were not a good mix.

Reluctant to break the mood, he held on to her even after the melody had ended. Songs and singers soon became meaningless blurs as they danced through one tune then another. Eventually, Eden raised her head from his shoulder to ask, "What time is it?"

Time? He hadn't kept track. Not when he had no place to be except here in her arms. Angling his wrist, he squinted at the illuminated face of his watch and reluctantly released his hold. "It's past one. I guess we should leave."

"Do we have to?"

Her answer surprised him. He took it as evidence she was beginning to trust him. It scared him. "I'd like to stay, but I'm afraid I have an early commitment I must keep," he lied.

No further protests on her end. Hand in hand, they returned to the table to pick up her purse and collect his jacket.

Conversation was almost nonexistent the whole way home. Noel attributed it to the lateness of the hour and fatigue that had set in. He smoothed her hair and focused on the road ahead.

As the silence continued, he popped an Anita Baker CD into the stereo, adjusting the volume low. Big mistake. Anita's melancholy crooning only served to make the memories surface. God, how he and his ex-wife had loved to listen to music. The attraction between them had been instantaneous. He'd met her on a flight during one of the rare times he'd managed to snag a first-class seat. She'd been intelligent, articulate, and gorgeous. A lethal combination. He'd wanted her immediately and fallen in love almost overnight. But that was a long time ago. Back then he believed in love. He'd been young, in lust, and gullible. Too gullible. He'd wised up quickly though, after returning from a job in St. Thomas to find his house empty and his wife gone. After that he'd vowed never to get involved. He'd adopted a "love 'em and leave 'em" attitude, and stayed clear of all globe-trotting females. Home and hearth were not in the plan.

Noel glanced in Eden's direction. She was asleep, her head resting on his shoulder. When he pulled up in front of her house, she was still dead to the world. Leaning over, he nuzzled her neck, stage-whispering, "Wake up, sleeping beauty."

"Where am I?"

Even groggy, she was totally beguiling. His fingers sought her cheekbones, outlined the tip of her nose, and traced the fullness of her bottom lip. She reminded him of Kahlua, soft and purring to his touch. His palm cupped her chin, tilted her head back and forced her to look him in the eye. Guileless brown orbs reflected gut-wrenching emotion before shutting down. Taking advantage of what he thought he'd seen reflected in those eyes, he probed her lips.

Eden kissed him back with an intensity he'd never guessed she possessed. Such undisguised feeling made him bold. He masterfully used his tongue to begin a slow exploration of her mouth. His hand sought the neckline of her dress, fingers plunging below to caress full breasts. Sweet Jesus, she wasn't wearing a bra. He would never be able to say good night now.

A thud on the bumper of the Camry jolted them forward.

"Holy . . ." Noel cut the colorful expletive short and turned in time to see a white Buick zoom by.

"Son of a—," he yelled, jumping from the car to

watch the Buick disappear amidst a screech of tires and burning rubber. It was too dark to read the license plate.

"What happened?" Eden asked, joining him. She touched his arm.

"Someone clipped us."

"We were parked?" Her voice sounded skeptical.

"My guess is it's a bunch of drunk teens."

She tightened her hold on his arm and inquired. "Aren't you going to inspect the damage?"

"I suppose I better."

Eden followed him to the rear of the car. An ugly dent ran the length of the Camry's rear bumper. In a tentative voice, she asked, "Were you able to get a good look at the car that hit us?"

Noel's hands slid across the rear bumper, fingering the damage. "It was a white, late-model Buick," he said tersely.

"Are you absolutely sure?"

"Positive. Why?" He straightened. There was something about the sound of her voice that he didn't like. What was it she wasn't saying. "It had tinted windows."

"Noel," Eden said, her voice strident. "Call the police. This isn't an ordinary hit-and-run accident. That car's been following us."

Eight

Noel held the cellular phone in one hand and punched in the numbers. He knew he would probably wake Gary up, but the way he looked at it, he could have called earlier this morning, right after the white car had hit them.

Gary's voice, still husky with sleep, growled. "This better be good."

Noel heard the phlegm in his boss' throat. It signified a long, hard night of boozing and smoking. He glanced at his watch, verifying the time. Seven o'clock would be an obscene hour for a man who partied on the weekends.

He could hear Gary's latest conquest shouting in the background, "Hang up and come back to bed, honey."

Immediately, Noel pictured the woman. Probably another one of those identical blondes Gary liked so much. A statuesque creature with a bra cup that overfloweth, and not much else upstairs. Even so, he was envious. At least his boss had a warm body to share his bed. Damn that white Buick.

"Hi," Noel said, drumming his fingers against his coffee mug and focusing on the present.

"Hey, bud, like I said, this better be good."

Noel sipped his Starbucks coffee and set the mug down. He tugged on the elastic band of his jogging shorts, settling it comfortably around his middle. "Hey, yourself." Without preamble he said, "You wouldn't have a clue why a white Buick would slam into me?"

"Nope, not a clue. You okay?"

"Fine. My bumper isn't though. The Sommers woman thinks that car's been following us."

"Gimme a license plate number and I'll run a check."

It was a logical response and one he'd anticipated. "Sorry, didn't get one. It was dark and the driver didn't stick around."

Gary groaned. "Too bad. I can't help you then, bud."

Noel had pretty much known that without a license plate number, he wouldn't have a shot. But he'd hoped that his boss would know if someone was after him again.

"Look, whoever hit me meant business. I've got at least two-thousand dollars in damage on the Camry. I was forced to make up a story about why I couldn't call the cops. I had to tell Eden Sommers that my insurance wasn't paid up. She already thinks I'm an unsavory character, that really put icing on the cake."

Gary guffawed loudly, hawking to clear his throat. Noel pictured Bambi in bed listening to her lover's vile noises. He grimaced, not envying the woman one bit.

Gary came back on the line. "Gimme a break, man. What do you really care? It's not like you're involved with the woman. At least you better not be. You more than anyone should know romance leads to heart-break." He lowered his voice and Noel clamped the phone closer to his ear. "Just boink the Sommers wench and get it out of your system, man."

"It's not like that with us." Noel bit back the words he really wanted to say. No point in getting into a heated argument with Gary. Nothing would change his boss' opinion of women.

"Look, I'll call you back at a more civilized hour. Together we'll figure this out. Until then, try to stay out of trouble." He hung up before Noel could say another word.

Eden peered over a gigantic Scotch Broom and watched Noel jog by. Drops of rain trickled from the rapidly graying sky and he'd succumbed to the heat, shed his long-sleeve T-shirt, and tied the sleeves around his neck. Sucking in a breath, she focused on the sweat and rain glistening against his mahogany skin. She moistened her lips and took several more composing breaths. How could the sight of one man's bare chest throw her into such a tizzy? It didn't make sense.

She'd never based her attraction on mere physical attributes. She'd always liked brain, *and brawn,* a little voice reminded. She continued to stare, following the progress of Noel's flapping shirt until it disappeared into his driveway. Only then did she return to her weeding.

The incident with the white car still troubled her. Why would someone follow them, and deliberately ram into Noel's bumper? His rear bumper had been severely damaged, yet he was willing to let a hit-and-run driver go free? He'd refused to call in the cops, reinforcing all she'd initially believed. The man was in some kind of trouble.

Nibbling on her lower lip, Eden plunged her trowel into a hard patch of dirt, hacked away, and unearthed a monstrous weed. Noel really must think her a fool, giving her a story about not paying his car insurance. "Hmmmph."

How could he be so utterly irresponsible? *But he was so sweet last evening. And we did have a good time,* the irrational voice in her head piped in. *No. He was utterly adorable.* Now how to explain this business about not paying his bills.

"Stop dwelling on Noel Robinson. Stop thinking about him," she admonished out loud. Squeezing her eyes closed, she focused on the weeds. After a half-hearted attempt to get the better of one resistant shrub, she gave up, glanced at a sympathetic sky, and anticipating the deluge soon to follow, scooped up her tools, and raced back to the house. She avoided the rain by seconds.

On the kitchen table, yesterday's mail remained unopened. Eden shuffled through the pile, discarded circulars and obvious junk and relegated the vast majority to the garbage. Slowly, she reviewed the three remaining items: a card from her mother, a manila envelope from work, and a magazine with a yellow forwarding label.

She chose to read her mother's card first, delighting in the thought that her brother, Bill, his wife, and kids would be visiting the United States shortly. Next she scrutinized the magazine with the yellow forwarding label, exclaiming when she realized it wasn't even hers. It belonged to 4907. The mail carrier had made a mistake.

Eden struggled to remember whether the numbers went up or down. She was 4905. Her elderly neighbors lived in 4903. That would make 4907 Noel's house. A thorough perusal of the magazine's cover confirmed her suspicions. It was his all right. Two senior citizens would hardly be interested in *Flight International* magazine.

Intrigued, Eden scrutinized the yellow label closely. The name Noah Robbins came clearly into focus. She repeated the name out loud. It was so familiar. Too bad her brain wouldn't cooperate. "Noel Robinson. Noah Robbins," she mumbled, "coincidence?"

To satisfy her curiosity, Eden inserted a thumbnail under the edge of the label. She peeled it back, revealing the original white label. She grabbed a pen and quickly jotted down the Maryland address. It would be a place to start. A dab of Super Glue took care of affixing the yellow label back in place.

She looked out floor-to-ceiling glass walls, noting the rain had eased; the downpour reduced to a steady drip. Acting on impulse, she grabbed her grandmother's bright yellow oilskin from the closet, slipped the hood over her head, and buttoned the coat. Picking up the magazine, she headed out. Time to confront Noel Robinson or whoever he was.

In a matter of minutes she was at Noel's front door.

Hand balled into a fist, she paused before knocking. In a purposeful delaying tactic, she dropped her hand to the snaps of the oilskin, and peeled the coat off.

A myriad of thoughts converged. What now? What would she say when he answered? How could she explain why his identity mattered? And what if he replied that none of it was any of her business? He could well accuse her of snooping and he would be right.

Taking a deep breath, Eden banged on his door.

Noel squinted into the peephole, waited for the face to come into focus, then threw the door wide.

"Eden, what brings you here?"

"Nice welcome," she said, shaking a bright yellow slicker in front of his face, showering him with raindrops. "Aren't you going to invite me in?"

"Of course." He took the raincoat and stood aside to let her pass.

As she headed for the sofa, he noticed that she carried a rolled up magazine in one hand.

Jutting his chin in the direction of the periodical, he asked, "Are you trying to train Kahlua or me?"

She flashed a teasing smile, crossed one long leg over the other, and made herself comfortable on his couch. "Do you need training?"

"Some think I do."

Another smile transformed her face. Given time, he could lose himself in those huge brown eyes. The crazy thought surfaced. He wanted this woman forever and ever. Obviously he'd lost his mind. Years ago, he'd made that costly mistake, marrying someone who looked like her, acted like her too. You'd think he'd know better than to get involved with wild, perpetually restless airline types. Travel to exotic locales made them think they were special. A mere man couldn't possibly satisfy their needs, not when they were on a constant quest for bigger thrills. He shook his head to clear it, dismissing the vision of Eden's perfectly toned body beneath his, her tousled mane of hair on his pillow. The smell of wildflowers in his nostrils.

"Earth to Noel." Eden waved the magazine to get his attention.

The motion snapped him back to the present. "Sorry, can I get you something to drink?"

She shook her head. "No thanks, if I have another glass of anything I'll float away." She clutched the rolled up magazine in one hand, twisted a lock of hair with the other, and changed the direction of the conversation. "What did you decide to do about last night?"

Noel flopped onto the couch beside her. He draped an arm around her shoulder and nuzzled her neck. "Last night? Did I miss an invitation." The comment was followed by a mock leer.

Eden shifted her position and his mouth grazed her shoulder. "That wasn't a proposition." Her tone grew serious. "Last night your car was almost destroyed, either one of us could easily have been hurt. The driver of that car slammed into us intentionally. I don't understand how you can sit idly by and let a hit-and-run driver go free?"

Noel decided not to address the last part of her tirade. Hoping to distract her, he wove his fingers through her mass of wild curls, and bought time. He yawned. "The hit was probably intentional. This close call has at least made me do one thing, I'm going to pay my insurance tomorrow."

Eden jabbed his middle with a pointy elbow. "Don't you dare patronize me. I'm not some little moron you can give a trumped-up story to. You're intentionally letting this person get away. I want to know why."

Even if her eyes weren't flashing dangerously, he would have known by her tone she was spitting mad.

"Eden, be reasonable," he pleaded. "We never saw the driver, nor were we able to get a license plate. Even if my insurance were current, what would we say to the police?"

"You could say . . ."

"Yes?"

She remained silent but he could see the wheels turning. Eventually she tossed the magazine on the coffee table, slapped her hands against his chest and conceded. "All right, already. You win."

He seized that opportunity to take possession of her hands, flip them over and kiss her soft palms. "Anyone ever tell you, you're one foxy mama when you're mad."

"Puh-lease." She pulled her hands away and jammed them into the pockets of her jeans.

It was time to steer the conversation in another direction. Flattery wouldn't get him anyplace, except in trouble. He'd have to try another ploy. Anything to divert her line of questioning. He hated to lie but if it came down to it, he had no choice. He couldn't tell her who he worked for and why he was here in Washington State. The last thing he needed were the boys involved, strutting their stuff, alerting everyone that he was hiding out in Seattle.

"Talk to me about Flight 757's delay," he said, instead.

"Why is it so important to you?" she countered.

His arm circled the back of the couch, centimeters from the nape of her neck and all that lustrous hair. "Just following another unexplored avenue."

He could tell a cutting remark was on the tip of her tongue, but somehow she refrained from voicing it. "What is it you'd like to know?"

Her question was an excuse to shimmy out of his reach and fix those glorious eyes on him. Her skittishness only made him sidle closer. He wanted to touch her, smell her, love her. His fingers plucked the wisps at her nape. Her feminine scent pulled at him. Damp skin and soap. He loved it.

His voice was more gravelly than ever when he framed the question. "How long was the flight delayed?"

Visibly she went back in time. He could have sworn she forgot he existed. "Some of the papers said an hour. In reality, it was more like two."

She'd gotten his attention. "You sure?"

She blinked once, twice, then focused on him again. "Yeah I'm sure. I sat in on the crew's briefing. I'm the person who sent the flight attendants on board to complete their safety and galley check."

His questions came like bullets now. "What was the official reason for the delay?"

Eden thought for a moment. "You know, I don't know. I don't recall. Air traffic, I think."

"You think?"

She winced. In his excitement, his fingers pinched her shoulders. "Ouch, you're hurting me."

"Sorry."

She leapt from the couch, rubbed at the spot where his overeager fingers must have left an imprint, and finally said, "Come to think of it, Rod mentioned something about waiting for a delivery. I'm positive that's what he said."

"Delivery?"

"Yes. They were holding for a box containing a cooler with dry ice."

Slowly it all came back. All the gory details she'd subconsciously suppressed. Rod's telephone call to the briefing room. His whispered plea to meet him upstairs for coffee so they could talk. When she'd turned him down, he'd kept her on the phone, pleading his case. She'd told him his hormones had done his thinking for him. He'd made his choice and would have to live with the consequences.

Eden felt the familiar tightening in her chest. The sudden need for air. The feeling of light-headedness. Now was not the time to have a full-fledged panic attack. Not here. Not in front of this man. She'd been doing wonderfully well these past few days, up until his prying questions had made these painful memories resurface. Now look what he'd done. Right now she'd kill for a cigarette. Not so much for the nicotine, but for something to do with her hands. It had been five whole days since she'd last smoked.

Taking deep breaths to regain her equilibrium, she suddenly realized that smoking wasn't even an option. In her haste to get to Noel, she'd left her purse behind. She concentrated on her reason for being here. She'd had a purpose. Noel's distracting questions had caused her to forget her goal. At last she snapped a finger, remembering. Ah yes, the magazine!

Conscious of Noel hovering, she made a U-turn and almost slammed into him. Then like a running back

evading his reach, she successfully retrieved the magazine and thrust it at him. "Who's Noah Robbins?"

His face betrayed his surprise. She pressed her advantage, simultaneously regaining her composure. Pointing an accusatory finger in front of his nose, she jabbed
air. "And don't even try to lie your way out of this one.
This," she waved the magazine, "isn't the first piece of
mail I've seen with Noah Robbins' name on it. But this
time it's addressed to you. Explain yourself."

Noel's face welded into the studied blankness she'd
quickly grown used to. He didn't blink an eye. "I'm
Noah Robbins."

"You're who?" she sputtered. She'd expected him to
lie, issue a feeble protest, and quickly concoct a story.

"Noah Robbins is my real name."

"Who's Noel Robinson, then?"

"That's also my name. It's the name I use for business."

This time he'd really confused her. "Why would you
need a pseudonym to run a furniture-design business?"
she asked, skeptically.

His voice, gravel on velvet, formed a smooth reply.
"Who's talking furniture design. I'm also a journalist
by trade."

A journalist! Who would have thought? Rendered
speechless by his revelation, she admitted it all suddenly
did make sense. The details he'd known about the
crash, his ability to afford an expensive home on Mercer
Island, his insatiable curiosity about the disaster. Even
the unrelenting questions thrown her way. Hallelujah!
The mysterious aura surrounding him was explainable.
He was researching a story. *And using her to do it.*

"You lied to me, Noel. . . ." she said, pointing her
finger at him.

Cutting off her protestations, he pulled her into his

arms. "No, I didn't. I just omitted telling the whole truth. I'm sorry, Eden."

Before she could get another word out, his head dipped to devour her mouth. Her hands pushed his chest. Then both hands dropped to her side. Noel's kiss was sweeter than she'd ever imagined. Despite her anger, she gave in to his hungry tongue as it danced, circled, and danced again. The connection was electric. Her response so unbelievably passionate, it would have been pointless to check. She'd been so wrong about him and his kiss felt so right.

Noel made noises in the back of his throat as he gathered her even closer. She could feel every masculine inch of him pressed against her thigh and God did she want him badly. As his kiss deepened, his hands circled the column of her throat, fingers caressing the hollows, then traveling downward to settle at her breast.

The thin cotton of her blouse proved an ineffective barrier for the heat of his hands. He molded the peaks gently. She wanted to leap out of her skin. In seconds, he'd worked the buttons free and a cool air-conditioned breeze blew against her bare skin, stiffening her nipples. In a quest to be free, her breasts pushed against the restricting confines of her bra. She wanted his hands all over her.

Against her lips, Noel groaned, "Oh, Eden, let me love you."

Love her? A nightmarish reality returned, and with it sanity. She wasn't ready for love, carnal or otherwise. She'd given it once and look where it had gotten her. She'd been betrayed, her trust violated.

But this isn't Rod, the little voice in her head shouted. *You want this man. You've been bonded to him from the moment you first met him.* And though she'd felt that way, truth was, she barely knew Noel Robinson. Up until now, he'd kept his dual identity a secret. What else hadn't he told her?

Eden stepped out of Noel's arms, determined to deny the feelings he'd aroused. She raised a tentative hand to touch her bruised lips while the other fumbled to secure the buttons that had come undone.

"It's too soon, Noel," she said, ignoring the plea in his eyes and her pulsating treacherous body.

"Eden," he rasped, scooping her into his arms again. "Tell me you don't want to make love with me."

"I . . ."

"Don't say it. You're a lousy liar." He silenced her with another mind-altering kiss, quickly undid the buttons she'd secured, and shifted his attention to her breasts again. Her heart welcomed his touch but her head said he should stop. Common sense told her nothing good would come of a one-nighter with Noel Robinson. And silly as it sounded, she didn't just want a quick roll in the hay. She wanted him forever.

Her cotton shirt remained bunched around her breasts while Noel's free hand fumbled with the snap of her jeans. She needed to stop him now before things really got out of control. They could easily live to regret this moment.

"Uh, Noel."

"What baby?"

The endearment made her feel special. Cherished. It had been a long time since she'd been held in a man's arms and caressed. Apparently too long, or she wouldn't be reacting like this. Like a foolish teenager in heat.

"Noel, I think we should stop."

Immediately, his hands ceased their roaming. He held her at arm's length and stared deeply into her eyes. "Do you really want me to?"

She was never good at lies. She didn't necessarily want

him to, more like she needed him to. She paused a beat too long.

"Oh baby, I'm taking you to bed." His warm breath seared her skin. He scooped her into his arms and headed in the direction of what must be his bedroom.

You Tarzan, me Jane, she thought, deciding to go with the flow.

In Noel's bedroom, she got a fleeting impression of champagne walls, oak floors, cathedral ceilings, and an old pot-belly stove. He set her down on a cream-colored comforter and got in bed beside her. Holding her close, his warm hands created patterns against her exposed flesh, stroking, probing, exploring. She no longer thought of the consequences, simply opened up to him.

Noel's hands were at the clasp of her bra, working the hooks free, releasing her aching breasts. The confining scrap of material he pushed high against her neck. His lips suckled her breasts and the tip of his tongue traced a sleek path from breasts to belly button. Eden squirmed against him, letting his hands cup her buttocks, pulling her closer. At last she could feel the full, glorious length of him. He was as excited as she was. She brushed her hand against his groin to let him know she wanted him.

His hand cupped hers, trapping further movement. The bulge she held in her palm served to make every nerve ending throb. Her body was on fire and only this man had the salve to ease that burn. She pressed her body even closer.

Noel's hands moved upward to cradle her face. She opened her eyes and found him looking at her, his expression unreadable.

"God, I want to love you, baby," he said in a husky voice.

"Love me then." She'd thrown down the gauntlet.

Noel paused, apparently surprised by her brazenness. "Help me undress."

She helped pull the polo shirt over his head, found the zipper of his Dockers, and when it was undone, lowered his shorts and briefs simultaneously. The expression on her face must have been priceless because he said, "Like something you see?"

She chuckled, embarrassed to be caught staring. "Very much."

Who was this gasping hussy? Certainly not her.

Noel's hands made short work of the open blouse and dangling bra. He practically pried her jeans off. She was left only in rose-colored lace panties. In seconds he straddled her, supporting the bulk of his weight on powerful arms.

Eden inhaled the clean, fresh smell of soap and subtle aftershave. Drakkar. She'd know that scent anywhere. Nothing smelled better on a man. Combined with Noel's own personal fragrance, she would need no further aphrodisiac. Slowly, he eased himself down the length of her, his hands performing magic on her body, making every sense come alive, every tiny inch of skin long for his touch. She let her mind go blank and from some far off spot, registered his fingers inching below the elastic of her panties, stroking, probing, loving. In response, her hand grasped his shaft, hips bucking against him in a sensual dance.

"Honey," Noel gasped against her lips, his breath a warm elixir. "I think we're ready. I just need to get protection."

Impatiently she watched him fumble through the drawer of the nightstand and remove a foil package. Barely able to hold on, she helped him sheath himself.

Noel entered her slowly as if she were a fragile piece of china he'd been entrusted with. When he'd filled her up, he started a series of slow strokes that quickly built in intensity. Eden wrapped her legs around his back, pulling him into her, forcing him to give her everything.

The shrill ringing of the phone cut through the noises of their lovemaking. What now? Eden's legs locked around Noel, slowing his movements.

"The phone's ringing," she rasped, pointing out the obvious.

"The machine will pick up eventually." His finger outlined the hollow of her neck. His lips burnt a brand against her skin.

"What if it's important?"

"Nothing's more important than you and me right now." The finger moved to her clavicle. He gave another thrust. "Admit it. You need me as much as I need you."

It was the *you need me* that got her. What the hell was he talking about? She'd never needed a man. Wanted them, yes. But need implied dependency. Implied you were unable to cope on your own. She had never needed anyone that badly. Not even Rod.

Though her body throbbed, she ground out, "Look, maybe this wasn't a good idea."

"Says who?"

"Says . . ."

The answering machine clicked on and a man's gruff voice blared over it, "Hey Rob, time to talk turkey, man. What's taking you so long to get that information? Just boink the Sommers chick, and get it over with man."

Nine

"Eden, please, it's not like it sounds. I can explain."

Tears blurred her vision as she pushed out of his arms, rolled off the bed, scrambled to find her discarded clothes, and quickly stepped into her jeans.

"Listen to me, baby. Gary's probably been drinking. He wasn't using his brain. He was just mouthing off."

Eden raced from the room, tugging on her shirt.

"Please, baby, hear me out," Noel called after her.

Tears streaming uncontrollably down her cheeks, Eden could barely concentrate on putting one foot in front of the other. She managed somehow to find his front door, fasten her hands around the knob and let herself out. Covering her ears with her hands, she shut out his pleas but not the terrible words she'd heard on his answering machine. Even as she raced down the front steps, she could still hear the man's voice like a warped CD repeating the words. *What's taking you so long to get the information? Just boink the Sommers chick . . ."*

She'd let him do that.

She'd bought Noel Robinson's bill of goods, hook, line and sinker. His interest in her had never been real. All along he'd been warming her up for the kill. He'd do anything to get his story. Even sleep with her.

She ignored his shouts, concentrated on not falling, and navigated her way down the stairs.

"Eden," Noel pleaded, "please wait up."

Fat chance of that happening. She kept going, knowing that time was on her side, that it would take him a while to struggle into his clothes and come after her.

Noel yelled louder, apparently not caring if the whole neighborhood heard. "Eden, I'm sorry. What can I say? My boss is an insensitive clod. It's not like it sounded."

His boss was an idiot. That much was obvious. Still, she wasn't about to listen to feeble explanations or more of his lies. What excuses could he come up with now that he'd been found out? It was crystal clear that he'd never really cared about her, that he'd been using her all along. He'd played on her sympathy, telling her that story about his friend who'd died in the crash. Most likely the whole thing had been made up. To think she'd just let him have her.

As she raced down the driveway, the tip of her shoe connected with a ceramic flowerpot. She pitched forward, and slid on the slick pavement. Grabbing at air, she went down hard and connected with the wet asphalt. Her palms throbbed. The ache was nothing compared to that of her shattered heart. How could she have come so close to falling in love with a sleazeball like Noel Robinson, or whatever his name was?

"Baby, are you hurt?"

He'd caught up with her.

Refusing to look at him, she grunted something unintelligible.

Noel crouched down, wrapped his hands around her waist, and eased her into a sitting position. His fingers brushed the tears from her eyes even as his large palms cupped her face, forcing her to look at him, "Tell me where it hurts?"

Disgusted at herself that his touch still had the power to evoke such strong feelings, she snapped, "Get your hands off me."

Ignoring her attempts to shrug out of his arms, he pressed her face against his chest, and stroked her hair. "I'm here for you, baby. Cry all you want. We can always talk later."

How smooth he was, insensitive too, pretending that he didn't know he'd caused her hurt. Still, the tears flowed freely. She felt like a fool. She let him cuddle her, not caring anymore.

A raindrop splattered her cheek, followed by another and another. A few seconds later the downpour came. Soon she was soaked to the bone. Oblivious that she was drenched, her head remained on his chest. She could not summon the strength to move, much less piece together the remnants of a heart that could never be whole again.

"We'll catch pneumonia," Noel eventually said, putting her away from him. "Why don't we go back to my house and talk?"

His voice and the craziness of the situation finally registered. Why was she clinging to a man who cared nothing about her? Why was she allowing him to comfort her? Why was she even listening to him?

"I'm going home," she sniffed, pushing away.

"Okay, I'll see you home then."

"Like hell you will."

Ignoring her outburst, he smoothed her hair and pulled her against his sinewy body into a standing position. "After you take a hot shower, we'll do some serious talking. You'll let me explain."

Despite her anger, her body pulsed. Eventually she regained her equilibrium, tugged out of his grip, and headed home.

"We *will* talk," he yelled, following her.

In her current mood she wasn't willing to talk, much less listen. Why devote the time? He'd just feed her an-

other pack of lies. Just like the story he'd told about
making a living as a furniture designer.

As she stalked toward her front door he caught up
with her.

"Dammit, Eden. Can't you bend a little. I'm willing
to apologize for something I didn't even do. Making
love to you wasn't some strategic plan. It was something
that happened. Something we both wanted. Why let my
jerk of a boss turn it into something lurid?"

Ignoring his pleas, she pushed the door open. The
phone was ringing as she entered. She'd forgotten to
turn the answering machine on again. Torn between
answering, and shutting the door in his face, she lingered too long on the threshold. Kahlua seized the opportunity to bound across the floor, scoot between her
legs, and jump into Noel's arms.

Eden watched Noel hug the feline close. So much for
getting rid of him quickly. She would answer the phone
and murder the traitorous cat later. A conversation with
anyone would buy her time and help regain her composure. She raced across polished wooden floors and
dove for the receiver.

"Hello."

Static crackled through the earpiece.

"Hello," she repeated.

"Last night was only a warning," an eerily familiar
voice said. "You and Robbins are going to get seriously
hurt if you . . ."

"Who is this?" her voice cracked.

"That's not important. What's important is that you
stop snooping. I know you got hold of the logs . . ."

"Why are you doing this . . ."

The sentence ended as she surrendered the receiver
to Noel's tugging hand. He set Kahlua down and although he said nothing, his eyes blazed fire. He listened
for a moment and without uttering a word, hung up.

Afterward, he stood facing her, the cleft in his chin even more pronounced. "How many of these calls have you gotten?"

"What?" She turned away from him.

"How many calls, Eden?" His hand rested on her shoulder. She could hear the concern in his voice and felt compelled to turn around.

"This is only the second. You were here when the first came." *Hang ups didn't count. Or did they?*

In a deadly quiet voice he said, "You'd better be telling me the truth."

She nodded and his fingers kneaded her shoulders. Her entire body sagged against him. He caught her just as her knees buckled. Her stomach lurched, indicating that she was about to be sick. She quickly covered her mouth.

"Where's your bathroom?" he asked.

She made a wild gesture toward the hallway. Half carrying her, he headed in the direction she'd indicated. They just made it.

Afterward, he held a cool towel to her forehead. "Feeling better?"

Embarrassed that he'd witnessed her weak moment she nodded.

"Want to lie down?"

"Yes."

He held her by the elbow and guided her along.

Too weak to assume he had an ulterior motive, she pointed vaguely up the hallway.

He picked her up like he would a child, carrying her in the direction in which she pointed. "Your bedroom?"

"To the right."

Using his shoulder, he pushed the door open.

"I'll get you a glass of water." He set her down on an

intricately woven comforter. "And a pail," he added as an afterthought, quickly retracing his steps.

After he left, the phone rang again. Eden felt her stomach muscles tense and another wave of nausea threaten. She still hadn't had time to turn the answering machine on.

On the fifth ring, Noel returned to her side, set the glass of water on the nightstand, and placed the pail she normally used for mopping next to the bed. "I'll get it, if you'd like," he said.

Eden nodded, closing her eyes for a brief moment.

"Hello." Noel covered the mouthpiece, looked over at her and whispered, "They're still hanging on. Hello," he repeated. Then after another second or so, "They just hung up."

He caught her by the shoulders, positioning her over the bucket as another wave of nausea hit.

Later that evening, Noel sprawled on his couch pretending to read a Stephen King novel. He stared at page after page, the print blurring before his eyes. This business with Eden still hadn't been resolved. He knew she must still be upset. But he hadn't had the heart to have an open, honest discussion, not when she'd been so sick. He'd stayed with her until she'd fallen asleep, figuring that tomorrow was soon enough to address the situation. Now he regretted putting off the conversation. Tossing the book on the coffee table, he paced the room and decided he needed air.

Outside, a balmy spring breeze greeted him. The smell of salt lay heavy in the air as he inhaled deeply. Lacing his fingers together, he placed his wrists against the railing of the terrace. What to do about Eden Sommers? When exactly had she become more than a means to an end? He'd already made a cardinal mistake, allowing her to get under his skin. Thoughts of her now filled every waking moment. It was that damn vulnerability that drew him, that, and an overwhelming need to hold her and protect her from all that was wrong with the world. He'd come to realize she was unlike his ex-wife, Gayle. Not much ever fazed that one.

Impulsively, he made up his mind. He would go to Eden, try talking to her. How long did nausea last anyway? He would get on his knees if that's what it took to convince her to accept his apology. Even so, was it worth it? If he did manage to smooth things over, wouldn't she eventually come to hate him? They were on opposing missions after all. For Ty's sake, he needed to prove that Rodney Joyner had played a major role in Flight 757's crash.

Eden, on the other hand, was equally determined to prove her dead fiancé's innocence. It was a no-win situation all around. Still, at the very least, he owed her an apology. Gary's words had been unnecessarily crude. They had hurt her badly. Never mind that they'd made him look like a scurvy dog. And despite his efforts to appear cool, Eden's opinion of him did matter.

Before he could change his mind, Noel raced into the house, tugged on a pair of Bass loafers and headed out.

The rain had stopped and a dreary black night greeted him. At the rear of Eden's house, Noel peered through sliding glass doors. He was surprised to find her in what had become a familiar position. She sat hunched over the kitchen table, sifting through what must be a week's worth of mail. Smoke curled from a crystal ashtray to her right. Noel grimaced.

An overhead light shone directly down on her hair, turning her wild mass of curls into interesting shades of copper and brown. A smile replaced his frown. He remained spellbound, captivated by the picture she made.

His hand reached out to rap on the glass but never made it. She seemed to sense his presence, looked up staring vaguely in his direction, her fingers twirling red-rimmed spectacles.

Time to make his presence known. He rapped softly.

A hand clutching her chest, Eden sprang from the chair.

Noel pressed his face against the glass and waved.

She approached the door cautiously. "Who's there?"

"Noel."

For what seemed a long time she fumbled with the locks, eventually sliding the door open. Arms crossed, she faced him. "What do you want?"

"May I come in?"

She seemed reluctant at first, then moved aside.

"Obviously you're much better," he said, looking in the direction of the smoking ashtray and sweeping a wisp of hair from her forehead. She swatted his hand away. He crinkled his nose. The acrid smoke from the smoldering butt hung heavy in the air.

Eden followed his gaze. "I only had one drag," she offered as explanation. "It made me nauseous."

Noel pursed his lips. "Perhaps you'll quit then." He took her hand, "Can we talk?"

She sighed, a long, drawn out sound. "What's there to say that hasn't been said?"

"You misinterpreted a comment earlier today. I want you to know how sorry I am. Those comments should never have been made."

"No need to apologize. There was no misunderstanding what I heard."

He squeezed her hand. "Look this isn't easy. Can we sit down?"

She waved in the direction of a chair. "If you must."

They both remained standing. To cover the awkward moment, he stubbed her cigarette out and put the ashtray on the counter. Keeping his voice low, he said, "I'm sorry you heard that message. Gary had no business saying what he did. At times he can be a real pig. I hope you know I would never discuss you in those terms."

"So you admit you have discussed me," Eden challenged.

He couldn't lie. There'd been enough lies between them. "Yes."

"Why?" Eden's eyes flashed dangerously.

"Gary knew that you and I were working together, trying to make sense of the crash. Unfortunately, he's one of these small men who has a difficult time understanding that women and men can be friends."

She fitted the red-framed glasses securely around her ears and stared at him. "And you believe that women and men can be friends?" She sounded skeptical.

He knew it was a loaded question and one that would require finesse to answer. If any other woman had asked him the same thing, the answer would have been a simple yes. He prefaced his response by saying, "In many cases, yes."

"In our case?" she stared at him.

Clearing his throat, he said softly, "That depends."

Refusing to look him in the eye, she intentionally shifted the conversation, picked up a manila envelope from the table, and waved it at him. "They want me back at work."

"When?"

"Probably within the next two weeks."

"We'll have to work quickly then."

Agitated, her fingers drummed the table. "What makes you believe that I still want to work with you?"

He moved in closer. She stepped back. "Why would you let one person's idiocy affect our mission? We have a mutual goal. And as I admitted to you earlier, I'm also a journalist. I've got lots of information at my fingertips."

Huge, brandy-colored eyes blinked at him behind trendy glasses. "How do I know I can trust you?"

Her words pierced his heart. She was right, yet so wrong. Hoping to convince her of his sincerity, he reached for her shoulders. She moved away, leaving his hands to dangle awkwardly at his sides. "You'll need to trust someone eventually, if you're to uncover the truth." Before she could frame a rebuttal he changed the topic. "What about that cooler you mentioned earlier? Any idea what it contained?"

She nodded. "It held a human organ; a liver or kidney, I'm not sure. It was scheduled for transplant."

Noel made a wry face. "The poor soul never got his transplant then."

The morbid comment elicited a tentative smile. "Not that time around." Gallows humor.

"You wouldn't by chance know what hospital it was going to?"

"I don't believe that was ever mentioned."

"Any idea how we can find out?"

Eden thought for a moment. "I'll have to call Lori."

"Can you do that first thing tomorrow?"

Hands on her hips she stood facing him. "Why is this so important to you?"

He desperately wanted to touch her cheek and reached over. She flinched, leaving his fingers stroking air. "Call it a hunch, intuition, whatever. I just have the feeling that the box—carton—whatever it was, is in some way linked to the crash."

An impish smile surfaced, giving him reason to hope that they could again be friends. "Does that mean you no longer think Rod's responsible?"

His thumb itched to outline her jaw, stroke those luscious lips. "I didn't say that."

The laughter left her eyes and she practically spat the words at him. "I can't wait to prove you wrong, then."

Ten

Over the anguished cries of passengers, Eden heard the staccato noise of sputtering engines. The plane plunged several feet and a tangle of oxygen masks dislodged. The people around her screamed. The woman in front of her sobbed, her gnarled hand struggling to make the sign of the cross. Other passengers remained frozen in position, unwilling or unable to pull the cords, bring oxygen to their noses and mouths. To breathe. They'd given up hope, convinced they were already doomed.

Eden searched the cabin looking for a flight attendant. Wisps of smoke lent a surreal effect to the scene around her. She could smell burnt rubber and God knew what else. Through the haze, she spotted Rod, wearing an oxygen mask and carrying an oversize package. Good, he'd come to save her. As he floated in her direction, panic became a tangible thing. Passengers scrambled upright, fighting one another for the coiled tubing. The yellow oxygen masks seemed to take on lives of their own and in a bizarre dance, gyrated out of reach, taunting the passengers to come and get them.

Rod's steps slowed next to her seat. Eden felt an immediate sense of relief. If anyone, he would know what to do about the rapid decompression and the crazy nightmare she'd been thrown into. She waited to hear the calming sound of his voice, see the reassuring smile that made her feel safe. Instead, grim-faced he handed over the package. She accepted silently, looking up, waiting for an explanation. The person bending over her *was no longer Rod. The man's eyes breathed fire; mouth rounded into a gruesome abyss. Rod had metamorphosed into Noel.*

Heart thudding in her chest, it registered. She was on her own. Noel Robinson didn't know a thing about airplanes, or so he said. What's more he didn't care about any of them, especially her. Eden squeezed her eyes closed and listened as the box she held ticked loudly. Oh God! It was a bomb. *A bomb could detonate at any moment. Eden let out a rip-roaring scream.*

A shrill sound reverberating in her ears as she forced her eyes open. The dream had been different this time, though exactly why, eluded her. Recognizing the jingle of the phone, she groped for the receiver. "Hello."

Silence.

Jolted into full wakefulness now, she felt the tremors begin. It had been a long time since she'd had a full-blown panic attack but the memories lingered. *Breathe,* she admonished herself, sucking in huge mouthfuls of air and eventually steadying her voice enough to repeat, "Hello."

A rustle of paper and the sound of labored breathing. "Hello?"

The breathing on the other end quieted. A familiar, warbling voice slurred, "Woman, I'm watching your every move. Better not forget that." Click, and the sound of a dial tone. Eden dropped the receiver.

Sitting up in bed, she hugged her shaking arms, pulled in huge lungfuls of air, and exhaled slowly. Later today she would have her number changed. It was time. But what to do now? Don't think. Just move. Keep busy. Make coffee. What time was it anyway? She squinted at the clock on the end table, surprised at the obscene hour. Not yet half past five. Clenching her teeth to stop the chattering, she made a quick decision. She didn't want to be alone. Not if someone was out there watching her.

Rising abruptly, she threw on the comfortable baggy shorts she'd flung over a chair days ago, then scrambled to find a T-shirt and clean pair of socks. After shoving her feet into an abandoned pair of sneakers left in the middle of the floor, she nuked a cup of water and added instant coffee to it. She drank the contents in three quick gulps. Grabbing a hooded sweatshirt, she raced from the house.

As Noel exited the bathroom, he heard banging at his front door. He hobbled toward the sound, simultaneously stuffing his feet into running sneakers. Someone must want him badly.

"Eden," he said, throwing the front door wide. "Is everything all right?"

"Fine," she said, throwing him a wobbly smile. "I'm here to take you up on your offer." Her hand made a wide arc pointing out his jogging ensemble. "Thought maybe you'd like company this morning." He detected the tremor in her voice and wondered why.

"I'm delighted you'd consider joining me," he said carefully. Then remembering last evening's smoking ashtray, and the previous disaster, added, "Are you sure you're up to it?"

Eden placed her hand on her hips, eyeballed him and smiled, though somewhat tightly. "Are you insinuating that I don't have the stamina?"

"I never said that."

"The implication was clear."

He bent over, tied the laces of his sneakers, and looked her dead in the eye. "Mind telling me what's really going on? You were pretty angry when I left last evening."

Eden squirmed uncomfortably. He kept his eyes trained on her face.

"I've gotten over my annoyance with you," she mumbled, not sounding as if she did. "How about a little wager?" The desperation he sensed tugged at his heart.

Noel smiled back, letting her off the hook. His gut told him that despite her bravado, something was obviously wrong. She wouldn't have forgiven him that easily. He pretended to think for a moment. "How about—if you don't complete the entire mile, you get to spend the day with me."

"And if I do, what's in it for me?" Her tone held an edge to it. Underneath the surface cool was last night's angry woman.

Even as Noel's smile widened, and he threw both palms in the air, he was determined to find out what had really brought her here. "I'm at your mercy then," he said evenly, "You get to call the shots all day."

A calculating look crossed her face. She tossed him another gut-wrenching smile. There would be hell to pay if she won the bet.

That smile threw him. He turned away to gather a towel and his composure. Eden Sommers this early in the morning had an unsettling effect on his libido. The woman oozed vulnerability. He sensed she was scared. One look into that heart-shaped face, those frightened cognac eyes, and he'd known something was wrong. Every male bone in his body longed to comfort her, draw her into his arms, and kiss away the terror registered on her face.

"Ready?" Noel eyed her shapely legs in the baggy black shorts. Men had been known to slay dragons for less appealing packages.

"Ready."

They started off slowly and quickly picked up the pace. Eden hung in there beside him. Over the sound of sneakers slapping pavement he heard her labored breathing.

"You okay?" He tossed the question over his shoulder.

"Fine."

"Want to take a break?"

"W—why? Do—you?" she puffed.

Noel shook his head. She'd begun to tire but he was pretty sure she'd make it back. "We're almost there. Let's keep going."

He rounded the home stretch, Eden at his heels. He could tell she was making a valiant effort to keep up and slowed his strides. Behind him he heard the sound of a vehicle accelerating. Instinctively he turned in time to see a white car barreling in their direction.

"Eden, look out!" he shouted. He got a quick glance at the first three letters on the license plates, then dove, pushing her out of the way.

Like human cannonballs, they rolled down the hilly embankment and came full stop in a muddy puddle. The car zoomed away leaving the occupant's raucous laughter in its wake. Rank water filled Noel's mouth and ears. Cursing softly, he spat out bilge and with some effort helped Eden to her feet. They'd come full stop in a gully. He wiped a smudge of mud from her nose and plucked at the twigs entangled in her hair. Despite her disheveled appearance, she had never looked more beautiful. At that moment he knew he would do anything to protect her. Even give her his heart and soul.

Rigid with anger, Noel hugged Eden to him. She was visibly shaken. "You okay, sweetheart?" He kissed the top of her head.

"M—my ank—le," she stuttered, holding on to him.

For the first time he realized that her gait was unsteady. He, in fact, supported most of her body weight.

"Let's get you home then." He settled her against his body.

She wrapped her arms around his waist, admitting, "Noel, I'm scared."

"Nothing to be scared about, baby." He drew her even closer, swearing softly. "One way or the other I'm going to get that sucker. And when I do, he'll be sorry he's alive."

Later that day, Eden lay on the couch, foot propped up on the same pillow Kahlua had claimed. Her ankle wasn't broken, thank God. Just a nasty twist. She put aside the pile of magazines Noel had bought her, and rubbed weary eyes. She didn't know what to think anymore. Noel had been gentle and thoughtful when he'd brought her home. He'd held her ankle in his hand, gently prodding, ascertaining that bones weren't broken. He'd practically spoon-fed her breakfast, lunch, too, as a matter of fact. Then he'd raced to the store, returning with epsom salts for the swollen ankle, a pile of magazines, and a large bottle of ibuprofen. After making sure she was comfortable, he'd left, citing business, promising to return later that evening.

Eden massaged her pounding temples, refusing to give in to the headache that had surfaced. Noel, Noah, whatever his name was, gave off such confusing signals. She wanted to hate him, but couldn't. He'd come through for her when she needed him. What could he hope to gain from being so attentive, other than a good story? Mulling his motives over in her mind, she closed her eyes and eventually succumbed to weariness.

The jingling phone caused her to bolt upright. It was a shrill reminder that she hadn't gotten around to changing her number. The foot still throbbed. She glanced at her watch, amazed that she'd slept more than two hours, and with baited breath waited for the answering machine to pick up. Kahlua had disappeared.

A chirpy female voice announced, "Eden, if you're screening your calls it's only me."

Forgetting about her headache and throbbing ankle, she grabbed the receiver. "Lori, how are you?"

"Wonderful. Can't say the same about you, though. What's going on?"

They knew each other too well. She would never be able to fool Lori Goldmuntz. Eden told her about the last few days, omitting nothing and ending with her twisted ankle.

"You poor baby, why would someone want to run you off the road?"

"I'm still trying to figure that out. Unless . . ."

"Yes?"

Unless someone wanted a reporter out of the way. Eden twisted the phone cord around her wrist. "Unless they're after Noel."

"Or both of you. Are you planning on calling the police?"

Eden shivered. She hadn't given that much thought. She'd discuss it with Noel later. "Noel feels the crash might be linked to the flight delay," she said, avoiding Lori's question. "Do you remember that carton the pilots were told to hold for?" Fragments of the dream niggled the back of her mind.

"Vaguely."

"Noel thinks the two are in some way connected. Any way to find out what hospital in Houston the cooler was to be delivered to?"

When Lori didn't answer right off, Eden wondered what thoughts were going through her mind. Her friend eventually said, "I'll check the briefing notes, talk to Michael and get back to you. Tell me something

though, it's been Noel this and Noel that, what's going
on between you two?"

Eden's ankle pulsed. She squirmed uncomfortably.
"Absolutely nothing. Our relationship's strictly business."

"And I'm Hillary Clinton."

Eden's voice rose a pained octave. "The man has no
interest in me, Lori, nor me in him."

"If you say so."

"How about over there?" Noel pointed to a redwood
chair facing Lake Washington. "We'll use one of those
tables as a footstool." He lowered Eden onto the seat
and moved the table closer.

Eden sank onto comfortable cushions. She winced as
he gently eased her foot into position. They'd just enjoyed a simple dinner and were planning to have coffee
on her back deck. Noel had put up a pot and the smell
of vanilla wafted its way outside.

"Isn't the sunset lovely," Eden chattered, as he
flopped onto the adjoining chair. His closeness made
her shift uncomfortably.

"Umm hmm."

"Sometimes I wish I were an artist so that I could
capture those lovely pinks and mauves on canvas," Eden
babbled.

No answer. A scrape of his chair and he'd moved
closer. Taking her hand, he searched her eyes. "Eden,
I think it's important we talk."

She looked at him, waiting for him to continue.

"About the other night . . ." He swallowed hard.

Holding her hand up like a traffic cop, she quickly
interjected. "No need to say more. It should never have
happened."

Noel linked his finger through hers. "But I wanted

it to happen. It's all I've been thinking of since I met you."

What audacity, to actually admit that he'd planned on sleeping with her! She was tongue-tied.

"What I didn't plan on was for something else to happen," Noel continued.

"Okay, spit it out. We're both adults. Why don't we admit it was a horrible mistake and move on."

He released her hand and took her chin in his palm, forcing her to look at him. "Is that what you really believe?"

For a second, their eyes held. That couldn't be real emotion she saw there. He was master of the con. She wouldn't let him get to her. She lowered her lids quickly, ignored the fluttering in her stomach and nodded. If only he wouldn't touch her.

He released her chin and turned away, pacing the deck for what seemed an eternity. Eventually he returned to her side and in a deceptively calm voice said, "Would you say it was a mistake to have fallen in love with you?"

Forgetting the damaged ankle, she was up in a flash. She swayed, wincing at the pain. "Coffee's ready."

Noel reached out, capturing her shoulders, easing her back into a seated position. "Coffee can wait."

"No it can't."

"Stop avoiding the issue, Eden. Whether you want to admit it or not, our lovemaking wasn't merely two animals mating. There were some real feelings there. Passionate feelings. . . ."

"Gee, and I thought we were just two healthy, red-blooded humans going at it," she mumbled, cutting him off.

Noel crouched beside her chair. He reached over and took her face in his hands. "Ugliness doesn't become you, Eden." Before she could say another word he'd covered her lips with his, his tongue intruding where her mouth formed an *O*. She was tempted to bite that tongue, but her treacherous heart overruled her head and she found herself responding.

One kiss led to another and another. When they finally surfaced for air darkness had descended.

"Tell me again about the two red-blooded humans going at it," Noel rasped, kissing the corner of her mouth.

"We're only . . ."

He cut her off with another earth-shattering kiss. Afterward he folded her into his arms and whispered, "So is it safe to say that you love me as much as I love you?"

She didn't dare answer.

Eleven

"I didn't get all of the license plate, just the first three letters, CZY." Noel said to the man across from him.

"And the make?"

"Late-model white Buick."

The man scribbled the information, eventually looking up. "I think we've got enough to run a check."

That's what Noel had been hoping. He rotated his shoulder blades, willing the tension to ease. The men seated around his kitchen table would do their best to find the Buick, of that he was sure. They were old friends and had gone through a lot together.

"So how you holding up, buddy?" the freckled man next to him asked.

Noel turned his attention to Jay. "About as well as can be expected."

Jay brushed a wisp of shocking red hair off his face and threw him a skeptical look. "I'd say you're a little ragged around the edges. Tell me, now that your cover is blown, will you be hanging around long?"

Noel's arms reached overhead in an exaggerated stretch. The last thing he needed was the third degree. He yawned, hoping everyone would get the message and leave. "Depends."

Ignoring Noel's signals, Carl, across from him, con-

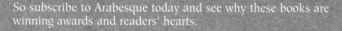

WE HAVE 4 FREE BOOKS FOR YOU!

ARABESQUE

(If the certificate is missing below, write to:
Zebra Home Subscription Service, Inc.,
120 Brighton Road, P.O. Box 5214, Clifton, New Jersey 07015-5214)

FREE BOOK CERTIFICATE

Yes! Please send me 4 *Arabesque* Contemporary Romances without cost or obligation, billing me just $1 to help cover postage and handling. I understand that each month, I will be able to preview 4 brand-new *Arabesque* Contemporary Romances FREE for 10 days. Then, if I decide to keep them, I will pay the money-saving preferred subscriber's price of just $16.00 for all 4...that's a savings of almost $4 off the publisher's price with a $1.50 charge for shipping and handling. I may return any shipment within 10 days and owe nothing, and I may cancel this subscription at any time. My 4 FREE books will be mine to keep in any case.

Name _____

Address _____ Apt. _____

City _____ State _____ Zip _____

Telephone ( ) _____

Signature _____ AP1198
(If under 18, parent or guardian must sign.)

Terms and prices subject to change. Orders subject to acceptance by Zebra Home Subscription Service, Inc. . Zebra Home Subscription Service, Inc. reserves the right to reject or cancel any subscription.

tinued to scribble. "Does that rather vague answer have anything to do with Eden Sommers?"

Noel tempered his reaction. He wasn't in the mood for taunting and that's exactly what would happen if he so much as blinked an eye. "Now where would you get that idea?" he drawled.

"Well she's not exactly a double bagger. You could do far worse."

"Double bagger? What's that supposed to mean?"

"Requires two paper bags over the head before you take it to bed."

Noel threw him a withering look as everyone laughed raucously.

A day later, Eden slammed down the receiver and glared at Noel. "Why wouldn't you let me call the police?"

Noel stroked Kahlua's fuzzy head before setting the cat down. "Because it's not necessary. I've got it under control."

Frustrated, Eden hobbled across the room. The swelling around her ankle had gone down, but her foot was still sore. She stopped short, almost tripping over Kahlua, and placed her hands on her hips. "What's wrong with you? A person rams into your bumper and you're perfectly content to let it go. Later, the same person tries to run us down and, despite your threats, you haven't done a thing about it. Why aren't you doing something about finding these people?"

"Where did you get the idea I'm letting anything go?" Noel said, coming up behind her and kissing the nape of her neck.

Despite the fact that her hormones were in overdrive, she spun around to face him. "Well, aren't you?"

He grabbed her by the shoulders, planted another

wet kiss on her neck and growled, "I'm a reporter, Eden. I don't necessarily have to get the police involved to feel safe."

Good point. Still, she would feel more secure if the authorities were informed. "Explain yourself."

"I have people looking into the matter."

Stony-eyed she challenged him. "People? Are you talking about those men who visit at night?"

"What did you say?" Fingers tucked in the loops of his jeans, he waited for her to go on.

"Don't play dumb with me. Ever since I've been here, two weird characters have visited you at odd hours." She chuckled dryly. " 'Course at first I thought you were dealing." Then realizing she'd let that slip, she clapped a hand over her mouth.

"You thought I was selling drugs."

She nodded.

Noel's eyeballs rolled to the ceiling. "Just my luck. The woman I've fallen in love with thinks I'm doing something illegal."

Eden's hand fell to her side. He couldn't be serious. His comments were meant to divert her from the subject, that was all. Just as she'd done previously, she ignored his admission of love and put the conversation firmly on track. "Who are those men, anyway?"

"Agents."

His answer floored her. *Agents, as in FBI? Could this be another lie?* "Why would you have friends who are FBI agents?"

Noel wrapped a strand of Eden's hair loosely around his fingers and looked her in the eye. "I don't remember saying FBI. Even so, it's not that unusual. Friendships run the gamut in my business. Diversity's the name of the game."

Eden slapped his hand and stepped back, forcing him to loosen his grip on her hair. She wasn't buying the story. "So what you're saying is that until your friends uncover these people's identities, we're to continue like everything's normal? We're to wait like sitting ducks till there's another attempt on our lives?"

Noel's fingertips outlined the curve of her jaw. "Did I say that?"

Eden tamped down her emotions. She needed to focus, to get a handle on the whole sordid mess. Noel's touch evoked irrational feelings and curtailed her ability to think. Despite his declarations of love, and a heart pumping like crazy, every instinct screamed he was lying.

"Why is it such a big deal to get the police involved?" she managed to get out.

The tips of his fingers outlined her lips. "Because I'm quite capable of protecting you."

He pulled her into his arms and kissed the top of her head. Over the fluttering in her stomach, she heard the beat of his heart. She would have followed him to Hades if he'd asked her.

The shrill ringing of the phone intruded on the moment. She'd had her number changed. Who could be calling?

"Want me to get it?" Noel groused.

"If you wouldn't mind."

He took purposeful strides toward the phone, hefted the receiver and growled. "Yeah?"

"It's for you," he said, angling the phone in her direction.

She accepted the receiver with more than a little trepidation. "Hello." A smile replaced her puzzlement when she heard Lori Goldmuntz's cheery greeting. "One mystery solved," she said after the conversation ended.

Noel quirked an eyebrow and folded his arms. "Well, are you planning on keeping me in suspense?"

Though tempted, she knew there would be no rest till she filled him in on the conversation. "I got us an answer. Some of the guys handling cargo have since been laid off. One of them told Lori's husband, Michael, that the organ was scheduled for delivery to Baylor Hospital. What's our next move?"

Noel chewed the inside of his jaw. "I think I'd like to find out who was responsible for sending it and who would have met the flight on the other end. Any hope of speaking with Michael's source?"

Eden tried to follow the way his mind worked while bits of the dream wormed its way through her thoughts. "I suppose I could ask. Do you think there was something else inside that box beside a human body part?"

"Perhaps."

She looked at him, at the same time grappling with his response. "Does that mean you no longer think that mechanical issues contributed to the crash?"

Noel stared out of the living room's floor-to-ceiling window before turning back. His words were measured. "Now did I say that? I just want to explore all the possibilities."

Eden continued to challenge him with her gaze. "Good. Because given the number of maintenance problems that aircraft had, it seems amazing there were so few delays."

"You've got a point. And that lead's definitely something worth pursuing, but not now." He left his position at the counter and sauntered toward her. "What say we let this whole thing rest temporarily and go out and have fun?"

Eden tossed him a skeptical look. "You couldn't possibly mean play hooky?"

"Just for a little while?" Invading her personal space, he touched his finger to her lips, anticipating her protests. The same index finger now traced the curve of her bottom lip and his breath caressed her neck. His closeness did funny things to her breathing.

"I'm thinking of taking the Zodiac out," he said. "Join me?"

It was an opportunity she could hardly pass up. She'd always loved the water and it had been years since she'd been out on the lake. Besides, she would be a liar if she didn't admit that being in the small, motorized boat with Noel held a certain appeal. "Okay."

Other people must have had a similar idea, because Lake Washington was dotted with assorted small craft when they set off. Using the space and time to observe him, Eden sat on the far side of the Zodiac while Noel manned the helm. He'd told her he loved her. She just wasn't sure she believed him. He'd also been deceptive about his career. What else was he hiding?

Noel guided the boat effortlessly out to deeper water. Eden's gaze drifted to the beautiful and expensive homes on the shores of the lake. Her fingers trailed the water, testing the temperature. Ice-cold. Logically, the lake's coolness should have provided a soothing balm to her overheated skin. Yet for some unfathomable reason she remained on edge, unable to shake the feeling they were being observed.

"Eden, see over there," Noel interrupted her thoughts. He pointed a slender finger toward the shores of Lake Washington. "That's Bill Gates' house."

Awed, Eden stared at the opulent mansion. "My God, it's monstrous."

"Forty-thousand square feet to be exact, and probably the equivalent in millions to build. Hey, are you okay? Are you cold?"

She shook her head to reassure him, suppressing the involuntary shiver that slithered down her spine. The day was brisk, but the sweatshirt should have warmed her, and the breeze should have felt wonderful on her face. Why then did she have the feeling someone had walked across her grave? "I'm fine," she lied. "It's just that I have this eerie feeling we're being watched."

"On shore, probably half-dozen pairs of binoculars are trained on us." He produced a thermos of coffee. "Try not to be so paranoid."

She shot him a withering look and gratefully accepted the Styrofoam cup. *Paranoid, huh! Was that really what he thought about her.*

"Try to relax and allow me to play tour guide," Noel said, his tone softer.

Eden sipped her coffee, refusing to look him in the eye. She focused on the cleft in his chin, resisting the urge to trace the indentation. He couldn't be in love with her. She quickly looked away; her attention now on the surrounding small craft; an interesting assortment, running the gamut from jet skis to expensive power cruisers. One boat in particular seemed to be closing in on them.

Eden realized Noel, too, was concerned by the big boat's proximity. Though seated, he'd taken on the stance of a prizefighter.

"Noel, do you think it's following us?" Eden's voice was barely a whisper.

"I'm not sure."

The speed of the Zodiac picked up as he aimed the boat toward the center of the lake. The Sea Ray Weekender followed at a more respectable distance.

Eden gulped her coffee, deciding that she'd let an overactive imagination get the best of her. Most probably the Weekender held a local family out for an afternoon of pleasure cruising. It had to be coincidence that they took a similar route. She turned on the boom box Noel had laid on one of the seats, found an R & B station, and said brightly, "Don't you just love Sade?"

"Actually, she's one of my favorites."

His response surprised her. So far they hadn't a whole

lot in common, except for this unexplainable physical attraction.

The tune ended and another one began. "Do you feel the same way about Ashford and Simpson?"

Noel smiled, a dazzling white smile, the ebony of his skin even more pronounced today. She resisted the urge to take his face between her hands, and feel the cool texture of his skin beneath her palms. What had come over her? All she could think about was him.

The Weekender behind them gunned its engine. Eden turned around. She got a glimpse of the man at the helm, dark brown hair drawn back in a ponytail, wraparound sunglasses covering his eyes. He looked vaguely familiar. The cruiser's speed picked up. No mistaking, it headed directly for them.

"Hold on, we're in for a rough ride," Noel shouted, getting her attention.

Stomach lurching, Eden clutched the handles on the sides of the Zodiac. She closed her eyes, trying her best to ignore the boat's erratic movements as it came down hard. No way could they hope to outrun the cruiser. Over the churning of her stomach, Eden heard Noel yell, "Can you swim?"

As the Weekender bore down on them, she managed a shaky nod. The bow was dangerously close now. Shiny chrome railings glinted in the sunlight. The man behind the wheel smiled, gunning the engine again.

"Good. On the count of three we're going over the side. One, two, three."

Icy water closed over Eden's head. She felt herself sinking but summoned all her willpower and came up kicking and sputtering. She shook water from her eyes and tried to focus. Floating beside her were the remnants of the Zodiac. The speedboat was long gone, only a white trail remained. Panic set in as she realized there was no sign of Noel.

After a second or so, when Noel still hadn't surfaced, her imagination went wild. He'd never made it out of the Zodiac. Were those little bits of him she saw floating beside the mangled rubber? Treading water and gulping mouthfuls of air, Eden looked up into a deceptively blue sky. Her heart beat wildly while fragmented bits of advice from her swimming instructors came in incomplete sentences. *Conserve energy—don't overreact—when tired float.* Had anyone even witnessed that they'd come this close to being murdered? What if no one came to their rescue?

Eden's body convulsed and the roaring in her ears filled her head. In moments she would be in the throes of a full-fledged panic attack and there wasn't a thing she could do about it. As the real world receded and shock set in, she was unable to make even minimal effort to keep her head above water. She gave in to the sinking sensation. Quite suddenly she was buoyant. Cognizance slowly returned as she drank in huge breaths of air, and fought the vise keeping her head above water. She hadn't survived to be taken down by the Loch Ness monster.

"Ouch! Take it easy." A familiar, gravelly voice growled. "You'll drown us."

Reality rushed back. "Oh God, Noel. You're alive," she said, her arms clinging to his neck.

"We're alive, baby. We're alive."

For the first time Eden realized that boats were coming to their rescue, closing in around them. The nearest, a sleek sailboat, held a chubby blonde, squeezed into a red bikini. She hung over the side next to a companion of equal proportions. The man held a life preserver. He tossed the ring in their direction.

Together they reached for it.

Twelve

"How you doing?" Noel asked, handing over a mug of piping-hot coffee.

"Fair to middling." Eden accepted the cup, set it down on the coffee table, and avoided his eyes.

"Only fair to middling. That doesn't sound good. Does the ankle still hurt?"

She shook her head.

Noel gingerly picked up her feet, eased into the vacant spot on the sofa, and repositioned her ankles on his lap. He made a place for Kahlua. The cat rubbed her head against Noel's arm, meowing coyly and he scratched the feline behind the ear. "Hungry, girl?"

"Hardly." Eden bent forward to stroke Kahlua's head. "More likely she's looking for attention."

"Just my luck to attract the wrong female," Noel muttered.

"What was that?"

He chose not to repeat himself, but instead concentrated on the purring cat nuzzling against him. Darting a glance Eden's way, he felt the tightness in his groin. She looked adorable, swaddled in an ancient terry-cloth robe; a towel concealing her hair. And although she made a valiant effort to pretend that she didn't know he was looking at her, her body language said otherwise.

"So how are you really?" Noel asked, noting the tight lines around her mouth.

Eden sipped her coffee. She took her time answering. "As I indicated earlier, the ankle's no longer a problem. I'm still shaken up though."

Noel ran a hand over the fuzzy socks covering Eden's arches. "And you have every reason to be. Imagine what would have happened if those yachters hadn't come to our rescue—"

"I don't even want to think about it."

"Did the police grill you like they did me?"

Eden nodded. "But I don't think they took me seriously. I think someone convinced them that the guy at the helm was drunk. In any case, they'd already made up their minds that it was an accident. Now you and I know that's bull."

Noel suppressed a sigh of relief. Despite the police speaking with eyewitnesses on several boats, his quick thinking and innate charm had saved his butt. God had most definitely been on his side, assigning him two rookie cops, so overwhelmed to meet the infamous Noah Robbins, they'd become tongue-tied. And when he'd produced the ID to support his claim, they'd done everything short of lick his boots. He'd even pretended to take them into his confidence and admitted he was undercover. That strategic move had ensured him friends for life. Cops understood the need for secrecy.

The story he'd given them wasn't entirely true. Still, they appeared to buy what he'd said. Had either of them watched the news on the east coast, they would have known that he was considered missing. At least that was the story the department had agreed to go public with. It beat saying that he was in hiding, or even worse, had been forced to take a vacation.

The real truth was that he'd been removed from the investigation. Gary's boss had decided that Ty's death had caused Noah to lose his objectivity. That he could no longer be impartial. In a sense that was true. Avenging his friend's death had consumed him and finding someone to blame was now a personal crusade. His ardor hadn't lessened one bit though he'd been taken off the case. He still meant to find Ty's killer, even if he had to identify the person posthumously. Not even Eden would stand in his way.

"Noel, you're a million miles away."

He shook his head to clear it. Day by day it had gotten easier to remember to answer to "Noel."

"What's that, honey?" He shifted his gaze and focused on Eden. Caught staring, she lowered her eyes. Had his endearment made her that uncomfortable? Taking advantage of her unease, he set Kahlua on the floor, ignoring the cat's angry meow, and lifted one of Eden's sock-covered arches to his lips. He kissed the instep.

"Noel . . ." Eden squirmed, attempting to free her foot.

Her ankle felt so tiny in his hand. He turned over her foot and planted a kiss on the sole.

"Stop it," she hissed, swatting his arm.

Noel's free hand captured her wrist. Slowly, he brought the palm to his lips and blew against the flesh. "Didn't you say you thought you might have seen the operator of the Weekender before?"

Eden's breath came in little gusts. "You're deliberately trying to distract me, quizzing me while I'm weak and vulnerable."

Noel could tell she was trying to make light of the electricity jolting off both of them. He suckled a finger. "Nope. Just curious. I thought maybe the man's identity had come to you." He sounded as if he were out of breath. He didn't care.

He captured her pinky in his mouth and bit down

gently, letting his tongue circle, then captured another finger.

He removed her feet from his lap and swung her into a sitting position. Taking her chin between his palms, he stared into her eyes. "Baby, that little incident scared the hell out of me. I don't know what I would have done if something had happened to you."

His admission gained her full attention. "Actually, I thought I'd lost you." He heard the catch in her voice.

Hiding his surprise, he pressed the point, sensing that she was now willing to listen. "Eden, I get this idea that you think I'm joking when I say I love you. You're responsive to my touch, yet you shut down almost immediately if I put my feelings into words. Am I rushing things? Are you still in love with Rod? If that's the case I'm willing to wait. It's not like I'm unreasonable."

For a moment her brandy-colored eyes seemed uncertain. He sensed she was about to say something. His ego desperately needed reassurance. He couldn't be that far off base. Instinct told him that she cared. His instincts had never failed him before.

Before Eden could look away, he dipped his head, claimed her lips, and probed gently, seeking an opening. An intimate dance began as their tongues melded, separated, and rejoined in an ancient game of hide-and-seek. He needed to find out how she really felt about him. His feelings weren't purely one-sided, that was for sure. His fingers plucked the belt of the terry-cloth robe, loosening the tie just enough to let him in. His hands stroked soft silk and he buried his nose in the hollow of her neck, inhaling her smell. Honey and almond. A nectar too sweet to resist. He wanted to drink her up. In an attempt to sate that need, he pressed his body against hers. She had to feel how much he wanted her.

"Noel." Eden's voice sounded throaty as she pressed against him.

Needing no further invitation, he lowered her onto the couch, covering her body with his. His hands roamed the smooth expanse of her chest, crested the hills, found the valleys, and plucked at the buds her nipples had become. He used his tongue to lave them, then moved his hands downward to caress her taut stomach. With the tips of his fingers, he explored the crevice of her belly button.

"God, Noel."

"What, honey?"

"We shouldn't be doing this. I was so mad at you."

He focused on the was. Must mean she'd forgiven him. "And you're not anymore." It wasn't a question.

"No, how could I be? You saved my life."

He didn't want gratitude. He wanted her love. Yet common sense flew out the window as it always did. He would willingly take her on any terms.

"I want to make love to you," he said, kissing the corners of her mouth.

"Make love to me."

She was willing to give him another chance. He yanked at the robe's belt quicker than it took to blink an eye.

As he'd suspected, underneath the heavy dressing gown she was completely naked. He expelled his breath in an audible sigh, feasting his eyes on all of her: Firm breasts that were definitely more than a mouthful, a trim waist, curly apex, and long, long legs. Perfection, if such a thing was possible. When he felt himself grow harder, he covered her hand with his own and let their joined hands touch his aching need. Eden quivered. Easing off her, he loosened his belt and quickly lowered his zipper.

The doorbell rang.

Rotten timing. "Don't answer it."

"What if it's important?"

"Nothing's that important."

The bell chimed again. This time for a longer period.

"Why don't I look out the window and see who it is?"

Noel groaned as Eden fastened her robe and pushed off the couch. He watched her pad to a nearby window, shift the blinds, and peer through the space. Turning back, she mouthed, "Federal Express. Might be urgent."

His erection now history, he muttered an oath then zipped his pants.

Approaching the door with some trepidation, sanity returned. She'd had a close brush with death. Capsizing had been a traumatic experience so who could blame her for losing her head? And emotions had continued to run high after she and Noel were safely on land. He'd held her, hugging her close, telling her a dozen times or so how much he loved her. She'd obviously let those three little words go to her head allowing them to color her judgment.

Grounded, Eden approached the door with purpose. "Who is it?"

"Fed Ex."

"Can I see some ID?"

Out of the corners of her eye, she caught Noel's nod of approval.

As she raised the blinds, the man in the gray walking shorts and light blue cotton shirt fished out his identification and held it to the windowpane. Eden pressed her nose against the glass making sure the face in the picture matched the guy holding the square plastic badge. Noel come up behind her. He imprisoned her with his arms, body pressed closely against hers.

"Looks authentic."

"Yes it does. Be with you in a second," she yelled.

Circumventing Noel, she moved toward the front door, opened it quickly and accepted the envelope. Hurriedly scribbling her name, she stepped back inside.

"Who's it from?" Noel asked.

For the first time Eden glanced at the return address. Her eyes met his and held. "My job. My guess is I'm wanted back at work."

Eden spotted the sign for the mall and made a quick right. She circled the parking lot, eventually finding space in the very last row. It had been a gruelling morning so far. She'd been forced to leave the relative safety of home to take care of things like replacing her driver's license. Her purse, containing credit cards and other essential documents, had been lost when the Zodiac capsized.

It had taken her two full days to get up the courage to go out. A driver's license was a necessity, symbolized who she was. Calls to various establishments had taken care of replacing credit cards, but a driver's license and Social Security card meant appearing in person, standing on line, and dealing with bureaucracy. Things she hated.

She'd left early that morning, avoiding having to explain her intentions to Noel. But as the day wore on, she regretted her impulsive decision to head out alone. Noel's presence would have made the long wait in line bearable. Much as she hated to admit it, she missed him.

Eden pushed the button on the remote key ring. Reassured to hear the click of the automobile lock, she set off. She planned to pop into the nearest department store, purchase a pocketbook and wallet, then head home.

Inside, cool air conditioning greeted her. She ignored the signs for Nordstrom and headed for Mon Caché.

"Can I help you?" An overly cheery voice inquired from behind a counter. A saleswoman peered at her through a maze of expensive-looking leather bags. The woman wore huge glasses and an oversize smile.

"I'm looking for a great big leather bag that will accommodate both my makeup and appointment book. Preferably Coach."

"I've got just the thing." The woman's eyes twinkled. She crouched down and reached into the display case. "How about this?" Standing, she held out a bucket bag.

"Perfect."

Removing the cash she'd gotten from the bank, Eden completed the transaction.

The saleswoman's eyes widened as she accepted the fistful of bills.

"Can I get you anything else?"

She'd almost forgotten. "Yes, a wallet. One that holds a checkbook. Same manufacturer please."

After looking at what appeared to be the entire collection, Eden finally made a choice. And again paid cash.

When the woman attempted to wrap her purchases, Eden declined. "It's okay, just give me the receipt and I'll put the wallet in my bag."

Impulsively she made a slight detour through the lingerie section, then decided it was a waste of time. Why would she need lingerie? Who would she wear the little black teddy for? Noel? She was being ridiculous.

The electronics department was close to the exit. The thought popped into her mind before she could stop it. Why not surprise Noel and replace the radio he'd lost when the Zodiac had gone down. She'd make a fast purchase then head home. Wending her way through assorted stereos, computers, and faxes, she eventually came to a section where small groups gathered around several oversize TVs. All were tuned to the same channel showing a baseball game in progress. Eden could tell by the sharp intake of breath and muttered cheers, the home team was winning. She continued, reaching the end of the row.

An uncomfortable feeling surfaced. She sensed she was being followed. Glancing over her shoulder did nothing to reassure her. Was that a person hiding behind the floor model to her right? For a long time, she stared in that direction. Then convinced that it was more a figment of her imagination than anything else, she continued down another aisle filled with TVs. Paranoia must be getting the better of her. That's what almost getting killed did to a person. She heard muffled footsteps and sensed the person closing in. Her skin crawled as she clutched the strap of her newly purchased pocketbook and darted a glance behind her.

Taking long, slow breaths to calm herself, Eden inhaled the scent of the perfumed interior. For an interminable moment, she stood still, gathering her bearings, and willing her heartbeat to slow down. With resolute steps she exited the store. A hand clamped down on her shoulder spinning her around. She jumped.

"May I have your bag, please?" The voice belonged to a long-haired fellow; a Fabio double. He wore tight jeans and a backward baseball cap. One hand held a walkie-talkie.

"Why?" Eden's grip on her purse tightened.

"Do you have receipts for that bag?"

Comprehension dawned. Tight-lipped, she said, "Inside."

Sensing the hostility blazing from those watery blue eyes, she fixed him with a scorching glare.

Here it was happening again. Lone black person in a predominantly white store and the store security immediately assumed you were a thief.

The man waited, hand held out.

Eden took a long time unzipping the bag. She reached in and withdrew the receipt.

"Here they are," she said, dropping the papers into his outstretched palm. She slid the bag's zipper closed.

A small crowd gathered. She could tell from the look on their faces that she'd been tried and found guilty. Catching the eye of a middle-aged mother with a portly teenager in tow, she was surprised to see the animosity flashing from those hazel eyes. The woman's lip curled and she knew that she'd already been labeled a thief.

Eden turned her attention back to the store detective. The look on his face was priceless. He scrutinized the small slips of paper and then grudgingly handed them back. "You paid in cash. Those are some awfully expensive purchases you've made." The last was said with a sneer. Eden crossed her arms and eyeballed him. Reluctantly, he added, "Sorry ma'am, no offense meant, just being cautious. You didn't come in with a bag."

He'd certainly been following her. She continued to glare.

"I'm only doing my job," the detective mumbled. "The salesperson should have removed the tags."

No true apology. Just a bunch of excuses.

"Do you have a boss?"

The man nodded.

"Then lead me to him. I have a good mind to sue you people."

As the crowd dispersed, Eden followed the man to the back of the store. She emerged a half an hour later, slightly less annoyed than she'd been. Apologies had been made but that had not compensated for her humiliation. And even though the store had tried to soothe her feathers by giving her a written apology and a fistful of coupons, she knew that would be her last shopping excursion in Mon Caché.

On her way out, she passed through the electronics department again. A crowd of skinheads were huddled around the same floor model where the detective had lurked. The tallest of the group held the remote and was busy surfing the channels.

An announcer's voice boomed, getting her attention. "Missing going on three weeks is ladies' man, Noah Robbins." Eden's head snap backed, she made a U-turn. "Our station has been flooded with calls from women all over—"

Abruptly the newscaster's voice trailed off.

Dare she ask the holder of the remote to flip back to the channel. One glance in that direction convinced her not to. Given her recent run-in, better to leave well enough alone. Quickly she looked around for another TV, eventually catching the eye of a Native American man.

"Would you mind?" she asked, motioning to the remote he held.

"Not at all." He handed her the rectangular object. Immediately she began to surf the channels. But by the time she'd found the station, the reporter had moved on to another topic.

Feeling like she'd been punched in the gut and her innards ripped out, Eden quickly left the store. She'd been right all along. Noel hadn't been on the up and up from the very beginning. Still, who would have thought he was a fugitive? And what did the reporter mean by, "Our station has been flooded by calls from women . . . ?

Then the awful thought surfaced: Could Noah Robbins be a criminal on the run?

Thirteen

Replaying the newscaster's words in her head, Eden ignored the scenery. She drove by rote, turning onto her block, her stomach still lurching.

"Please God," she whispered, "Don't let Noel—uh—Noah, be out on his deck waiting for me."

She needed to digest the news and wasn't ready to face him yet. What had she been thinking of, getting involved with someone she barely knew? No sirree. It wasn't as if she hadn't known that something about the man didn't add up. She'd just refused to listen to the little voice in the back of her head, and she'd totally ignored her gut. A confrontation right now was absolutely out of the question. She simply wasn't up to it. She'd need time to rehearse, plan what she would say.

Eden pushed open her front door to a ringing phone. Kahlua padded across the floor to greet her. While she attempted to block the door and impede the cat's progress, the answering machine clicked on.

A tentative female voice inquired, "Eden?"

A stranger had her new number? She waited for the woman to speak.

As the woman stumbled over her words, barely making sense, Eden frowned. "Eden uh . . . it's Mrs. Moss. Your mother's uh . . . next-door neighbor."

Forgetting Kahlua, she left the door wide open and bolted for the phone. "Yes, Mrs. Moss."

"Oh Eden, thank God you picked up."

"What's wrong with Mommy?" She hadn't called her mother that in years.

"Well uh . . . that's why I'm calling. There's been a slight uh . . . accident."

Eden suddenly felt faint. She waited for the room to settle, clutching the nearest chair for support. She rode the first wave of nausea.

"Eden, are you there?"

Taking deep breaths, Eden focused on the ceiling. Now wasn't the time to fall apart. Her mother needed her. "I'm here Mrs. Moss. I'm here. Is she all right?"

A beat later. "The doctors say she is, but they're keeping her overnight for observation."

"She's in the hospital?"

"Yes, Downstate Medical. Earlier today she was crossing the street. Using the pedestrian crossing if you please, when this white car flew out of nowhere and just about mowed her down. Thank God for quick reflexes, only the edge of the bumper caught her or she'd probably be—look she's okay. Just bruised up real bad and the doctors think she might have a slight concussion."

A white Buick, Eden thought, processing the information. "I'm coming home, Mrs. Moss," she said before the woman went off on another tangent.

"I thought you would want to. Bill's flying in as well. He called the apartment when I was getting some of your mother's things so I told him what happened. He's agreed to take the next plane in."

"My brother's coming from Germany?" It had to be more serious than Mrs. Moss was letting on. Bill didn't disrupt his life for anyone.

"Umm hmm. Says he can easily move his vacation up

a week or so. He was coming to the States anyway, didn't you know that? That boy is just so loving. A real devoted son."

And I'm a cold slab of liver. The words hung unspoken in the air. "Thank you, Mrs. Moss. Thanks for letting me know."

"Don't mention it."

After obtaining the hospital's number, Eden hung up. She brushed back a tear. Her extended leave had just ended. It was time to go home. It wasn't like she could have pushed Pelican Air off forever, anyway. Not if she wanted to keep her job.

"Hey, Rob, you ready for this?"

Noah propped the cordless phone between his ear and shoulder, waiting for his buddy to go on.

"I think I found your white Buick."

"Yeah?"

Excitement coursed through Noah. He suddenly wished Eden were with him to hear the news. After jogging, he'd stopped by her place and found her gone. Initially he'd been worried. As the hours ticked by, his anxiety grew and he'd become frantic. Had Eden been there right now, she would have seen Joe Cool dissolve before her eyes and a nervous wreck take his place. Glancing at his hands, he realized they'd fisted. He closed his eyes and imagined his grip around the neck of whomever had hurt her. One twist. One wring. Christ he could even hear the pop. No, he had to stop his wayward thoughts. He'd never been a violent man, not until someone had deliberately set out to kill him and Eden. Messing with him was one thing. Messing with Eden, another. He planned on doing everything in his power to ensure they stayed alive.

"I ran a check on the license plate just like I promised," Freckles boomed.

"Get to the point."

"It's a stolen vehicle."

Noah let out a long, low whistle, every muscle in his body tensed. His voice was harsh when he responded. "Who's the owner?"

A beat went by, then two. *Drumroll please.* Freckles had an annoying habit of dragging out a response.

"Well, that's the thing. It's a company-owned vehicle registered to Pelican Air."

Noah felt another wave of excitement engulf him. It didn't serve to display too much interest. Freckles, sensing a rapt audience, only provided trickles of information. "Go on," he said, making his voice deliberately testy.

"Pelican filed a stolen car report several months ago. Kinda strange that the vehicle would show up on the other coast. . . ."

Noah didn't have time for irrelevant chitchat. "Has the car been impounded?"

Another pause. "Well, that's the thing. The automobile's still missing."

Noah bit back a crude oath and ended the call. Hopes of wringing the vermin's neck evaporated. He'd even fantasized about doing it publicly. Eden would be there to watch and he'd be her hero.

Instinct told Noah all the pieces were finally coming together. It would only be a matter of time before he unraveled the puzzle. Right before the end of most cases he was usually pumped, but this time he was angrier than he'd ever been. It had been so easy to attribute the crash to pilot's error, now he wasn't so sure. His gut told him that something about the way the plane had literally fallen out of the sky stunk. It had felt good to be able to pin Flight 757's crash on someone. That way he hadn't felt so helpless about his friend's death. Ty was the closest he'd come to having a brother.

But why the attempts on his life? Why the threats to Eden? They must be on to something. Somebody undoubtedly had something to hide. The attempts on his life had intensified after he'd been on TV, though he'd merely been doing his job, just like he always did.

Noah mentally ticked off all the avenues he and Eden had explored so far. They'd considered the poor maintenance angle. They'd even gotten hold of the logs and reviewed the plane's mechanical history. Hitting a temporary dead end, they'd then focused on the flight delay. When Eden had revealed the surprising news that the plane had been held awaiting the arrival of a cooler, he'd been hell-bent on finding out who had ordered the delay and which department had accepted responsibility. Any day now, Eden's friend should have that answer.

Noah suspected that Eden had been the last person to speak with Rodney Joyner. What had the pilot's demeanor been like? Had he said something seemingly insignificant, but extremely vital to the case? Dead men couldn't speak and Eden seemed the logical person to pursue, up until he'd gone and foolishly fallen in love with her. He'd been told she'd been Joyner's lover and confidante. Acting on a whim, he'd sensed she'd be heading cross country and he'd been lucky to rent the house next door. Initially, he'd hoped that with some subtle questioning, she'd break and admit that Rodney Joyner was the drunken playboy the papers had made him out to be. But she'd remained loyal. True-blue in fact. He liked that quality in a woman.

Noah heard scratching at his back door. He frowned, then realizing it was Kahlua, cracked a smile. Hustling to answer the cat's call, he scooped the feline into his arms and nuzzled her furry head. Desire suddenly pulled at him. He needed to see Eden. He'd camp on her doorstep all day if that's what it took. If she didn't show up, he would call the police.

Eden ignored the buzzer. She already knew who was on the other end.

The ringing persisted. It sounded like someone had put their shoulder to the bell. Dumping the contents of the lingerie drawer on the sofa, she took her time sorting through flimsy underwear. Muttering, she thrust bras and panties into an open suitcase and turned her attention to another drawer of clothes.

The ringing continued.

"Go away," Eden muttered, "Just go away."

"Eden, I know you're in there. Your car's parked out front."

The sound of Noah's voice made her shiver. This made no sense at all. She'd just received confirmation the man was in hiding. He could be a serial killer for all she knew.

"Eden! Let me in." The racket almost deafened her. "Want the entire neighborhood to hear your business?"

That did it. Eden flung a pair of black lace bikini panties on top of a bright red teddy. Confrontation time! She stomped her way toward the door and flung it open: Denim and attitude filled her doorway. Noah held Kahlua out, his lopsided smile tugged at her heart. She wouldn't weaken. Wouldn't let him get to her.

Eden accepted the cat and grumbled, "What do you want?"

"You."

Refusing to make eye contact, she focused on the cleft in his chin while the clean, fresh smell of him filled her nostrils. *Stay strong, Eden.*

"Aren't you going to invite me in?"

"I hadn't planned on it."

Another devastating smile and she was a goner. He gently moved her aside and without waiting for an invitation strolled in.

"You can't come—"

"What's this?" Mouth welded into a grim line, his hand gestured to the half-filled suitcase.

"What does it look like?" Eden set Kahlua down.

Noah arched an eyebrow. Using his index finger, he picked up the black lace bikini panties and swung the tiny scrap of lace off the tip. "Going somewhere?"

"Home." Eden remained at the open door, one arm crossed over the other, eyeballing him.

Crumpling the panties in his palm, Noah eyed her warily. "That's awfully sudden." He waited for her to say something.

Sick of parrying, Eden challenged, "When were you planning on telling me, Noah?"

She watched for his reaction but he didn't even flinch. "When was I planning on telling you what?"

His nonchalance infuriated her. Losing it, she pointed a finger at him. "You're on the run, aren't you? You're hiding out. That must mean you're in some kind of trouble?"

The panties fell or got tossed into the open suitcase, she wasn't sure which. The same finger holding them now stroked his chin. He stared at her for what seemed a long, long time. "What makes you think that?"

Eden moved in closer. She wanted to see his eyes. Her mother once told her that you could tell a liar by the way their eyes shifted. "I went shopping today—"

"Yes?"

"I walked into the electronics department. The news came on. The newscaster said you were missing."

Noah's index finger made stroking motions against his chin. "And so you immediately concluded that I'd done something evil, that I must be wanted in several states."

He'd verbalized exactly what she'd thought. "Well are you?"

Noah crossed the room, looming over her, his fingers pressing into her shoulders. She ignored the warm, tingly feeling starting in her toes and working its way upward. She wouldn't let her treacherous hormones betray her.

"Lady, what does it take to gain your trust?"

Honesty. "Noah, if you're in some kind of trouble, why can't you just admit it."

His hands dropped to his sides. His eyes pleaded for understanding. "Would you believe me if I told you that I have no prior arrest record, nor am I on the FBI's most-wanted list?"

This time she answered his question with a question. "Why should I?"

Her response apparently floored him. His bravado all but disappeared. He raised a tentative hand to grasp her arm. "Eden we've been through hell and back together. By now, surely, you must have some sense of the type of person I am."

Determined not to let emotions get in the way, she ignored both fluttering stomach and fast beating heart. "What's a girl supposed to think? All I know is that you've lied to me over and over. First, you introduced yourself as Noel Robinson, said you were a furnisher designer whose best friend was killed in the Pelican crash. After I found some incriminating evidence telling me you weren't who you'd said you were, you reluctantly admitted to being Noah Robbins, reporter extraordinaire—"

Noah's smile filtered through. "I never said that—the extraordinaire part, that is."

He was trying to make light of the situation but she

wasn't about to let him off the hot seat. She fixed him with a stony glare. "Don't try to play me."

"I'm not. It would be useless. You've already made up your mind that I'm a criminal."

He was right. She had tried and sentenced him. Every instinct told her he was hiding something.

Noah removed his wallet from his trouser pocket, rummaging through, he took out a business card. "Here," he said, tucking the card into her palm. "Call Detective Young, he's one of the police officers we spoke with after the Zodiac sank. He'll vouch for me."

Eden stared at the plain white card. Should she call his bluff? She doubted the police would agree to testify he was an upstanding citizen if he weren't on the level.

Still holding the card in hand, she forced herself to apologize. "Look, I'm sorry. It's just that I heard your name on the news and I made the obvious assumption."

"It's okay, you're forgiven," Noah said, quickly. Too quickly. "Now tell me why you're going home."

And although she knew he'd subtly shifted the conversation, she found that she needed to talk to someone. So she told him all about the call from her mother's next-door neighbor, Mrs. Moss. About how she suspected her mother's little mishap was no accident, ending with how scared she was. Ten minutes later when she began to cry in earnest, she let him wrap his arms around her.

Fourteen

They were seated in the passenger lounge of the American Airlines terminal. Eden, traveling standby, waited for a boarding pass. "I'm going to miss you," Noah said, snuggling her in his arms.

"Promise we'll stay in touch." She traced his lips with her fingers and a wave of desire flooded his belly. He couldn't let her walk out of his life like that. There was much too much unfinished business between them.

Impulsively, Noah added, "I'll do better than stay in touch. Perhaps I can drive your car back. You did say that you were having it trailered. That's probably costing you a bundle." He tapped the pet carrier at Eden's feet. "Kahlua would enjoy a nice comfortable ride home instead of being stuck under some airplane seat." As if to confirm the truth of his statement, the cat peered from between the metal grids, looking shell-shocked. She meowed pitifully.

"Just look at my buddy. She's petrified. That's no way to treat a lady." Noah pretended to glare at Eden, then winked. "You didn't even tranquilize her."

"I couldn't bear the thought."

Sensing Eden weakening, Noah decided to press the issue. "Kahlua might be less scared if I drove her. If I get a friend to drive my car, we could form a caravan and see some of the good old U. S. of A. at the same time. How about it?"

"I'd hate to put you through that trouble."

He almost had her. "No trouble at all, as long as you don't mind the mileage. Besides, I'll look forward to Kahlua's company. I love your cat—love her owner too." Noah kissed Eden's cheek and buried his nose in her hair. The cloying smell of wildflowers filled his nostrils. It was getting more difficult to put her on that plane. "I'm going back to work in a week or so," he muttered, attempting to disguise the frog in his throat. "It's not like New York's really out of my way. It's in the general vicinity of home."

Startled cognac eyes flashed him silent questions. Her bottom lip quivered. "You report to an office? I'd assumed you were a freelance journalist."

He would have to tell her the truth, and soon, before she found out from a stranger. Not now though, not when she was about to board a plane to see her injured mother. It would wait until the next time they met.

Funny, but before meeting Eden, he hadn't thought much about deception. He'd merely been a man with a mission, subscribing to the code, any means to an end. Ironically, that callous outlook had turned around to bite him. Now how to tell the woman he loved that he'd been stringing her along? That his entire life was a lie and he had a whole other identity? Eden would never understand his reasons when even he wasn't clear.

"I don't freelance," he said, answering her question. He wrapped her tightly in his arms and held her trembling body close. "Ssssh. Relax, the flight will be over before you know it."

Around them the sounds of shuffling feet and sniffing good-byes grew louder. The boarding process had begun.

Noah looked at the passengers at the gate. Students,

professional types, and mothers with young children jostled for positions on line. Standing off to the side, was a man with lank brown hair and a droopy expression. For a brief moment their gazes met, then the man fumbled in a knapsack and hurriedly put on a pair of tinted sunglasses. Noah focused his attention on Eden again although he couldn't shake the uneasy feeling that they were being observed. It had been constant ever since the Zodiac episode.

He took Eden's shaking hands in his and rubbed them vigorously. Her palms were clammy. "Honey, you're a strong woman. You've survived losing your fiancé, and I haven't seen you light up a cigarette in days. Jesus you've even tolerated me," he joked, attempting to pull her out of the black funk she wore like a cloak. "We're only talking about a little old plane ride. You know how airplanes work. They're one of the safest modes of transportation. Heck, annually more people die in car accidents. You'll get on board, order a glass of wine, and kick back."

Eden visibly gulped air. "I know you're right. I'm going to have to get a handle on this somehow. Flying's part of my job. I can't afford to fall apart every time I get on a plane."

"Spoken like a true champ. Trust me, the more you fly, the more you'll conquer the fear. I have every confidence in you." He hugged her tighter, before carefully posing the question. "Tell me, do you associate airplanes and terminals with memories of Rod?"

The vein at the side of Eden's neck pulsed. She made a quick recovery. "Why do you ask?"

The question hung in the air. Talk about feeling like a rat.

"I thought it might help if you told me about the last time you spoke to Rod. You mentioned that he'd called you minutes before his plane took off."

"He did."

There was such a look of abject pain on Eden's face, that he almost didn't say it. "I don't want to upset you, Eden. But maybe if you focused on the tender things Rod said to you, his professions of love—"

Eden squared her shoulders and stood up abruptly. He'd gone too far. Pushed her to the limit. She retrieved the pet kennel at her feet and set Kahlua on top of a chair. The cat purred loudly.

"Professions of love?" Her words were followed by a derisive snort. "I don't believe Rod was capable. At least not in the traditional sense. Monogamy and Rodney didn't exactly go hand in hand." She picked up the carrier and headed toward the counter where a representative in a navy blue jacket punched buttons on a computer keyboard.

"Eden, wait!"

When she turned back he was surprised to find her dry-eyed. Crossing the space separating them, he placed his hands on her shoulders, shifting her body to face him. "How about telling me what really happened that evening. Start at the very beginning."

He could tell she was struggling with the decision, vacillating. Maybe if he gave her one more push.

A slightly nasal voice boomed over the intercom, "Standby passenger Sommers, please approach the podium."

With a pinched expression on her face, Eden headed in that direction. She accepted the boarding pass from the agent and returned to his side. "Looks like I have to go."

Noah took possession of the kennel. Kahlua purred. If he had anything to do with it, he, Eden, and her cat would not be apart long. Draping his free arm around her shoulders, he walked with her toward the departure gate. It was the shortest walk of his life. Deciding to drop his line of questioning, he said, "Perhaps we can talk about this some other time. Maybe when I drop off Kahlua."

"Maybe."

"Last call for passengers boarding flight 296." The same nasal voice announced.

Eden's footsteps faltered. She undid the clasp of her purse, and fumbled inside. "I really appreciate your offer. I thought I had an extra key to my car but I'll have to Fedex you the spare. Tomorrow I'll call the towing place and cancel, and I'll call you with directions to my home." She gazed at him, blinked rapidly, and continued in a ragged voice. "Thanks Noah, I've really enjoy—"

His finger grazed her lips silencing her. "Don't say it. This isn't good-bye, Eden. We'll talk soon—tonight." Pulling her into his arms, he unleashed all his pent-up emotions in that kiss.

Eden Sommers might not be aware of it, but she and he had only just begun.

Hours later, Noah took his time punching out the digits, simultaneously composing what he'd say in his head. He'd put Eden on that plane what seemed an eternity ago. Already he missed her terribly. The phone rang and rang, rattling his already overwrought nerves. Finally, an answering machine clicked on.

The recorded message ceased and Noah spoke. "Hey Gary, I was hoping to catch you at home. We need to talk about getting me back—"

He heard the sound of a receiver being picked up on the other end, then his boss' voice. "Lay it on me, boy."

Noah grinned. Gary, the crafty bastard screened his calls, hardly unusual given their line of work. Noah fin-

ished what he'd been about to say, adding. "I'm ready
to come home and more than ready to go back to work.
There's gotta be an assignment out there with my name
written on it."

His boss chuckled. "Try assignments, Rob. Your little
vacation followed by that forced leave of absence did
us in. I've got plenty to keep you busy."

"I look forward to being busy."

"Good. Incidentally, we should be publishing our
findings and recommendations about that Pelican Air
crash soon."

"The hell you will." Noah bit back an ugly oath. Gary
was baiting him. He'd known that though officially off
the case, Noah'd been conducting his own investigation.

In an all-out effort to appease him, Gary's voice lowered in a conspiratorial whisper. Noah knew when he
was about to be snowed. "Lighten up, man, we've had
a lot of pressure to wrap things up. You didn't seem to
be making much progress so we had to move forward.
Congress was breathing down our necks, families of the
victims screaming. The world's premier accident investigation agency has to stay on top of things."

Noah counted to five then said between clenched
teeth, "And what did the agency conclude?"

"We'll discuss that when you get back. Hey, what's
with you and the Sommers chick? She wouldn't be the
reason you have this sudden desire to work?"

Noah bit back the invective and through clenched
teeth snapped, "That's none of your business."

"Ah ha! So your sudden willingness to return does
have something to do with the bimbo stewardess."

"Eden is a quality assurance supervisor, not a flight
attendant." Noah decided to let the adjective go, what
would be the point calling his boss on the "bimbo"
part. It would only ensure a heated discussion. The man

had never been politically correct in his life, simply didn't care to be. Besides, he'd already accomplished his mission. He'd gotten Gary to agree he could return to work.

For the first time that evening Noah smiled. His return to the Washington, DC area would serve a dual purpose: he'd keep an eye on Eden and at the same time conduct in-person investigations with Pelican's staff. Though it might take some doing, he'd make sure that the reports didn't get published until he and Eden had a handle on this thing. That just meant they'd have to work like demons.

Eden woke up shivering. Underneath her, the sheets were soaked. Sitting up in bed, she brought a limp hand to her forehead and wiped away the dampness. The dream had returned. This time in living color and with a macabre twist to it. She'd been seated on that plane, listening to the screams of terrified passengers; feeling desperate and hopeless, the acrid smell of smoke filling her nostrils. There had been no Rod or Noah sightings this time. The dream's focus had been a little black box. A package, actually, the type you'd mail to a friend. The box had been stowed in the galley. She'd noticed it during a trip to the bathroom, it had been sitting on the counter. Sensing it was no ordinary package, she'd given it more than a second look.

As the dream progressed, the box had become larger and larger, taking on almost humanoid proportions. At one point it had grown feet and come dancing down the aisle, even taking the seat right next to her. But when the box spoke, an annoying ticktocking obscured its words, and it had been difficult to understand. Frustrated, she'd yelled at it, and in front of her eyes, it had self-destructed, dissolving into millions of pieces.

A walking, dancing, ticking box? What a ridiculous thought. There'd been too much talk of flight delays and coolers. She was bone-weary, that's what it was. Too many late nights watching scary movies were taking their toll. Tiredness did strange things to a person, she'd heard, even made them hallucinate. For too long, she'd been operating purely on nervous energy.

Knowing that their mother needed no additional stress, especially that caused by hyperactive children, Eden had convinced her brother and family to move into her apartment temporarily. Once Carrie had been released from Downstate Medical Center, Eden had moved into the brownstone on Avenue J. The doctor had mandated nourishing meals and plenty of bed rest, and Eden aimed to make sure his orders were followed.

Squinting, she focused on an ornate jewelry box on top of the dresser. She rubbed the sleep from her eyes, and peered through splayed fingers at the red box. After a minute or so, she swung her legs over the edge of the bed and waited for the fog to recede.

One eye remained centered on the box. It's bright red lacquer and heavy brass lock got her attention. Grandma Nell's legacy had been sitting there all night, in full view. No wonder she'd dreamt of boxes. The jewelry box had been left to Eden's mother. It held all the expensive baubles her grandparents had picked up in their travels. Eden doubted her mother had opened it recently, much less worn any of the gems it held.

Eden shook her head in another attempt to clear it, her thoughts now on Noah. She should try reaching him, she supposed. Though he'd said he would call her, she needed to take the initiative. She hadn't given him her mother's number. Dismissing the thought soon after it had surfaced, she mentally ticked off a list of items that needed to be accomplished today.

Yawning, she peered at her watch. She'd overslept

again. This was becoming a bad habit especially since she was due back at work in a few days. Time to grab a cup of coffee and go call Bill and Helga.

"Eden," the whispered inquiry floated through the closed door.

"What are you doing up? You're supposed to be in bed," Eden whispered back.

Her mother's head emerged through a crack in the door, followed by her entire body. A brightly colored scarf covered her wild mop of hair. She smiled brightly. "I made a pot of coffee." She waved an empty mug in Eden's direction. "Want some?"

"Thanks. But I'll get it. You need to get back to bed."

"Says who?"

"Says me." Eden pointed an imperious finger. "I'll call the doctor if you don't."

An unintelligible grumble followed. Holding her ribs with one hand, the cup in the other, her mother made a U-turn. Eden felt a pang of guilt. "Tell you what. We'll sit at the kitchen table just for a few minutes, enjoy our coffee, and catch up."

"Sounds good to me." Cognac eyes so like her own sparkled with mischief. "Good, we can talk about that fellow you're seeing."

"What fellow, Mother?"

"You know. The one who answered your phone." Cassie took a seat at the table and waited for Eden to join her. "What's he look like?" she asked the moment Eden sat down.

In a delaying tactic, Eden sipped the steaming brew.

"Is he a—stud muffin? That's what you young people call the hunks of today."

Eden sputtered and set the coffee cup down. "Gawd, mother. You've been watching too many soap operas."

"Well is he?"

Eden knew there would be no peace for the weary. "Yes, Mother. Noah's very good-looking."

"Is he nice? There's something about the name, Noah, that's got strength to it. See, even hearing his name brings stars to your eyes."

"I don't—"

The phone rang. Glad for the interruption, Eden rose to answer. She glared at her mother, picked up the receiver, and covered the mouthpiece. "Go back to bed." Removing her hand, she said, "Hello."

"Hey, little sis. How's it going?"

A smile tugged the corners of her mouth. Ever since she was old enough to remember, Bill had always called her "little sis."

"We're managing. How are you and the little ones holding up? Finding everything okay?"

"Yup. Your niece and nephew are having the time of their lives. I caught them out on the terrace yesterday about to water-balloon some poor old man."

Eden's laughter rippled. "Thank God that's all they were doing."

"Got a couple of messages for you."

Eden held her breath. Was it the one she waited for?

"Some woman called Sinclair Morgan says you need to get in touch with her. She wants you to either get a physical or go see the company doctor. I'm not sure. I'll have to listen to the message again."

Eden exhaled. "No need to. It's been handled. I'm going back to work on Monday."

Bill groaned. "Are you really ready, Eden? Don't let anyone railroad you." She could tell by his voice he was concerned.

"It's time. Besides, I'm going to need money soon."

"I'll give you some."

They went back and forth.

Bill continued, "You've gotten quite a few phone calls. When I pick up there's no one on the line."

"Most likely wrong numbers," Eden said with more conviction than she felt. Oh God! It was happening all over again.

"And another thing, some guy called a couple of times. I didn't quite catch his name. He left a uh—personal message on your answering machine."

Please let it be Noah. "What did he say?"

"Something about loving you and missing you—I—uh—saved it." Bill cleared his throat. Sounding rather embarrassed, he continued, "He called back late last night, but said he was on the road and couldn't be reached. I gave him mom's number. Sounded like a nice guy."

"He is."

Fifteen

Noah knew he was in the city by the size of the buildings and the way traffic picked up. Behind him, and in the lane on either side, cabbies in yellow taxis honked their horns rudely. The drivers zipped from one lane to another, narrowly missing cars to the right and left of them. He glanced at the clock on the dashboard noting the time. A little after three. Not quite rush hour. Hopefully, Eden's apartment was close by, still it wouldn't hurt to call just to be sure.

Minutes later, after fighting the guy to the right of him, Noah was able to pull over. He eased into a space at the curb just as another car slid out. Fumbling for the cell phone on the dashboard, he positioned the instrument between ear and shoulder. Kahlua's contented purr filled the car's interior. He tossed the cat in the cage beside him an affectionate glance, stuck his fingers between the metal grid and scratched the feline's ears. "You'll see your mother soon, hon."

Where was that number Eden's brother had given him? He located the scrap of paper in the glove compartment and dialed the 718 area code. After a couple of rings someone picked up.

"Hello."

The woman had a European accent, the voice definitely wasn't Eden's. Must be the sister-in-law she'd mentioned. Inflecting enthusiasm into his voice, Noah tried not to let his disappointment show. "Noah Robbins here. Is Eden in?"

"Ah, Noah." The warm, friendly response boosted his confidence. She knew who he was. "Eden's not here. She's back at her apartment. Do you need the number?"

"I have it." He thanked the woman and rang off.

Noah placed the second call, simultaneously struggling to gain control of his emotions. He hadn't earned the name Joe Cool for nothing. He, more than anyone, knew that it didn't pay to show a woman that you cared too deeply. You'd only get hurt. And he knew all about hurt. Wasn't he the one who'd come home to an empty apartment, found his furniture gone, and a Dear John letter tacked to the refrigerator. Still it had been ten long days since he'd seen Eden and he missed her so badly it hurt. Just thinking of her made him tremble with longing.

A breathless "Hello," and Eden was on the line. A television blasted in the background. He couldn't find his voice and she repeated the greeting.

"Hi, there," he said.

"Noah? Where are you?"

Lowering the car window, he scanned the area looking for signs that would reveal his location. "Fifty-seventh," he said, eyeballing the post on the corner.

"And?"

"Lex—"

"Lexington. Close to Bloomingdale's."

Only a woman would make that association. He smiled, spotting the imposing concrete high-rise, streams of people swinging through the glass doors. "Yeah that's right."

"Busy section of town."

"I noticed." Why was she stalling? "I'll need directions."

"Is Kahlua all right?"

"Fine. She's been wonderful company."

She seemed to hesitate then eventually said, "I'm on the west side. Take—"

Noah jotted directions as Eden gave him the details. She sounded like he felt. Nervous and edgy.

No sooner had Eden hung up, than the phone rang. She lowered the TV's volume and raced to answer. Must be Noah again.

Jorge, her Puerto Rican doorman's thick accent, filled her ear. "Mees Sommers, you have an envelope at the front desk."

Eden ran through her options. Pick up the envelope or change clothes and touch up her makeup? Vanity prevailed. It was probably only Pelican anyway, and she'd told them she'd be in on Monday.

"Tell you what, Jorge. I'm expecting a visitor in about—" Eden calculated how long it would take for Noah to get there, figuring in traffic and parking. She added, "Twenty minutes. His name is Mr. Robbins. Give him my envelope, after you announce him."

"Sure thing, Mees Sommers."

Even that short conversation had cost her valuable time. She raced for her closet. What to wear? What to wear? Nothing too fancy. Nothing that would make it look like she'd been primping. Still, something dynamite. In her excitement she stepped over the open suitcase of soiled garments on the closet floor and almost went flying. Steadying herself, she flicked through the racks, mentally examining and discarding options.

Outside, the day hinted of the warm summer to come. A light breeze blew through the open windows, bringing with it a hundred city odors: the noxious fumes of backfiring trucks, the mouthwatering smells of street vendors, and that indescribable smell that only New Yorkers knew. Humming a popular tune, she smiled at her reflection in the mirror.

Suddenly, it came to her. She'd wear red. Red made her feel good. It was a power color she'd once been told. Impulsively, she shimmied into a thigh-high red mini-dress that clung to her curves. It was the kind of dress you'd throw on to go shopping or if you were meeting a girlfriend for lunch. Sticking her feet into flat red sandals, she headed for the bathroom and makeup. Ten minutes later, she emerged, hair secured in a knot at the top of her head, cheeks and lips slightly tinged red.

Eden cast a cursory glance around the apartment. Despite the fact that Helga and Bill had left it neat as a pin, she plumped up the cushions of the old-fashioned divan, then stooped to pick up a piece of lint from the dark wooden floors. The ringing phone made her jump.

Noah, so soon! She wasn't ready. *Breathe, Eden. Breathe.*

So as not to appear anxious, she let the phone ring once, twice, then counted to five.

"Yes, Jorge?" she finally said.

Nothing on the other end.

"Jorge? Hello?"

Click.

She felt the nausea build, saw the room fade and come back into focus. Was she overreacting? No one knew she was home except for her family, Lori, and Sinclair. Bill had said he'd gotten a number of hangups, was that pure coincidence or a veiled warning? Either way, time to get her number changed.

The phone rang again. Eden's panic built. Pressing a hand to her chest, she debated not answering. But what if it was Noah?

What if? She somehow managed a tentative, "hello."

"Mees Som—"

"Yes Jorge?" Her thudding heart accelerated.

"Meester Robbins is here to see you."

"Send him up," Eden said more curtly than she meant, "and don't forget to give him that envelope."

Elation took the place of anxiety. Noah was in her lobby. He'd brought her cat. The warm fuzzy feeling in the pit of her stomach had little to do with Kahlua. Who was she kidding?

She gave the place a quick once-over and tried to view it with an objective eye. Not more than 600 square feet, the apartment was small, tasteful, and cozy. Since she'd been big on privacy, she'd added an attractive divider and turned the L-shaped studio into a one bedroom. In the living room, a cream-colored canvass couch ran the length of one wall; its light color a delightful contrast to highly polished wooden floors. A smattering of handwoven rugs covered dark mahogany floors. Ivory walls held a collection of primitive art, running the gamut from African masks to musical instruments.

The doorbell rang.

She couldn't do it. Couldn't put one foot in front of the other to answer. But the truth was she wanted her cat and desperately wanted to see Noah.

"Eden," he called.

Even his voice made her shiver. "I'm coming," somehow got lodged in her throat.

An invisible hand pushed her toward the door. She struggled with locks and fumbled with the safety chain. At last the door swung open.

"Well, hello."

He was there bigger than life. And despite her doubts, her misgivings, nothing about her feelings had changed. She wanted him just as badly as she had before.

"My God, you look wonderful," Noah said, stepping inside. "Tell me you didn't go through all that trouble for me." He slid past and began circling her.

She would neither deny nor confirm his statement as all six-foot-four of him invaded her space, making her apartment appear smaller than ever. She could barely breathe, much less answer him. Carrying the cat's kennel by the handle, he pulled her into his arms. She closed her eyes enjoying the feel of him, the familiar clean smell of him. His soul-searching kiss actually made her knees buckle. She'd almost forgotten the emotions that his kisses unleashed. Reality check. Kahlua's kennel whacked her back. An angry hiss reminded them of the forgotten cat.

"Better let Kahlua out," Eden whispered, reluctantly breaking the kiss.

"Sure thing." Noah set the carrier down. He released the latch freeing the cat. Kahlua, tail at half-mast, stalked off, stopping only to toss a baleful glare over one shoulder. "How's your mother?" Noah asked, straightening up.

"Recovering. The police still can't find the person that ran her down."

Noah shook his head and made a *tssking* sound. After a while he turned his attention back to her apartment, planted both hands on his hips and looked around. "Nice setup."

"Thanks. I did my best."

He whistled. "And a remarkable job it is. Eclectic, tasteful, and very much you." He surveyed the room again, missing nothing. "Now before I forget." He retrieved a crumpled envelope from his pocket and handed it over. "Your doorman asked me to give you this."

Eden glanced at the plain white envelope. The handwriting, a spidery scrawl, was not one she recognized. Clutching the unopened envelope, she asked, "Can I get you something to drink?"

Noah flopped onto the couch and stretched out his legs. He stared at the images on the silent TV then back at her. "A beer, if you have one, and something to munch on if it's not too much trouble. God, I forgot just how brutal New York traffic can be. DC's a piece of cake in com—"

She jumped on his words. "So that's where you're from. I suspected as much."

Noah blinked, but made a quick recovery. "You did, did you? Where's that beer with my name written on it?"

"Coming up in a minute."

She gave him a mock curtsy and headed for the kitchen.

Eden returned with a tray holding a platter of cheese and crackers and two Michelobs, the envelope propped between the bottles. Noah relieved her of the tray, setting it down on an exquisite coffee table, an intricate combination of wrought iron and glass.

"Are you planning on opening that envelope?" he asked. For some inexplicable reason, he sensed she was delaying that task. The first rush of jealousy hit him. Could the note be from an old boyfriend, or current one for that matter? They'd never discussed previous involvements. He'd simply assumed that Rodney Joyner's death had left her single and available.

"Eventually."

He took a swig of beer and bit into a cracker. "Don't sound so enthused."

"All right I'll open it."

She slid a perfectly manicured nail under the flap. He focused on her face watching for a reaction. When

she unfolded the note and scanned its contents a per-
plexed look registered.

"Something wrong?"

Eden nibbled her lower lip, perusing the letter again.

"Eden?"

"Yeah?" She looked up, but didn't really see him.

"What is it?"

"Hmm."

Forgetting his hunger, he slid off the couch and
placed his arm around her shoulders. "Don't give me
that B.S. Something's the matter. Is that a love letter?"
He tried to make light of the situation though every
muscle in his body revolted at the thought. He'd rip
off the eyelids of any man who tried to lay claim to her.

"Here, see for yourself." She handed the note over.

"Shall we sit." Tension slowly eroding, he gestured
to the couch, waiting for her to sit. Glancing at the
crumpled paper then back at her, he continued. "This
is Xeroxed."

"I know that."

"Why would someone send you a cargo manifest."

She took a tiny sip of beer and set the bottle down.
"It's not just any old manifest, look at the date."

"May 5, 1998," Noah repeated. "The date of the Pelican crash."

"Exactly." Eden picked up the bottle and swigged the
liquid. "Look closer. Look at what's listed."

"Alright. What am I missing?"

She slid next to him. A delicately colored nail pointed
out item by item. The smell of wildflowers enveloped
him as cheek to cheek they pored over the crumpled
paper. "Nowhere does it say anything about Baylor Hospital or a human organ for that matter." The last was
whispered.

"You're good." Her closeness had made it increas-
ingly harder to think, much less keep his hands to him-

self. In his excitement, he kissed her. "We're on to something, girl. Was there a letter? An address, maybe?" As if he didn't know the answer.

"No." But for good measure, she turned the envelope upside down, examining the front and flap.

He traced patterns against her cheeks with the tips of his fingers. "God, did I miss you." So much for keeping his cool.

"Me too."

Her admission, lukewarm at best, served to encourage him.

He kissed the nape of her neck and trailed his hands down her arms. Time to tell the truth. He couldn't put it off much longer. When she wrapped her arms around his neck and sighed softly, thoughts of serious conversation were temporarily put on hold as ten frustrating days of loneliness took their toll. This time he kissed her holding nothing back.

Eden tugged at his shirt, located the buttons, and undid them one by one. She slid her hands inside the opening, running her fingers through the curly hairs of his chest. Oh, God! Just the touch of her palms drove him wild. He kept his mouth on hers as he lowered her onto the couch and pressed himself into her. Their desire grew into a live, tangible thing.

"Oh God, girl. I've missed you so much."

"Not as much as I've missed you."

Eden's legs imprisoned him, pulling him closer. There would be no turning back now. He managed to free himself, lower his zipper, and fumble for the foil packet in his wallet. His other hand slid the flimsy scrap of fabric she called underwear aside.

"Help me," he said, ripping open the seal.

Eden slid the sheath on him and helped him into position. Like custom gloves, they fit perfectly. Each thrust elicited a series of ecstatic gasps. Sliding the shoulders of her dress downward, he captured her breasts, molded them gently, then nibbled at the peaks.

"God, Noah!"

"I'm hardly the almighty, baby."

In a simultaneous outpouring of passion they toppled over the edge.

Spent, Eden emitted a contented sigh. Her nose lay in the hollow of his neck. Only a slight movement of her head indicated she was alive. He kissed the soft wooly hair. What would it be like to have her in his life forever and ever? He dismissed the thought, concentrating on the cargo manifest. Who would have sent the list? And what had been their purpose? *Think, Noah. Think. You're rusty, old boy. Someone's trying to tell you something.*

The phone rang. Eden stirred beneath him. The ringing continued and still she made no effort to get up.

"Do you have your answering machine on?" Noah whispered, his tongue teasing the lobes of her ears.

"Umm hmm."

"Umm hmm, yes? Or umm hmm, no?"

She looked at him through glazed eyes, her body language subtly changing, tension slowly returning.

Comprehension dawned. "Jesus, Eden." He leapt off the couch and strode purposefully toward the phone. "Why didn't you tell me it's happening again?"

Adjusting the red dress, and simultaneously avoiding his eyes, she propped herself into a seated position, staring at the silent figures on TV.

Noah picked up the phone and a soft click resounded in his ear. He swore softly. "Dammit!"

Heading back the way he had come, he noted that Eden's concentration was now riveted on the television. Judging from her expression, something or someone had totally captured her attention. There was such a look of abject disbelief on her face that he wanted to go to her, hold her, and assure her that whatever it was couldn't be that bad. Curiosity and his own need for reassurance made him come closer. He froze in his tracks, any thoughts of comforting words fleeing from his head. There he was, a microphone thrust under his nose, bigger than life on her twenty-five-inch screen.

Impulsively, he grabbed the remote and clicked the power off.

Sixteen

"Hey, why did you shut off the TV?" Jumping up, Eden glared at Noah.

"Because we need to talk."

Looking into Noah's solemn face, she was torn between hurling accusations and hearing him out. "Who are you?" she whispered.

"Can we sit down."

"No. I'm comfortable standing."

He reached over to touch her arm but she stepped back, putting distance between them.

"Eden, it's a long story."

"I have all day." Expression bleak, she folded her arms across her breasts. "I'm waiting."

"My real name is Noah Robbins."

"I already know that."

"I'm really not a furniture designer."

"Surprise, surprise! Yet you fed me some story about a deprived childhood apprenticing with a carpenter. Or was it a furniture designer?" She clicked her tongue. "This vocation later became a hobby." She tapped the tip of her shoe against the wooden floor. "Your latest story is that you're a reporter."

"Actually I'm a—"

The phone rang, cutting him off mid-sentence.

Distracted and torn between hearing Noah's latest

fabrication and the person waiting on the other end of the line, she darted a look at the offending instrument.

"The machine will eventually pick up," Noah said. "This talk is long overdue."

They stared at each other. The tension in the air was so thick you could literally cut it with a knife.

The answering machine clicked on and Eden's recorded message filled the room. "Sorry, I'm not available. But please be sure to leave your name, telephone number, and a brief message, I'll call you back as soon as I can." *Beep.*

Heavy breathing on the other end, then a muffled voice. "Mind your own business, witch. Next time you won't be around to hear this."

Taking rapid strides, Noah crossed the room. He grabbed the receiver and shouted into it. "Who the hell are you?" After a second or so he mumbled, "Damn coward, hung up." He slammed the phone down and turned back to her. "Look, Eden, I swear no more lies. If you hear me out this once, I'll tell you everything and at the end, if you decide you want nothing to do with me, I'll understand."

Despite the fact that she was angry with him, very angry, curiosity prevailed. "All right, talk," she said, seating herself on the sofa.

He came to sit next to her, but she sidled away. She couldn't let him touch her, not if she wanted to keep a clear head.

"Eden, I'm a safety inspector. I work for the National Transportation Safety Board. Those men you saw visiting late at night are friends on special assignment at the Seattle branch."

His admission made her sit up and listen. Every airline employee knew who the NTSB was. The agency, based in Washington, DC, was charged by congress to investigate civil aviation accidents throughout the

United States. Was this another one of his stories? "Go on."

"I was the inspector assigned to Flight 757."

No wonder his name and face were familiar. He would have been in the paper and on TV.

"You know our agency has a reputation for impartiality. Since I was fully aware that my best friend was on that plane, I should have refused the case. But I wanted to be a big guy. I was gonna handle it." His voice broke.

So there had been a friend. She wanted to reach out and touch him but steeled herself against making contact. He hadn't lied just once, he'd lied over and over.

"Initially, I figured I'd just do my job, write my report, and that would be that."

"Why didn't you?"

"My gut told me there was something wrong from the very beginning. Most accidents occur during take-offs and landings and airplanes don't usually fall from the sky, especially when they've been airborne for more than an hour. Then when the black box was found—"

"The black box was found?" She must have missed that particular news article.

"Yes, the cockpit voice recorder, not the FDR."

"The Flight Data Recorder's still missing, then?"

"Yes." Noah cracked his knuckles and for the first time Eden realized that telling her this wasn't easy for him. She desperately wanted to believe him, but how could she trust anything he said?

"Was there something on that recorder that made you believe that Rod was to blame?" she probed.

"Yes." Noah wasn't able to look at her. His fingers massaged his temples and he stared straight ahead.

"Why was it so important you find me?" She held up her hand, silencing whatever he was about to say. "Don't deny it, your move to Mercer Island was deliberate."

"I—" Noah darted her a quick look, wincing at her unsmiling face.

"It was hardly a coincidence that you moved next door."

"I was taken off the case and forced to take vacation," he said, cracking his knuckles again. "The powers that be felt that I'd become too personally involved. And I'd begun receiving death threats. That vacation later became an extended leave. So when I learned through friends at the agency that you'd be moving to the Pacific Northwest, I thought maybe if I talked to you, I'd be able to put closure to this thing. See, I knew you were the last person Rodney Joyner spoke to. I thought you might be able to confirm that he'd been—"

Eden stood up, her voice trembling. "Drinking? Let's not play games. You've always thought he was drunk. That's why you questioned me and made those inferences about him being a party boy. That's why you wanted to crucify him. Let me tell you something." She pointed a finger close to his nose. "I was fully aware of Rod's faults. But one of them was not drinking and piloting. I must have spoken to him dozens of times before a flight, in fact moments before takeoff. This particular evening was no exception. Yes, Rodney was upset, but he was coherent, considering that I'd broken things off with him." The last slipped out, she hadn't meant to say that much.

"You'd broken up with him?" Noah's green eyes fixed on hers.

"I know what you're thinking," Eden continued. "Impaired judgment. Sorry to blow your theory, but Rod knew it was coming. He'd had weeks to adjust. I'd threatened to break the engagement when I found out—well—look, he wasn't perfect, but he wasn't half as conniving as you. You used me, Noah. You skillfully worked your way into my pants, just so you could get the information you needed. That's despicable." She felt herself tear up. She couldn't let him see her cry. Wouldn't.

"Eden that's not—"

"Eden, nothing," she said, refusing to give in to his pleading or his woeful looks. The man was a con artist. "Shouldn't you be thinking about leaving?" She threw him a pointed look.

He stood, examining the wrinkles in his khakis and brushing an imaginary piece of lint off his knees. "I had my friend drive my car home. I thought I'd take the shuttle back." He moved as if to comfort her, but she stepped out of his reach. "Eden, I'm sorry."

"Not sorrier than I am. If you catch a cab right now you might make the seven o'clock shuttle. May I have my keys please." She held out her hand.

Noah's emerald eyes burned a searing path across her face, the muscle of his jaw twitching. His warm hand brushed hers as he curled the key ring into her palm.

The connection was electric. She stepped back before she could be short-circuited.

"Eden, whether you choose to believe it or not, I love you."

"Please leave."

She waited until the door closed before letting the tears come. When would she get it through her thick skull that the entire male gender couldn't be trusted?

Lori Goldmuntz entered the crew lounge, a pot of coffee in one hand, two pieces of fattening danish in the other. "Shall I top that off?" she pointed to Eden's half-empty cup. When Eden nodded, she poured the liquid in the cup, and set the danish down. She took a seat opposite Eden. "Why so glum? You've only been back a couple of days. Sinclair couldn't have gotten to you already?"

Eden managed a watery smile. "Sinclair has nothing to do with my mood."

"Cigarette?" Lori shook a Dunhill from a red pack.

"No, thanks. I quit."

"Good for you. You were smoking like a chimney for a while, especially after Rod died. Oh, I'm sorry." Perfectly manicured nails flew to Lori's mouth. "How insensitive of me."

For the second time that morning, Eden managed a wobbly smile. "Just goes to prove anyone can quit."

Her friend's bottle-blond head wagged back and forth as she busily attacked the danish. Looking up, she spoke between bites. "Michael's having the hardest time finding out who brought the cooler to the airport. Even worse, none of the guys seem to remember delivering it to the plane. Michael's stumped. Nowhere in the system is that thing registered. He's going to try to contact his source. You know, the guy that's been laid off."

The news was hardly surprising considering neither cooler nor organ had been documented on the cargo manifest. Eden was now convinced that the cooler wasn't just any old cooler. Her nightmare had helped to drive home that point. Wisely, she kept her thoughts to herself, remembering what Noah had once said. He'd felt that both Lori and Michael relayed the details to too many people. "Lori, do you think our ex-employee would be willing to speak with me?"

"Let me check with Michael. If it's cool, we'll set something up."

Eden switched the subject. "Did you ever find out who the delay was charged to?"

"Yup. It was coded a flight-crew delay."

Eden spoke hesitantly, "That would mean—the plane was held—waiting for one of the pilots."

"Either that, or the decision to delay the flight came from someone in the cockpit."

"Gee, I hadn't thought of that." Joining Lori, Eden bit into her danish. They were onto something at last. Should she call Noah? An impossible thought. Their business together had concluded. She couldn't trust the man.

"On another note, whatever happened to Noel Robinson? I could have sworn that was a budding romance waiting to bloom."

Did the woman have ESP? Eden sputtered and took several seconds swallowing. Lori patted her back. Eventually she answered, "Noel Robinson's history, Lori. Actually the man was a fraud. Last I heard he claimed to be Noah Robbins, National Transportation Safety Board inspector."

Lori bounced in her seat. "Eden, you sly dog! You've been dating Noah Robbins. The Noah Robbins."

"What's that supposed to mean?"

"Where have you been hiding, kiddo, under a rock? There isn't a woman from here to Timbuktu that doesn't salivate over that man."

Eden tossed her a puzzled look. Why did Lori make it sound like she'd been hanging with Denzel Washington? "I've always thought the name was familiar. Is he famous?" she held her breath.

"Noah's the National Transportation Safety Board's hunk of the year. Knowing that television ratings will soar, the NTSB trots him out every time there's a plane crash. He gets his fifteen minutes of fame and the newscasters just love him. He's even been interviewed by Oprah." Lori raised a hand fending off Eden's interruptions. "Let me give you his profile. Six foot four, skin the color of deep mahogany, a body built like the proverbial brick—well you know. Buns that remind you of an onion. You could cry just looking at them. Wait there's more. Man's got a smile that lights up the world, cheekbones carved from pure granite. Top that off with being thirty-something and single."

"Noah Robbins is some kind of national stud?" Eden's heart plummeted. She'd been taken in by a master.

"In the same league as the playgirl centerfold of the year."

"Eden." A voice from the back of the room interjected.

Eden turned to see Sinclair Morgan heading their way. How much she'd overheard was anyone's guess.

Sinclair glanced at a piece of paper in her hand, frowning slightly. "A couple of guys from the NTSB are coming to look at our operation tomorrow. They've asked to have you show them around."

"Me?"

Sinclair winked. "Yes, you. Looks like you made quite the impression on that stud. He'll be here tomorrow, eleven A.M. sharp."

Practically clicking his heels, Noah stepped off the shuttle and into the crowded departure lounge at LaGuardia Airport. In a few minutes he'd see Eden again. Never mind that they hadn't spoken since that horrible evening. While being apart from her had been brutal, it had given him time to think, to put his life into perspective and his priorities in order. Deep down he knew they were meant to be together. But where would that lead? Marriage was clearly out of the question. He didn't intend to get hurt again. No sirree, he wasn't about to stick his key in a lock, come home to an empty apartment, and find his wife gone. And it wasn't like Eden was exactly geographically desirable. Dating her would mean work, commuting on weekends perhaps.

Paco, the inspector accompanying him, fell into step. "Hey, Robby, what's on your mind, man?"

"Nothing related to the job."

They headed for Pelican's check-in counter where they were to meet Sinclair Morgan. With each step, Noah's excitement mounted. He'd been lucky to get this assignment. Actually lucky wasn't the word. He'd engineered it by volunteering, hoping to get Eden's ear and plead his cause.

Initially, Gary had been somewhat suspicious of his motives. But he'd convinced his boss that since they were only days away from publishing their findings on the Pelican crash, what would be the harm. This would be a routine inspection. He'd complete the assignment, look at Pelican's safety practices and see the woman of his dreams. By appealing to the carnal side of his boss' nature he'd been virtually assured the job. Hell, he'd even stashed a pair of clean underwear and toiletries in his briefcase, just in case. He could wish, couldn't he?

A woman wearing a bright smile and equally bright jacket stood at the counter. She crossed the lobby, meeting them halfway, extending a hand. "Hi, I'm Sinclair Morgan, Pelican's base manager. Jack described you perfectly. He told me you'd be coming in on the ten o'clock shuttle."

Jack was the airline's chief pilot, they'd been told.

Both men shook Sinclair's hand then followed her to the right and down a flight of stairs. On their way, Sinclair acknowledged the greetings of both cleaners and pilots. Noah had heard Pelican's operation was small, but he hadn't guessed it was that small. They stopped in front of a closed door.

"Our offices and briefing rooms are back here," Sinclair said.

Noah's heartbeat quickened.

Sinclair punched in a code, jiggled the knob and pushed the door open. "You requested Eden Sommers show you around."

"I did."

Sinclair raised a quizzical eyebrow. "How do you know, Eden?"

Was it his imagination or was the woman smirking. "We've worked together in the past," Noah said, hoping that the woman wouldn't ask for specifics.

"Is that so?"

"Ms. Sommers' professionalism impressed me. She's one bright lady."

Sinclair beckoned them inside. "Eden's waiting in the Atlantic briefing room. Please follow me."

Eden's fingers twisted the ends of the burgundy scarf around her neck. Why had Noah asked for her? Hadn't she made it clear that there was never going to be anything between them? Now he'd placed her in a difficult position. She could hardly say no to the NTSB.

With her free hand, she smoothed the material of the pencil-thin, ankle-length skirt, then glanced at her watch. Eleven o'clock. The ten o'clock shuttle from National would have landed by now.

The sound of footsteps in the hallway forced her to pull herself together. She pasted on a phoney smile and with her professional mask in place, turned to greet the arrivals.

Oh God! The man looks better than ever. She saw the familiar cleft in his chin as he smiled directly at her, green eyes sparkling.

Sinclair beamed from ear to ear making introduc-

tions. "Eden, this is Paco Hernandez. Noah, I assume
you know."

Eden tried to block out Noah's presence, grasping
the outstretched hand of a tall, handsome Latino man.
His warm brown eyes roamed over her. "Nice to meet
you, Ms. Sommers."

"Eden." Noah's gravelly voice called her name.

Calling on the Almighty to get her through this moment, she faced Noah. "What a surprise to see you, Mr.
Robbins. Where would you like to start?"

"The name's Noah."

Wasn't he cool. Plenty of practice she assumed.

"I leave you in good hands then," Sinclair said, slipping from the room.

Eden repeated the question, this time directing it to
Paco. "Was there a particular area or department you
wanted to begin with?"

"I'll leave that up to Noah. Is there a men's room I
can use?"

Eden gulped. What rotten timing. Had the two of
them planned this? Now she'd be left alone with Noah.
"Out in the hallway. Hang right. It's the third door
down."

"Thanks."

The door closed behind Paco and she faced Noah.

"I've missed you," he said, moving in and taking her
hand.

Jerking her fingers from his reach, she stepped back.
The smell of a spicy cologne lingered in the air tickling
her nostrils. She'd never seen Noah dressed for business; this new look was very appealing. The double-
breasted gray suit, fitting to perfection had to be
Armani. A crisp white shirt and red power tie completed
the look.

Another step forward and he'd invaded her space. "I

can understand why you're still angry. But Eden, be fair, you never even heard me out."

"Heard you out? Isn't it enough that you lied to me repeatedly. Do you always use the people you claim to love?"

"I do love you, Eden. Intensely. Passionately. Staying away from you has been one of the most difficult things I've had to do."

Wavering on the brink of throwing herself into his arms, she remembered Lori's words. Noah was a lady's man, used to women lusting after him, fawning all over him. She couldn't let her heart get in the way.

"Look, this isn't the time or place to have this discussion," Noah said. "After we're done, I don't have to rush back to DC. We'll go someplace, have a drink, and talk. I'd say dinner but you'd only say no." He raised a hand, stilling her words. "Eden, listen to me, there's something you should know. I've read the Pelican report. I now believe Rod's innocent."

Seventeen

Eden perched on the edge of a bar stool looking as if she would rather be anywhere but there. Noah sat next to her nursing an almost empty beer bottle.

A trim waitress in a micro-mini and punk haircut leaned over to deliver their second round, giving Noah full view of ample cleavage. Smiling at him, she set the bottle down. "One Corona and a Robert Mondavi for the lady." She placed the glass of wine in front of Eden.

The airport lounge Eden had chosen did brisk business. Noah could barely hear himself above the buzz of professionals networking. Grateful that Eden had agreed to meet with him, he wasn't about to complain.

He picked up his full bottle of Corona and clinked it against Eden's glass. *"Salud."*

Without acknowledging his toast, Eden took a tentative sip of wine and set the glass back on the faux marble counter. Swiveling her bar stool ever so slightly, she turned to face him. "Where did your sidekick disappear to?"

"He left on the six o'clock shuttle."

"Oh?" a tiny pink tongue flicked out as she sipped the Mondavi. He longed to capture that tongue in his mouth and taste her sweetness. Eden's expression hardened as she caught his eye. "What is it you wanted to tell me?"

Her voice was cold. Uncompromising. A far cry from the practiced politeness he'd been subjected to earlier. Business was over with, and she no longer wished to play the game.

"We'll get to that soon. Look, there are some things I need to tell you, if we're going to move forward."

"Move forward?"

"That's what I want."

"Am I supposed to believe anything you say?" Eden said brutally.

"Touché." He knew he deserved it, but her jab still hurt. He swigged his Corona. "Look, much of my work is undercover, I'm not in the habit of announcing to the general public I'm with the NTSB."

Eden wrinkled her nose. "And I'm the general public?"

"I didn't say that."

Frustrated, he drummed his fingers on the bar. "Eden, this isn't exactly easy for me to say. I was removed from the case and technically on vacation. Later I was placed on leave of absence. My boss knew that I couldn't let this thing rest so he stuck his neck out, supporting me, basically going against his own boss' mandate. Had I walked up to you and introduced myself as Noah Robbins, NTSB inspector, would you have been receptive to meeting me?"

"Probably not."

An elegant man in a navy blue suit and cream-colored tie climbed onto the stool next to Eden. "Hi," he said, flashing her a megawatt smile. "Can I buy you a drink?"

"The lady's not interested," Noah snapped, tossing the man a look that would freeze water. Noah scooted his seat closer to Eden. She drew back, careful not to let their sleeves touch. The man in the navy suit turned his attention to the blonde on his right.

Noah angled his head, forcing her to look at him.

"Eden, I already said I was sorry. I've even acknowledged that I waited too long to come clean. Look, I was
wrong, I admit it, but there just never seemed to be a
good time." Her hand clutched the edge of the bar,
knuckles almost popping from their sockets. He covered her hand with his and continued. "When I first
met you, I had one purpose in mind. Get whatever information I could and run like hell. But you had the
most unsettling effect on me—and then I got to know
you. Talk about the best laid plans backfiring. You see,
I'd promised myself I would never fall in love again."

"Were you that badly burned?"

She was at least talking and hadn't removed her hand.
That was good.

"Scorched. I was married for five years to a flight
attendant. Gayle was a woman I trusted and loved more
than life itself."

Eden's golden eyes flickered in the light from the
wall sconces. Now that he had her attention, he kept
talking. "We'd recently renewed our vows. Imagine
coming home one day to find your wife had run off
with a pilot?"

"It must have been painful." Eden slid her hand out
from under his. "I'm sorry."

"Painful isn't the word. I was devastated. After our
divorce it took me almost a year to want to ask a woman
out."

"I would imagine." The tips of her fingers made circular motions against his balled fists. "So how come
you're considered the NTSB stud of the year?"

Lowering his eyelashes, he glanced at her surreptitiously. Eden's expression revealed nothing but curiosity. Curiosity and compassion. Perhaps she was ready to
believe him. "That reputation has no foundation and
I've never encouraged it. Why is it women seem to fall
so easily for the handsome face instead of the qualities

that make for a good relationship? Now here I go getting maudlin. Can we go someplace and talk? Someplace I can buy you dinner." He could tell she was about to protest, and his index finger touched her mouth, silencing her. "That cafeteria meal earlier today wasn't really food. Let me take you someplace where the steak's at least edible."

When he sensed Eden weakening, Noah pressed his point. "Look, I need to talk to you about the NTSB's findings, and this really isn't a good place. We could be easily overheard."

Eden picked up her purse and stood abruptly. "Okay."

"Eden, wait."

"I said okay. What kind of food would you like?"

Eden and Noah were led to a table in the back of the restaurant by an overzealous owner. Eden had chosen the little restaurant because the fare, though hardly classifiable as fancy, stuck to the ribs. Located in nearby Woodhaven, the restaurant was a stone's throw from the airport.

"Youse okay with this?" The portly restauranteur waved them in the direction of a table for two in a recessed corner. Fake silk plants created the illusion of privacy.

"Is this good?" Noah asked Eden.

"It's fine."

"Flag the waiter down when youse are ready to order," the owner said, departing.

Noah unfolded his napkin and settled it on his lap. Even from across the table, he could smell her perfume. "Now where were we?"

"You were going to tell me what you found out."

"Ah, yes." The smell of spring flowers tickled his nostrils, conjuring up visions of another time and place. He struggled to remember his topic. "I previewed the NTSB report, the one that's about to be released." No reaction on Eden's part. "I did mention the cockpit voice recorder was found."

"You did."

"Well, a committee consisting of our guys, the FAA, the plane's manufacturer, and the pilots' union all listened to the recording. . . ."

"Just tell me what was found." Eden's voice remained neutral.

Noah arranged and rearranged his forks and spoons in one straight line. He'd have to eat humble pie on this one. Still, the longer he dragged this out, the longer Eden would spend in his company. "Engine noises seemed normal, communications from air traffic control indicated nothing out of the ordinary, and conversation between pilots seemed routine."

Eden didn't even crack a smile. She just sat there prim as a nun, graciously not saying, *I told you so.* "What's considered probable cause?"

"Sabotage."

"God, Noah, no!"

Though he'd reinforced what she'd initially believed, Noah knew she must be hurting. He grasped the hand gripping the edge of the bar and waited until she'd taken several deep breaths. The news had affected him the same way but at least he'd had several days to deal with it. The thought of all those innocent lives lost nauseated him. How could anyone be that cold, that uncaring?

"Ready to order?" Their waiter poured two glasses of water and stood pen in hand.

Reality at last filtered through. "I'm sorry," Eden said nodding vaguely in his direction.

"Eden, have you decided?" Noah resisted the urge

to give her a hug. Maybe later. Maybe later when they were alone.

"I'm not very hungry."

"Soup and salad?"

She nodded, and let him order for both of them.

When the waiter departed, Eden took a long, cold drink of water. "Noah," she said, "I think I have a lead. Lori tells me the guy that's been feeding Michael information is willing to talk. He's been laid off for more than six months and times are lean. In the next couple of weeks I'll be hiring people for a temporary base. If I guarantee him a job, he'll talk to me."

"What are we waiting for? Call Michael, see if this man will meet us."

"Now?"

"Now's as good a time as any." Noah handed her his cellular.

He drummed his fingers against the table while Eden dialed the Goldmuntzes' number. She waited for someone to pick up. A child's piercing greeting eventually echoed in her ear. "Hello."

"Is your mommy or daddy home?" Eden lowered her voice, hoping the child would follow suit.

"Daddy is."

"Good. May I speak with him?"

When Michael came on, Eden went through the obligatory inquiries about health before stating her purpose.

"Where are you right now?" he asked.

Eden gave Michael the restaurant's name, glanced at a book of matches on the table, and provided the exact address.

"I'll try reaching Kendall Alexander. Do you have a number if he's agreeable?"

She gave him Noah's cell number and ended the conversation.

The waiter set down their salads and a basket of warm rolls. Eden reached for the bread eagerly.

"Got your appetite back?"

"Umm hmm." She bit into a crisp bun.

The phone rang just as Noah's entree and Eden's soup were served. Clamping the phone to her ear, Eden listened to Michael. "He'll do it! He'll meet us!" she whispered to Noah. "Oh Michael, that's wonderful news. Course we'll feed him and pay his cab fare. Do you even have to ask?"

An hour passed and still no Kendall Alexander. They'd long completed their meal and downed several cups of coffee.

"Do you think he got cold feet?" Eden asked Noah.

Noah gazed at the rapidly thinning dinner crowd. The few people remaining lingered over nightcaps. He shrugged his shoulders. "Who knows? Did Michael happen to mention where the guy lives?"

"Brooklyn."

"And we're in Queens. I don't suppose an hour travel time is unreasonable, especially if there's traffic." He glanced at his watch, then back at Eden. "He'll need to get here soon though, or I'll miss the last shuttle to DC and you'll be forced to put me up." He winked at her.

"There's always my nice comfortable couch," she said brutally.

Wow! She hadn't exactly said no. Her backhanded invitation, though totally unexpected and unplanned, warmed him. He decided to push it. "Thanks. Being in bed with you would be a whole lot more comfortable."

"If it's a comfortable bed you seek, then a hotel's always an option."

A man with skin the color of burnt pecans, dressed in denim from head to toe, rushed through the door.

He scanned the restaurant and smiled when Eden waved at him. She rose, beckoning him over.

"Hi, Kendall. We've never formally been introduced. I'm Eden Sommers."

"Noah Robbins." Noah stood up, offering his hand. "Ken."

The man's handshake was weak. "Please sit down."

"Michael didn't mention anything about a Noah," Ken said shooting Eden a wary look. "Can I trust this guy?"

"With your life. Noah's a friend of mine. He's with the National Transportation Safety Board."

"Yeah?"

"Hungry?" Noah asked after they sat back down.

"You buying?"

"Yeah." Noah waved over the waiter and had him bring Ken a drink and menu. He waited until the man placed his order. "Michael tells us you may have some information that could be helpful," Noah began.

Ken sipped his drink, eyes darting around the room. "What's in it for me?"

Noah opened his mouth but Eden beat him to it. Her voice was gentle even soothing. "I know you've been out of work for some time and Michael thought maybe we could help each other. We're opening a temporary base in a couple of months. We've got plenty of positions. If you're able to give us the information we need, I'll guarantee you a job."

"Will I get that in writing?" Ken knocked back his drink and signaled the waiter for another.

Eden cocked an eyebrow. Her face had begun to take on the expression Noah had come to associate with, "Don't push me." "My word's good enough. Either you want the job or you don't?"

"I want it." The waiter returned, set down a steaming bowl of soup and an enormous basket of rolls. Ken dove for the bread, biting into a crisp roll as if he hadn't eaten in weeks. He shoveled heaping spoonfuls of chicken noodle into his mouth and chewed. "What do ya want to know?"

Gesturing with her hand, Eden turned the conversation over to Noah.

"This is hard for us. Eden and I both lost friends in the Pelican crash. We're still trying to make sense of it."

Slurping soup, Ken opened his mouth. "Yeah, plenty of people died. That bothered me."

"Were you working that evening?"

"Hmm umm."

Noah could tell they were getting nowhere fast. One syllable answers wouldn't cut it; he needed more. He tossed Eden a helpless look, but she was digging through her purse and didn't catch his eye. She scribbled on a tiny oblong square and slid her business card across the table. "Here, Ken. Call me in two weeks for an interview."

Ken stopped spooning soup long enough to grin from ear to ear. "Thanks Ms. Sommers." He pocketed the card. "Yeah, I worked that evening. Me and a bunch of guys who've since been laid off."

"Anything unusual happen that you can remember?" Eden asked.

"No, same old garbage. One night's pretty much like another. Then we went back to the break room to play cards."

"When did you find out the flight was delayed?"

Ken allowed the waiter to take the soup bowl and replace it with a gigantic platter of ribs. Digging in, he said, "When the announcement was made, one of the guys tossed his cards down and raced from the room like his tail was on fire."

"What was wrong with him?"

"All night he'd been acting weird. We thought it was on account of him being pink-slipped. Guy never saw it coming. He came back later mumbling something about having to get a message to the purser. Till then we'd all thought the flight had left."

"Was it unusual to take a message to a flight attendant?" Noah asked.

"Not really, ramp guys and flight crews are pretty tight. I had plenty of flight attendants." Ken hesitated. "I think he lied though. This buddy of mine ran into him carrying a box."

"What was in it?"

Ken shook his head. "Don't know. Probably swiped some cargo. Sure acted even stranger when he got back. He was weird to begin with. Every penny went up his nose, if you get my drift." Ken placed his index finger on one nostril while snorting with the other. "The guys knew he was looney tunes but no one wanted to rat him. We all felt bad. Union people tend to stick together. He had no seniority and they cut his water. He was first to go. They at least had the decency to give him two weeks' notice. We knew our turn would eventually come. But after this whole thing went down—" Ken's voice wavered, "I been thinking . . ."

"You been thinking?" Eden's voice was deceptively low.

Ken spoke through a mouthful of ribs. "Thought maybe he had something to do with the crash. Could have gone over the edge and lost it. Stuff happens. I mean the guy was out there, you know. Everyone knew blow was a problem, but no one wanted to turn him in. It wasn't only the union thing that held them back. He was connected, chief pilot's nephew, you know what I mean?"

"What did he look like?" Noah's voice was dangerously low. Eden immediately knew what he was thinking.

"Tall and skinny. Greasy brown hair, whatever was left of it. Major attitude problem, showed on his face." Ken cleaned his plate with the last morsel of bread then wiped his mouth on his sleeve. "We done?"

"One more thing. What's this guy's name?"

Ken folded his arms across his now bulging stomach. He winked at Eden. "Tell you in two weeks when I get my job."

Eighteen

"We're close to solving this thing. I can feel it," Eden
said, shoving two neatly folded towels into Noah's hands.
When the tips of her fingers grazed his flesh, she jumped
back, electricity surging through her veins. "Give me a
couple of minutes and you can have the bathroom," she
babbled. Uncomfortably aware of Noah's bigger-than-
life presence, she bolted for the safety of the bathroom.

Noah had missed the last shuttle, and call her stupid,
she hadn't the heart to send him to a hotel. Gratitude
and guilt had plagued her. How would she have gotten
through the conversation with that slimeball if he hadn't
been around? Eden ran the tap, cupped her palms and
let the cold water trickle. Splashing her face with cool
water, she willed her racing pulse to settle. Only a shaky
and rather ineffective door separated her from this man
she'd had no business bringing home. What a glutton
for punishment.

Ten minutes later, having brushed her teeth, she was
still in there, hunched over the washbasin gazing at her
reflection. *Face it, Eden, girl, you're just too scared to go out.*
How would she handle it if she found him stark naked
in her bed? Would she have the strength to resist him?
Even worse, what if he forced himself on her?

"Oh, Eden," she raged out loud. "What happened to
your common sense?"

"You okay in there?" Noah called.

She wanted to tell him she wasn't. That his presence had created havoc with her libido. "I'm fine. Be out in a minute." Taking deep breaths she counted to ten before leaving the room.

Noah leaned against the wall, arms crossed. He'd stripped down to his shirtsleeves. The towels she'd given him were held in the curve of bulging muscles. Her mouth went dry just looking at him. The white T-shirt stretched across his hard chest and fit snugly around his tapered waist. Lord have mercy! Eden moistened her lips, "Bathroom's all yours."

"Thanks." Their eyes held momentarily. It took all of her willpower to break that gaze. She needed to remain strong, to remember how badly his deception had hurt. Relationships were built on trust and he'd lost hers. Noah glided past her, giving her one final searching look. In his wake, the smell of spring lingered.

This was madness. The man was a liar, yet her feelings for him hadn't changed one bit, if anything they'd grown stronger. How to explain this?

Keep busy. Refuse to think. She fetched sheets from the closet and began creating a makeshift bed on the sofa. As she tucked in edges of sheet, her eyes were drawn to the shirt Noah had draped over the arm of the couch. Did it smell like him?

She couldn't stop herself. She needed to touch that shirt. Wrap herself in him. Pulled in that direction by an unknown force, she reached over, retrieved the white shirt, and slowly brought it to her nose. Draping the sleeves over her head, she hugged herself tightly and closed her eyes. She was held in his powerful arms, minutes away from being loved by him. Fantasy, certainly not reality, given everything they'd been through. Still, how was she to get through the night knowing that only a flimsy divider separated them? Sheer willpower just wasn't enough.

"Just what are you doing?" Noah's voice penetrated. He sounded amused.

Embarrassed she whipped the shirt off her head, crumpled it in her palms, and turned to face him. Bare-chested, he confronted her. She swallowed hard. The best defense was a good offense she'd once been told. "What's wrong with you? You scared me, creeping up on me like that." Her eyes roamed his hard pectorals and again she moistened her lips.

"I didn't mean to," he said softly.

The depth of passion she saw in his eyes scared her. "I made up a bed for you. Do you need anything else," she babbled.

"Yes, there is one other thing I could use. You."

"Use being the operative word." Ignoring his blatant come-on, she shoved pillows at him. Noah's tongue was a silken web, she needed to remember that. "I'll see you in the morning, then."

As she headed for her bedroom she heard him call her name. "Eden."

"What is it?"

"Wouldn't it be much easier to admit we want each other." He held a hand up anticipating her interruption. "Look, nothing's going to happen tonight unless you want it to happen. I've never forced myself on a woman and I don't intend to start now."

Sorely tempted to go with the flow, she sighed softly. She'd only regret it in the morning. "We've got a lot to work out."

"Ain't that the truth." He quickly covered the space separating them and laid his hands on her shoulders. "I understand why you'd be angry. But try to forgive me. Put yourself in my place."

"I've tried," she said, "what I don't get is why the charade went on this long."

He seemed unable to give her the response she so desperately needed. The truth.

Later that evening despite the cool breeze flowing through the apartment's window, Noah tossed and turned. He hadn't had a wink of sleep since he'd laid down. It had been sheer agony lying awake knowing that only a tiny divider separated them. Why hadn't he just gone to a hotel instead of taking her up on her halfhearted offer to provide him a place to stay? Truth was, he'd hoped that she might forgive him. He stretched out one foot and acknowledged the animal nesting next to him. Kahlua, loyal beast that she was, licked his ankle. At least he still had one woman's trust.

The blast of an occasional horn and the rattle of early morning cabs filtered through the window. Noxious exhaust fumes, the shouts of garbagemen and the scrape of gigantic brushes against pavement indicated cleaners already at work. What a difference from DC where life seemed to end after midnight.

Eden's piercing shriek caused him to bolt from bed. The sudden movement sent Kahlua flying. He pushed the divider aside and flipped on the light. Eden writhed amidst a tangle of bedsheets. It was only a nightmare, thank God.

"Eden, honey, wake up," Noah urged. He sat on the edge of her bed, grasped her shoulders and shook gently. She moaned, uttered a guttural sound, and struggled to free herself. "Easy, baby. Now come on, open your eyes."

She came to slowly. First one eye opened then another. "Noah," she said, reaching out to him. He was too surprised to do anything but wrap his arms around her back and pull her tightly against his chest. She clung to him. By her body's jerky movements he knew she'd begun to sob. He kissed the top of her head.

"Hush, baby. Hush," he said, tightening his arms around her.

"God, Noah it was awful."

"It was just a dream, sweetheart. Would it help if you talked about it?"

He could feel her chest expand and deflate as she gulped air. At last she managed, "It's a recurrent nightmare. But this time it was god-awful."

"Tell me about it?"

In husky tones Eden recited, "I'm on a plane that goes down, kind of like the Pelican crash. People are panicking all around me and my only hope is Rod, or at least a man that looks like Rod. Sometimes the face is fuzzy and sometimes I think the man's you. Lately, the dream focuses on this peculiar little box . . . God, you're going to think I'm nuts." She swiped her nose with the back of her hand.

"Try me."

Eden sniffled. "This box, well . . . it has human qualities. It walks and even tries to talk."

Still holding her, Noah slid into bed and gathered her close. "What does the box say?"

"That's the thing. It makes unintelligible noises. Sort of a ticktocking."

"I don't think you're crazy at all, Eden," Noah said, squeezing her tight then kissing both cheeks. "In fact I think you're on to something."

"I am?" She'd stopped crying.

"Think, Eden. Think. The NTSB has ruled this thing sabotage. You're having peculiar dreams about a box. What's his name?" he snapped his fingers. "Kendall Alexander mentions this ex-Pelican employee was seen carrying a box. Must mean something."

"You don't think . . ."

"I do think we need to find this guy and soon."

Five hours later, Eden and Noah entered Pelican's terminal. Noah had already advised Gary he'd be arriving at work late. He now planned on catching a mid-morning shuttle.

"Do you have time for coffee?" Noah asked, tweaking the nape of Eden's neck.

"I suppose, although I do have a ten-thirty meeting."

Holding Eden by the elbow he guided her through long lines at the check-in counters and up an escalator. When she looked at him questioningly, he patted his pocket. "Ticket's right here. I don't have luggage so I'll check in at the gate."

Upstairs, in front of a tiny specialty coffee shop sporting the name Runway Cafe, Noah stopped to pick up a newspaper before leading her inside. "Is this all right?"

"Fine."

They were escorted to a table by a smiling waitress of indeterminate age. "Coffee?" the brunette asked, heading for the station where several pots perked.

Eden inhaled the heavenly aroma. Subtle scents of vanilla, coconut, and burnt almond filled her nostrils. She yawned, then flexed her neck, trying to get the kinks out.

"Did you get any sleep at all?"

Nodding, she refused to tell him that having him in bed made the world of difference. She'd slept better than she had in a long time.

Their waitress returned carrying two coffeepots. "Care to try the Palermo or something else?" she jiggled the pot. "It's one of our most popular brews."

"Palermo's delicious," Eden confirmed, watching Noah unfold his paper.

"Holy . . ."

"Sir, would you prefer another flavor? I can . . ." Their waitress eyed Noah curiously. Ignoring her, he continued to peruse the paper, muttering to himself.

Eden quickly said, "Why don't you go ahead and pour." She shot Noah a questioning look. Something in that paper had upset him badly. She waited for their server to depart before asking. "Well?" When he didn't answer, she cleared her throat several times to get his attention. "Noah, what's wrong?"

A muscle in Noah's jaw worked overtime as he folded the newspaper into four and slid it across the table. "Plenty. See for yourself."

Deliberately delaying reading, Eden sipped her coffee. Her fingers trembled when she finally picked up the article. Whatever it was, wasn't good news. She glanced at the photograph, her hands shaking so badly that coffee sloshed all over the picture. Rod's face took up most of the front page. She forced herself to read the caption. *Sabotage Caused Flight 757's Crash.*

"How, Noah, how? I thought the National Transportation Safety Board wasn't set to release their findings until next week."

"That's what I understood. Must be a leak someplace. That wouldn't be the first time we've had one. What makes me mad is . . ." he jabbed his finger at the article. "The NTSB is very careful about the way that releases are worded. They'd never sanction something like this knowing that it would upset the families of the deceased and cause the general public to panic. You should read that thing. Talk about sensationalism."

"I don't think I want to."

"It's pure speculation, some journalist's bid to get the crash on the front page again, and make a name for himself," he ranted. "One source is attributing the fatality to a middle eastern terrorist group. Another, to some militant group that Rod was supposedly a member of. Even the old missile theory has resurfaced. Are you okay, Eden?"

She shook her head, unable to stop the tears spilling. "I'll be fine. Look you gotta go, your plane's leaving in a few minutes."

"Forget about my plane," he said, surprising her. "I'm not leaving you in this state."

"I'll be fine, really I will." Eden opened her purse and fumbled for a tissue, but Noah was quicker. He retrieved a snowy white handkerchief from his breast pocket and handed it over. She blew her nose, crumpled the linen in her palm, then tossed the cloth into her purse. "I'll wash it and mail it to you."

"No you won't. You'll hand it to me in person. New York's a five-hour drive. It's even shorter by plane and you've got flight benefits. I . . . well I can always manage to ride a jump seat and if all else fails . . . I'm a private pilot . . . I own a small plane with a couple of buddies."

Private pilot? But hadn't he told her that there'd been no money for flight lessons? She replayed his words, struggling to remember. No, what he'd actually said was he'd wanted to be a commercial pilot. It hadn't worked out.

Blinking back the moisture, Eden forced herself to smile. "Now scram. You have to get back to work and I've got a meeting to attend."

Noah rose reluctantly. "Only if you're sure. Meanwhile work on that Ken person, see if you can charm him into releasing his buddy's identity. If all else fails I'll be forced to put on the pressure." He winked at her. "I'll call tonight. Stay sweet and try to stay out of trouble." He blew her a kiss, picked up his briefcase and exited.

* * *

After Noah left, Eden entered the In-Flight conference room to find a solemn group waiting. "Am I late?" she asked, glancing at her watch.

"I looked for you," Sinclair hastily inserted, "to let you know that we'd moved the meeting up."

Eden's glance took in the various department heads seated around the horseshoe table. Also present were the chief pilot, legal counsel, public relations people, Loss Prevention representatives, and various layers of management. Eden slipped into the chair Jack, the chief pilot, held out. "Thanks. What did I miss?"

"Not much. We just got started."

Sinclair, who was seated next to Jack, unfolded a newspaper. "Did you see this?"

Eden managed a nod. "Yes, it was pretty upsetting especially since there's no credence to it." She'd gotten everyone's attention.

"How do you know that?" Philip Feiner, Pelican's P.R. person, jabbed a stubby finger to make his point. "Says right here, this is a preliminary release by the NTSB."

"Does it really? What does it actually say, Phil?" Eden challenged.

The rotund man made a harrumphing sound, cleared his throat and read from the paper. "Says preliminary findings from the NTSB indicate—" He held one hand up. "Okay, okay I'm wrong."

Connie Messina, Pelican's legal counsel spoke, getting everyone's attention. "People, can we get to the real reason we're here?"

"Rumor control?" Sinclair offered.

Tim, the person heading up the communications department added. "Something's obviously got to be done. Our telephone operators are going nuts and we've been flooded with calls from the moment this newspaper hit the stands. Every phone line's lit and though my folks have been fielding calls, we're overwhelmed."

"Plus we're losing money. Business is almost nonexistent. Passengers are canceling like crazy." That pronouncement by the reservations director made everyone sit up and listen. "Don't you think a spokesperson from the NTSB should call a press conference."

"To say?" this from Jack.

"To deny these supposed findings."

"What if there's nothing to deny?" Eden's voice broke as she posed the question. "As far-fetched as some of these stories sound, are we certain that sabotage is clearly out of the question?"

"It's a ridiculous assumption," Jack said firmly. "There's some perfectly good explanation for what caused the crash. That plane had a history of mechanical problems. Are we going to give in to hysteria? I vote we make no statements and the whole thing will eventually blow over."

"I beg to disagree. Silence is not the answer. This headline has already created quite a stir and we have an obligation to the flying public to provide some kind of statement. A press release is a must." Connie Messina again. "We'll need someone with exceptional presentation skills and a certain amount of credibility to deliver the message. This thing should be nipped before it gallops way out of control. If our president and an NTSB representative appear on TV together, we at least stand a chance. How about that Noah Robbins? He's got lots of charisma and when he speaks women literally sit up and listen."

Tim offered his support. "I think you're onto something, Connie."

"Then we'll do it. We'll contact the NTSB and garner its support." Phil Feiner was already up and halfway out the door. Jack threw him a sour look. A master at recovery, he quickly changed faces when Phil said, "How's your nephew, Aaron? Has he found a job yet?"

The picture of affability, Jack smiled. "Not that I'm aware of."

Eden noted the chief pilot's flushed face and stilted answer. His nephew, Aaron was obviously not a topic he enjoyed discussing. She remembered bits and pieces of last evening's conversation. Ken Alexander had mentioned Aaron had substance abuse problems and was the chief pilot's nephew. No wonder the discomfort. What a stroke of luck though, Aaron was hardly a common name and if she enlisted Michael Goldmuntz's help, it should be easy finding out his last name. Even better, she'd simply ask Jack.

Eden caught up with Jack just as he was exiting the room. When she touched his arm, he swung around, flashing her a brilliant smile.

"How have you been, kiddo? We've missed you." His voice was warm, welcoming.

"I'm fine."

Jack touched her lightly on the shoulder. "We were all sorry to lose Rod. My men still talk about him. He was one helluva pilot."

Eden nodded. "Thank you for saying that. It would have meant a lot to Rod to know he was highly regarded." She switched the subject. "I didn't know you had a nephew that worked here?"

The light disappeared from Jack's eyes. "Used to work here. Aaron was laid off with the first set of cutbacks."

"That's too bad. Has he found something else?" Jack shook his head and suddenly seemed anxious to leave. But Eden planted herself firmly in his path. "The reason I ask is because we're opening that temporary base in Newburgh. I'm going to need lots of people and there's a good possibility the positions may become permanent. By the way, do I know Aaron?"

The chief pilot shrugged. "You might, though he looks nothing like me." Jack patted his ample stomach "He's thin as a rail, has dark brown hair, wears it pulled back in a ponytail."

Eden frowned as an image of a man surfaced. The description was identical to the man who'd almost run them down with his boat. "What's Aaron's last name?"

"Kilpatrick."

"Can you ask him to call me?"

"If you're sure. He's got a bit of a reputation as a troublemaker."

Nineteen

Seated at the table in the Pelican cafeteria, Michael Goldmuntz cupped his large fists around a steaming cup of coffee and waited for Eden to speak. When several seconds elapsed and small talk dwindled, he prompted, "Okay spill it. What's up?" Eden had seemed preoccupied for the ten minutes they'd sat there. Michael took her hand, squeezing gently. " 'Fess up, kiddo, something's bothering you."

"How would I get in touch with one of your guys?" Eden asked softly.

Michael raised an eyebrow, joking. "Business or pleasure?" He winked at her so she would know he was pulling her leg.

Eden scowled at him. "Business of course."

"Who are we talking about?"

Eden sipped the steaming brew and set down her cup. "Aaron Kilpatrick."

"What do you want with him? The guy's bad news."

"So I've heard."

"Believe me the man doesn't have one redeeming quality. From the day he'd been hired he'd been a major pain. Guy was as paranoid as they came, rebelled against authority, and acted out every chance he got. He's been in and out of rehabilitation programs. I've referred him to Employee Assistance so many times I've lost count . . ."

"Must be Kilpatrick you're talking about." One of Michael's ramp agents pulled up a chair and sat, smiling vaguely in Eden's direction.

"Hi Glenn," Michael greeted. "You know Eden."

Glen nodded. "Yes, of course. What's Kilpatrick done lately?"

"Nothing that I know of. You still in touch with him?"

The ramp agent shrugged his shoulders. "He used to call me every now and then. Loved to play poker. But I haven't heard from him lately. Someone told me he left town."

"Where did he go?" Eden asked.

"Don't know. Petey, in cargo services, says someplace out west. Alls I know is he let Petey stay in his place while he was gone. Was a real dump I hear. Petey had to get his old lady to come clean it. Roaches everywhere."

"Does Petey still live there?" Eden probed.

"Nope. Couldn't wait to get out of Hollis. Moved back to the Bronx weeks ago. Kilpatrick done something to you?"

"No. I'm just trying to help him. I heard he's the chief pilot's nephew and I've got openings to fill so I thought I'd give the guy a break. You wouldn't by chance have his phone number?"

"It's disconnected. But I have his address." After a while, he said, "You know there's a whole lot of guys laid off. I'd offer any of them a job before Kilpatrick. He's a lazy slug and he's got a mean streak to him."

"Kilpatrick's the one I'm interested in."

Glenn opened a worn address book, ripped out an equally soiled back page and scribbled on it. "There." He slid the scrap of paper in Eden's direction. "That's his last known whereabouts."

"Thanks." Eden pocketed the paper and pushed back her chair. "You've both been extremely helpful."

Back in her office, Eden placed the paper on her desk, smoothing out the creases. Talk about lucking out. She'd hit the jackpot getting Kilpatrick's address. She glanced at the piece of paper, noting the address. Hollis, Queens. Fifteen maybe twenty minutes away. She could easily make it there and back before the close of business. No she couldn't do it alone. What if this guy was . . . too bizarre a thought. She'd call Noah. He deserved to be filled in.

Digging through her purse, Eden located the business card Noah had given her. She dialed the number before she could change her mind.

"Hello." The sound of his gravelly voice made her toes curl. Around her the world wobbled on a none-too-steady axis.

"Hello," Noah repeated.

"Noah?"

"Eden." He made her name sound special. She wondered if the longing in his voice was purely her imagination. "How are you?"

"Fine. Actually better than fine."

"And your mother?"

"Almost fully recovered."

Next she told him about her stroke of good fortune and how she'd managed to get Kilpatrick's address.

"That's wonderful, hon. Soon as I'm through with this press conference I'll hop the next shuttle. Stay put, and don't do a thing until I get there."

Eden calculated rapidly. Three hours was a long time to sit idle and wait. Even if Noah rushed through the interview, grew wings and literally flew, he'd never make it to New York before nightfall. Not that she couldn't keep busy. Her in-box was full to overflowing and she'd been playing catch-up ever since she got back. Was Kilpatrick listed in the phone book or was the number disconnected? That information she could at least find out on her own.

Eden dialed 411 just as Lori walked in. Acknowledging her friend with a nod, she responded to the automated voice on the line. "Hollis. Last name's Kilpatrick, first Aaron. Six twenty-one Lenox Avenue."

After a considerable hold, a live operator took over. "Sorry the number's unlisted."

"Are you sure, operator?"

Receiving confirmation, she slammed the phone down and railed at Lori. "Would you believe the guy's got an unlisted number?"

"Whoa, who are we talking about?" Lori took the seat facing Eden.

Eden, realizing that she wasn't making sense, began to explain. The phone rang. "I'll have to get that." She tossed Lori an apologetic look.

"Hello."

A TV blared in the background. "I hear you been looking for me," a slurred voice said.

"Who's this?" The tone was strangely familiar though she couldn't quite place it.

Silence. The man cleared his throat and after a while said, "You wanted me to call you about a job."

Eden felt her pulse rate quicken. Hallelujah! The mountain had come to Mohammed. "Aaron Kilpatrick?"

"Depends on who's asking."

"Eden Sommers. I spoke with your uncle, asked him to have you call. When can we get together?"

The volume of the TV almost drowned out her words. She could hear a newscaster about to introduce Noah and Vernon Bond, Pelican's president. She'd have to wrap this up quickly. She wanted to see that broadcast.

"This an interview or a definite job?" The same slurred voice quizzed.

"That depends on you, Aaron."

Aaron grunted. "How much ya paying?"

Eden debated telling him. But what if he decided it was too little. She'd possibly blow her only opportunity to speak with him. "We can discuss the details when we get together. Meanwhile I'd like to ask you a few questions."

"No questions unless they relate to the job."

"But Aaron . . ."

"And we talk on my turf. Just you and me, babe. No one else. Plan on next Monday, seven o'clock sharp. I'll be in touch."

She hung up and, forgetting about Lori, rushed from the room. She needed to find a TV and fast.

A small group of flight attendants, pilots, and ramp agents huddled around the TV in the lounge. Spotting Eden, one of the flight crew vacated his seat, motioning her over. She smiled gratefully, thanked him, and sank onto the lumpy sofa.

On-screen, Noah and Vernon Bond made scripted statements. Eden's eyes remained on Noah. No wonder he'd been labeled the NTSB stud of the year. The cameras obviously loved him, playing up his best features. His brilliant white smile, flashes of ivory against ebony, tugged at her heartstrings. What presence the man had. The flight attendant seated next to her sighed and crossed her legs. Eden focused on the screen. Noah was a walking, talking Adonis, all right. Could he really be hers if she wanted him? Where did that come from? Noah was hardly hers nor did she want him. *Liar!* Her eyes roamed his body taking in every detail of the expensive navy suit, burgundy tie, polished black shoes.

Tuning in to the sounds around her, she realized why women salivated just hearing his name.

"God, he's gorgeous." The leggy blonde seated next to her confirmed.

"An understatement," the flight attendant sitting catercorner to her added. "He's not exactly the kind of man you'd throw out of bed."

Eden felt herself blushing. If only they knew that she was in the position to confirm what they'd said.

The chattering ceased as everyone focused on Vernon Bond's words.

Eden caught the tail end of his sentence. ". . . though we have reason to believe that foul play may have been a contributing cause of Flight 757 . . ."

Pandemonium broke out as everyone began talking at once.

Much to the chagrin of the man behind him, Noah slowed down. "Do I make a right or a left here?" He was driving Eden's jeep.

Eden peered at the map as the horn behind them blasted. "Right, I think."

Noah gestured for the driver to go by. "Sorry, buddy."

On their way to the city, they'd decided to detour and doubled back to Hollis.

"Read that address to me again," Noah said.

Straightening out the crumpled piece of paper Eden complied. "621 Lenox."

"Road or avenue."

"Avenue."

They continued on, Eden supplying instructions whenever she was asked. One block seemed shabbier than the other and Eden ventured, "Noah, do you think it's a good idea to keep going. I mean it's starting to get dark and this doesn't look like the safest place."

He squeezed her shoulder. "Agreed, but we need to scope out the neighborhood. No way am I allowing you to meet this guy alone after seeing this—" He gestured. "When are you supposed to meet him?"

"Next Monday?"

"Great. I'll take the day off and fly up. Better yet, I'll drive up on Friday and spend the whole weekend."

"Noah, you can't. Aaron Kilpatrick's not going to talk to me if you're present." Even as she tried to dissuade him, the thought of having him to herself for the whole weekend was too tempting. Still, what would be the point of encouraging him. Their relationship was headed nowhere. Even if she were prepared to forgive and forget, a long-distance romance came with its own set of problems.

Noah's hand left the wheel, covering hers. "Who said anything about being visible. Present doesn't mean visible." The smile he threw her made her body tingle.

"Oh you. Hey, Noah slow down. You just missed it. Lenox is right back there."

After consulting the rearview mirror, Noah reversed the car. He made a quick right and they turned down the block. Littered with garbage and rusted cars, people huddled everywhere taking advantage of the warm evening. Some sat on broken chairs having hair braided. Others were on stoops looking vacantly out at passing traffic. A depressing sight, four men slouched under the streetlight drinking from brown paper bags while a group of teenagers whizzed by on skates.

"Nice neighborhood. Can you see the numbers?"

"If you'd slow down I could."

Noah complied. The men under the streetlight eyed him warily. "Probably think I'm a cop," he said to Eden.

"Wouldn't you. We're acting suspiciously and my jeep sticks out like a sore thumb. We just passed four fifty. I'd say we need to go several more blocks. Kilpatrick's

is an odd number, so it will be on the other side of the
street."

"Smart girl." Noah patted her head.

They continued up the road. If anything the neighborhood worsened. A sour smell of rotting garbage invaded the car. "Pugh!" Eden said, holding her nose.
"Turn up the air-conditioning."

Slender brown fingers hastened to do her bidding.
In the twilight, broken streetlights looked like emaciated arms, reaching out for help. The tiny houses they'd
passed previously were now replaced by four-story
brownstones. As they stopped to read the numbers, an
occasional torn curtain shifted.

"You may have gone too far," Eden said, spotting a
misshapen mailbox with the number 656 in script.

Noah steered the car into the next parking lot and
made a U-turn. "Keep your eyes peeled."

"Okay slow up. I think this is it."

Noah stepped on the brake. They skidded to a full
stop in front of a Tudor-style brick home that had at
one time housed the middle-class. The brown lawn was
untended and what little of it there was, held broken
implements. Someone had cleared a path to the front
entrance.

"There's a side door as well," Noah said scoping out
the building. "Looks like it may house two families."

"Possibly three. There's a basement." Eden pointed
to a corrugated hatchway entrance. "Wonder which
one's Kilpatrick's."

"I bet you dinner it's the basement."

"You're on. What do we do from here?"

"Sit for a while and see if anyone goes in and out."
Noah turned off the ignition. He caressed her shoulders lightly, responding to her questioning look. "You
know I'd give anything to talk to the man. But we don't
want to scare him away."

"Then why are we parked in a visible spot, shouldn't we at least be across the street?"

"Nope. Out in the open's much better. It will only create more suspicion if we appear to be casing the joint."

"Okay, you know best." Eden tugged at her earlobe, the uneasiness she'd had all along surfacing. She'd been debating telling Noah her suspicions, foolish as they might seem. "Noah," she began.

"What is it, honey?"

"Jack, our chief pilot, described Kilpatrick to me. . . ."

"And?"

"You're going to think this is stupid but he sounded like the spitting image of the guy driving the boat. The one who ran us down."

Noah took both her hands in his, squeezing them gently. "It's not stupid at all. Something about this guy's strange. Think about it. His history with the airline leaves a lot to be desired. He's not a real stable type and losing his job may have pushed him clear over the edge."

Just then the front door pushed open and a slightly built light-skinned man emerged. He headed their way.

"Let me handle this," Noah said out of the side of his mouth.

Up close, the man's acned complexion was truly revolting. "Hi," Noah said before the man could speak. "Would you know how we'd pick up the Grand Central?"

"You lost." He eyed them warily.

Noah nodded. He pointed to the crumpled map Eden still held. "The wife wasn't feeling well so I made a little detour to find her a rest room. Next thing I know we ended up here. When I spotted Lenox, boy was I relieved. We used to have a friend that lived here.

We tried calling to see if he was still around but his number's no good. Guy by the name of Kilpatrick. Used to live in your house."

"You ain't cops or dealers?" The acned face came closer, eyes scanning their clothing.

Noah shook his head. "Nope. Do we look like cops or dealers?" He patted Eden's stomach. "The wife here's pregnant. She'll need to use a bathroom."

Reassured, the man snorted, jutting a thumb in the direction of the Tudor. "You sure as hell don't want to use his. That bastard, Kilpatrick still lives here. Place is a real mess."

"No kidding. Son of a gun, hon, Aaron Kilpatrick's still here. Why don't we ring his bell? I know you have to go babe, perhaps you can close your eyes and use the facilities."

Their informant quickly interjected. "I doubt he'd welcome you with open arms. He's been on a week's binge and that basement apartment's got more booze bottles and junk than the law allows. Hardly the best place for a pregnant lady. I'm the landlord, I should know. Hope you ain't too good friends, I'm goin' evict him. Had that white car parked on my front lawn towed to a junkyard. Needed to get my money one way or the other. Try the gas station at the corner. They've got a bathroom." He pointed down the block.

Noah put the car into drive. "Thanks for filling us in. Like we said, we haven't seen the guy in years."

"Wait!" Kilpatrick's landlord called after them. "I can give you directions to the Grand Central."

Twenty

Eden glanced at the clock on the wall, synchronizing the time on her watch. In two hours she would meet with Kilpatrick. She shifted uneasily, anticipating the upcoming meeting. From everything she'd heard, the man was a loose cannon. No wonder she was edgy. That morning he'd called to confirm the time and place and had given her directions to a neighborhood coffee shop.

Of course she'd called Noah at his hotel the moment Kilpatrick hung up. He'd driven up from Maryland just as he said he would, and they'd spent the entire weekend together. A delightful one, she'd had to admit. He'd been the perfect gentleman. And they'd had a perfect two days together. The weather had been beautiful and they'd spent the majority of the time outdoors: walking in Central Park, renting a little boat and rowing around the lake, and in-line skating. They'd even enjoyed margaritas at a charming sidewalk restaurant and taken in Broadway shows at night.

It had been fun to experience what a date with Noah Robbins was like. The real Noah Robbins. Based on the weekend's experience she had no complaints. The man had all the right moves. And though their physical contact had been limited to a few chaste kisses, she wondered how different their relationship would be, had there not been lies?

But what if he'd lost interest in her? Just the thought had made her want him more. Would he really have driven this distance to be with a friend? And why would he be willing to follow her to Hollis and back? *For Ty's sake. Closure for his story,* the little voice at the back of her head reasoned.

"Hey, Eden, you're a million miles away. Want some coffee?" Lori Goldmuntz's voice penetrated.

Eden looked up from the same personnel file she'd been reviewing for more than two hours. "Sorry. I didn't hear you."

"Coffee?" Lori brandished a pot.

Eden pushed her mug across the desk. "Yes, please."

Her friend poured the liquid and reached into a small refrigerator against the wall. Retrieving cream, she turned back. "Rumor has it you're leaving early today."

"I have an appointment."

Lori eyeballed her. "That appointment have anything to do with Noah Robbins?"

Eden remained silent, debating whether to tell Lori the truth. The Goldmuntzes had phoned over the weekend to invite her to dinner, but she'd turned them down cold, citing Noah as her reason.

"Okay be like that. Tell me I'm getting too personal. Just say your feelings about Noah Robbins are something you don't care to share. I'll back off."

Had it not been for Lori and Michael, she would never have gotten this far with her investigation. She owed them. "I'm meeting Aaron Kilpatrick at a coffee shop," she said.

"Alone?"

"Noah's following me. He'll keep an eye on things just to make sure Kilpatrick doesn't get crazy."

Lori slurped her coffee. Over the rim of her cup her

eyes met Eden's. "You be careful, girl. That boy's nutso. I've heard it said he's a real unsavory character."

The phone on Eden's desk rang. Anticipating Noah on the other end, she quickly picked up the receiver. She was not disappointed.

Noah skipped the customary greeting. "I'm on my way. Be there in fifteen minutes."

"The man himself?" Lori questioned the moment she got off.

"Umm hmm."

Lori swallowed her coffee and gave Eden a knowing smile. "Are you two getting serious?"

"Nonsense."

"Then why is it every time you speak to lover boy you get that dreamy look on your face?"

"Just your imagination," Eden mumbled, flipping through the personnel file in front of her.

Half an hour later, Eden was in her jeep with Noah trailing her. His automobile maintained a respectable distance, several car lengths behind. She kept an eye in the rearview mirror, reassured by the Camry's presence, and occasionally glanced at the paper on which she'd scribbled Kilpatrick's directions. She would need to exit soon. Signaling, she swung off the expressway, relieved to see Noah's car do the same.

Managing to avoid a series of potholes, she maneuvered the car down rutted side roads. Kilpatrick had assured her that it would be at least fifteen blocks before her turnoff. She glanced out her window and grimaced. A few tired looking garden beds did their best to brighten the front of small homes lining the street. On one corner, kids called instructions to each other as they kicked a ball back and forth. Two more blocks, and the area turned commercial, brick high-rises replacing small homes. Eden spotted a supermarket and knew she was close. She glanced at the rearview mirror, reassured to see Noah three cars behind. She signaled left, hoping he would see her.

In the parking lot of the coffee shop, dozens of cars managed to find space amongst overgrown weeds and rotting debris. The Eatery, a long, low, fifties-style diner, seemed a popular place. Eden glanced at her watch. Quarter to six. She minced her way across the parking lot, casually looking around, exhaling with relief when she saw the Camry cruise by.

Eden entered the crowded restaurant. Potential patrons stood on line waiting to be seated. A buxom blonde bearing a none too clean menu bore down, slapping a menu into her hand. "Party of how many, hon?"

"Two." Eden looked around to see if any of the men on line fit Kilpatrick's description.

"It's going to be a twenty-minute wait, hon, unless you're willing to sit at the counter."

"Counter's fine." She'd get the information from Kilpatrick, then figure out what to do about placing the man. He was hardly the flight-attendant type and most definitely bad news at the check-in counter. A back-of-the-house type of job might do. Cleaning crew could be the answer.

Toting her menu, Eden followed the blonde to the counter. "Coffee or something stronger, hon?" The blonde wielded a pot.

"Coffee's fine."

After the waitress left, Eden's hands shook as she raised the cup to her lips and sipped the murky brew. God-awful!

Forty minutes and three cups of coffee later, she was still sitting there, waiting. Angry that she'd allowed herself to be royally had, she pushed off the stool. An obese waitress, sporting elaborately braided hair and a shiny gold tooth, intercepted her progress. "You Eden Sommers?"

"Yes."

"You got a call." The woman's braids fanned out as she jerked her head in the direction of the pay phones. Noting Eden's puzzled look, she added, "Sorry, boyfriend didn't gimme his name."

Eden brightened considerably realizing it must be Noah. Good, she'd feel a heck of a lot better knowing that he was out there, somewhere, looking after her. She picked up the receiver and said, "Where are you?"

"Plans changed. I got stuck. Couldn't make it to the coffee shop."

She recognized the slurred voice. "Aaron?"

"Yeah. Meant to call before but got held up. Come to my house."

"What?"

"Look, I got to be someplace in an hour. It's either my house or nothing. You tell me about the job and I'll answer your questions. Whole thing will be over within ten minutes."

"Fine. You'll need to give me directions."

He told her and she hung up.

Eden zoomed out of the parking lot leaving the smell of burnt rubber behind. Noah put the car in gear, and maintaining a discreet distance, followed. Something was wrong, he could feel it. Kilpatrick had obviously not shown up, and Eden was heading somewhere, speeding like a bat out of hell.

Periodically, she slowed the jeep and glanced down. The vehicle swerved erratically. It took Noah moments to realize that she was looking at a piece of paper. Directions perhaps. Could Kilpatrick have found a way of reaching her? Just then, Eden made a quick right. Noah remained sandwiched in the middle lane with no out. He was forced to go two blocks until he was able to execute a U-turn. Driving back the way he had come, he made a left where Eden had made her right. The jeep and its driver were no place to be seen.

Keeping his eyes peeled for Eden, Noah continued down the road. Surely, she couldn't have just disappeared into thin air. He cruised the next block, eyes fixed on the upcoming street sign, hoping it would give some clue as to his location. Lenox Avenue! He'd hit pay dirt. Whistling, he swung the Camry onto the street.

Little had changed since he'd been there last. Though not quite sunset, hair was still being braided and drunks resided on the corner. Much as Noah tried, he couldn't shake the uneasy feeling that something horrendous was about to go down.

Aaron Kilpatrick was obviously playing games. He'd sent Eden on a wild-goose chase. But why arrange to meet her at a diner when he had no intention of showing up? And why make her come to his house? Every instinct told Noah not to trust Kilpatrick. He would make sure he did not let Eden out of sight.

Slamming the car into park, Eden got out in front of the Tudor-style home. Dusk had fallen and there wasn't a light to be seen or movement inside. She treaded her way through a litter-strewn path, plodding toward the side of the house. She'd feel more comfortable knowing for certain Noah was behind her. Hopefully he'd seen her leave the coffee shop and followed. Smiling grimly, she acknowledged he'd been right all along, Aaron Kilpatrick rented the basement apartment. She'd have to buy Noah dinner.

Dismissing her fluttering stomach and ignoring the buzzer, she raised a tentative hand to knock on the door. When seconds elapsed with no response, she tried again. What game was Kilpatrick playing?

"Aaron," she called, this time banging. "It's Eden Sommers."

Was that a noise, some movement she heard, or was it purely her imagination?

"Aaron, it's Eden," she repeated.

"Hold on." Footsteps approached. The clang of a chain being removed from the front door. "Are you alone?"

"Yes, I'm alone."

He threw the door open. A shadowy silhouette loomed, though she couldn't make out his face. Hovering on the threshold of the dark vestibule, she squinted.

"Get in."

"It's awfully dark. Do you have lights?"

"No use in announcing to the whole neighborhood I'm home. I'll turn them on once you're inside."

A strange answer. A strange man. Every instinct screamed not to enter. But curiosity won out. What if he had the information she needed? It could help put an end to her guilt. Though officially she'd denied it, she'd always felt a little responsible. Would Rod have been alive if they hadn't had their talk? Eden left the safety of the doorway and took a step inside. The metallic lock clicked behind her.

She followed Kilpatrick's frail form, sidestepping obstacles on the floor. *Please Noah. Please be outside.* Her host slowed and reached up to yank at something overhead. A weak light illuminated the room; a lone lightbulb swung from side to side. Eden barely made out the back of his head; lank brown hair tied back in a ponytail. Could he be the same man who'd tried to kill them? Dismissing the thought as ridiculous, she focused on her surroundings.

What a dump! She wrinkled her nose as an odious smell made her gag. In all her life, she'd never seen so much junk. Stuff everywhere in strange combinations: stacks of yellowing newspapers, cans, fuses, bags of fertilizer, fuel oil. Open cartons of leftover takeout perched on top of the piles. Ancient shotguns strewn across a stained mattress. An odor of old food and unwashed clothing permeated the place.

"Sit," Kilpatrick ordered, suddenly swinging around. He made room for her with one hand, toppling piles of magazines off a rickety chair.

Eden sat.

Kilpatrick's face, craggy, gaunt, unsmiling, frightening, searched hers. His eyes, dark murky pools, held not one hint of compassion. His emaciated body, cadaverous almost, leaned against the grimy wall, arms crossed. At that moment Eden knew this man had no conscience. He would just as easily hurt as talk to her.

"Tell me about the job," he said, his voice actually making her tremble.

"I'll get to that. I wanted to talk to you about the Pelican crash."

"What about it?"

"My source says you worked that night." She could tell by the flicker in his eyes she'd hit a nerve, and even though she'd never been so scared in her life, she pressed her point. "What do you know about a box scheduled for delivery to Baylor Hospital?"

"Not a thing," Kilpatrick snapped. The back of his hand swiped his nose.

And even though she risked making him more angry, she couldn't let it go. "But someone saw you carrying a box to the plane."

Like a snake he uncoiled his body and slithered closer, his arms imprisoning her on the chair. Yellow teeth bared. "That someone was wrong. I wasn't carrying anything."

Kilpatrick's sour breath hit her squarely in the face.

He was the voice on the phone. She was in trouble. Big trouble.

"Okay, so you weren't."

He squatted down beside her, his voice barely a whisper. "Don't patronize me, girlie. You're playing a dangerous game."

Think Eden, think. Keep your head. Don't let him rattle you. "Look, Jack said you needed a job. I thought perhaps we could help each other out—"

"That's a good one. Jack, top dog, chief pilot, recommending me?" This time Kilpatrick brayed.

"You help me. I help you. For God's sake, I'm appealing to your humanity. My fiancé died in that crash, I need to know what happened." Unplanned as it was, she began to cry.

For a second or so, Kilpatrick actually seemed stumped. She thought that perhaps she'd gotten to him. He rallied, sending her hopes plummeting. "Don't try conning me, bitch." Springing upright, he kicked the legs out from under her chair, sending her flying. She landed inches away from a sawed-off shotgun. "Your fiancé had his job. I had nothing," he screamed, lunging.

Eden's jeep was there, thank God, meaning she was obviously inside the house. What could have possessed her to take such a risk? It wasn't as if she knew or trusted the man. From everything they'd been told, he was bad news.

Noah circled the block, once, twice, debating what to do. He had to check on Eden, see for himself what was going on inside. He swung down a side street and pulled the Camry next to the curb. Leaping out of the automobile, he wavered only to set the car's alarm.

A sixth sense had told him to dress casually and com-

fortably. So he'd opted for navy blue sweats, high-top
sneakers, and a red cap. Now he could easily be mis-
taken for any homeboy. He approached the Tudor-style
home, his eyes searching the exterior of the basement
apartment. A weak light came from the hatchway. Stopping to examine his options, he paused again. What
good would it do to go barging in there alone? What
if Eden needed help? Best to let someone know where
they were.

As he unsnapped his cellular phone from the waist-
band of his sweats, and punched the programmed number, he hoped Lori Goldmuntz was still at the office.
The phone rang and rang. He cursed, biting off ugly
words when someone finally picked up.

"Pelican In-Flight Services office."

He didn't know her well enough to assume. "Lori
Goldmuntz, please."

"This is Lori."

"Noah Robbins here . . ."

"What's wrong with Eden? Did that man . . ."

He sensed panic in her voice and hastened to reassure her. "Eden's in Kilpatrick's apartment, I think. I'm
outside . . ."

"Good God! Give me the address."

He provided Kilpatrick's address.

"Take my cell number," Lori pleaded. "If I don't hear
from one of you within an hour, I'm calling the police."

Twenty-one

It was pitch-dark by the time Noah ended the call. He looked over in the direction of the Tudor to determine whether anyone other than Kilpatrick was home. It might take up valuable time but he'd feel a helluva lot better if a neighbor knew he was on the premises.

"Let the first floor not be vacant," Noah muttered, staring at tightly drawn blinds. He mounted four steep front steps and was faced with a closed screen door. Now what to do? Push the buzzer or knock? He knocked. Impatient when several seconds elapsed with no response, he placed his shoulder against the buzzer.

"Nobody in, 'cept for the militia in the basement. Landlord's got a night job." The voice came from behind him, making him jump. Noah spun around and squinted as a flashlight played across his face. Blinking, he barely made out the gangly youth on the end. "Neighborhood patrol. You got ID?"

Noah placed a hand in the pocket of his hooded sweatshirt.

"Not so fast, man. Get your hands up or I'll blow your butt away."

"I'm getting you identification," Noah said, withdrawing his hand quickly. Palm up he turned over the laminated square.

The youth lowered the flashlight long enough to scru-
tinize Noah's ID. "F-f-f-f-for real. You the guy on TV?"

"Yes. I'm an inspector with the National Transportation Safety Board."

Again the flashlight beamed in Noah's face, blinding
him. He blinked rapidly. "Lower that thing."

"Cool! You the guy that tells the people about the
crash."

"Yes." Why bother giving "neighborhood security" a
job description.

The flashlight lowered as Noah's inquisitor moved in
closer. "Kareem Warner, I'm an Angel. Always wanted
to be like you. What you doing here? What you doing
in Hollis? Investigating a case?"

Noah thought quickly. Opportunity presented itself.
The Angels were self-appointed do-gooders who pa-
trolled neighborhoods, subways, and public areas, looking out for crime. He would get the starstruck kid on
his side. "Came to find a friend. Perhaps you've seen
her." He described Eden.

"The fine brown-skin lady that climbed out of that
Cherokee." Kareem waved the flashlight in the direction of Eden's jeep.

"You've seen her then?"

"Couldn't miss her. She's some babe. Came by 'bout
twenty minutes ago. Made me and my buddies drool—
oops, she your woman?"

"Yeah."

"Sorry, man." Then after a second or so, "I think
she went to visit that nut in the basement."

Noah reached in his pocket for his wallet. He counted
out several twenties and though his street vernacular
was rusty, managed, "Do me a solid, man. Come with
me. I'm gonna grab my woman before she get into
trouble. I don't want her hangin' with no user." He
stuffed the bills in the kid's hand.

"Nah. I can't take this, man. This my job."

"Take it."

Noah began walking toward the side of the house. Kareem followed.

Trapped under Aaron Kilpatrick's body, Eden inhaled the smell of stale marijuana and unwashed armpit. Fragile as he looked, the man weighed a ton. She tried not to panic, tried not to flail at him. She needed to keep her wits. She'd seen a shotgun only moments before he'd tackled her. Could she remember its location? Aaron Kilpatrick's erection pressed against her belly. She was in trouble. *Talk to him Eden. You've been told before you're an excellent negotiator.*

"Aaron," Eden began, "why would you want to hurt me?"

His fetid breath hit her square in the face. She could feel him getting more excited. "You're not that stupid, girlie."

"I've done nothing to you, except try to help you. I'm here to offer you a job."

"Sure you are."

"Why wouldn't you believe me?"

" 'Cause you and that nosy boyfriend of yours have stirred up a mess of trouble."

"What does Noah have to do with this?"

"Plenty." Aaron pushed himself into a sitting position and straddled her. His erection pressed against her leg. She could at least breathe again. Aaron's hand played with the button at her neck.

Eden opened her eyes and stared into red-rimmed blues. "Please stop."

"Stop me. I get off on wild cats." He laughed evilly. She felt the walls closing in. It had been a while since she'd had a panic attack. "Not a damn thing you can do now, girlie."

She had to keep him talking. "What did we do to you?"

The button on her shirt gave. She heard Aaron's sharp intake of breath even as he worked another. "You had to go asking questions, poking your nose into things that don't concern you."

"You mean the crash."

"Yeah," he shouted, showering her with foul spittle.

"Why would you care?"

His face grew serious for a moment; the eyes glazed, as if he'd been transported to another time, another place. "Everything had gone down good till you two got involved. I'd planted a couple of bottles of vodka in the cockpit. They would have thought the flight crew was drunk." Vacillating he slurred, "You know they gave me some B.S. story, told me I was junior, that's why they let me go. They'd been better off telling me the establishment didn't care. And my uncle, fancy title and all, let them boot me." Aaron raised a grimy hand, wiping his dripping nose. Simultaneously, another of Eden's buttons popped.

His gaze shifted to her chest. Knowing that her lace-covered breast peeked through the opening, she tried to control her breathing. She needed to keep him talking.

"Victoria's Secret," he said, leering at her.

"But why us? We didn't know about you," she jabbered.

Aaron's hands cupped one breast. He leered at her. Eden squirmed, twisting her head from side to side, "I think I'm going to be sick."

His hand whipped out. She heard the scratchy sound of something being dragged along the linoleum floor. The blunted edge of an object nudged her into a sitting position. "Okay you can get up and use the facilities, but don't try nothing funny, or I'll blow that pretty head right off your shoulders."

She found herself staring down the barrel of a sawed-off shotgun and realized she was dealing with a lunatic. With trembling fingers she tried to do the buttons that he'd freed.

"Nope, don't touch 'em. I want to look at 'em." She slapped a hand across her mouth and he moved quickly out of her path. "Bathroom's over there." Keeping his eyes trained on her lace-covered breasts, he gestured with the gun's barrel.

No way would she escape. Six foot of wiry man would certainly overpower her. Maybe she could distract him.

Aaron followed her into the filthy bathroom. Overcome by the rank odor of stale urine, Eden gagged. Closing her eyes she knelt on the grimy floor and forced herself to place her head over the bowl. *Summon up your imagination, Eden. Think of lilacs in the field, the smell of a fresh spring rain, the aroma of freshly baked bread.* Even her imagination didn't stretch that far. When she picked up her head and darted a look backward, he was still standing there staring at her, the gun trained on her head.

"Can I have a little privacy?" she managed, "I have to—you know—go."

"Then go."

She had no choice. He wasn't going to be decent about it. She picked up her skirt an inch and saw such a look of want in his eyes she had to look away. When she made eye contact again, he licked his lips and the gun trembled.

Though she risked making him angry she had to know. "You killed those passengers Aaron, didn't you. And you ran down my mother?"

His upper lip beaded with sweat. "Didn't mean to. Didn't want to. The company made me mad."

Eden lifted her skirt another inch, revealing slightly more thigh. "Do you always do horrible things when you're mad?"

He licked his lips but kept the gun level. "All my life I been a nobody. The only thing I was ever good at was building things with my hands. This time I showed them." He pounded his chest with his free hand. "My hobby paid off. I'm famous."

She could care less about his hobby, but if she kept him talking he'd at least keep his hands to himself. "What hobby is that?"

"I make bombs. Started selling them as a teenager."

Aaron took a step closer. She hiked her skirt higher. "I can't go with you looking at me."

He stepped back. She'd bought herself time at least for the moment. She crossed over to the filthy sink, fumbled with the faucet and let the water trickle.

"Move." He nudged her with the butt of his gun. She had no choice but to precede him. He stopped in front of the soiled mattress. "Take off your clothes."

"Aaron," Eden said, "tell me about the bombs. How do you make them? Was it a bomb that brought down Flight 757?" If she kept him talking about a subject he enjoyed, she'd learn something and have time to come up with a plan.

"No, you don't. No delaying tactics." His voice took on a sing-songy tone. "Quit stalling and get out of your clothes." He pointed the gun at her head.

Kneeling to squint through a grimy windowpane, Noah whispered, "How long has Kilpatrick lived here?"

"About a year and a half."

"And has he always been this strange, Kareem?" Noah

pried his eyes from the dusty glass. "I wish I could see what's going on in there."

"Wait." Using the untucked tail of his shirt, Kareem scrubbed at the grimy pane. "That's better."

"Slightly." Noah made out a single lightbulb swinging off a none-too-steady string. An orangy glow cast shadows within the dingy room. How could any human being live like this? He'd never seen so much filth. No sign of Eden though, nor Kilpatrick for that matter. His heart rate escalated. What had the monster done to her?

Kareem's shirttail went at it again, this time clearing a bigger spot. "Guy was odd. Collected guns and things, scared the hell out of the neighborhood children." His newfound friend pressed his nose against the glass, then turned back. "I think I see them."

Noah practically knocked him out of the way. Following Kareem's example he used the edge of his sweats to scrub the glass. He thought he saw movement but couldn't be sure.

"Try over here." Kareem said, from his new position. "You ain't gonna like what you see though."

Noah took the spot Kareem vacated. As he sized up the scene, his left eye ticked and a lump grew in his chest the size of a football. Eden, clad only in bra and panties, stood in the middle of the room, Aaron Kilpatrick's captive. The man pointed a shotgun directly at her head. There was no mistaking the animal's intent.

"I gotta get in there," Noah said, clenching and unclenching his fists.

"Easy man." Kareem laid a hand on his arm. "We can't just go barging in. We've got to think of somethin'." He patted his pocket. "I got my piece."

Noah shrugged the hand off. "Where's the nearest entrance?"

Kareem pointed to the hatched doorway. "That's the only one I know of."

Noah pinched the nape of his neck. "Tell you what. Make a racket. Toss pebbles against the window or something. Do something to distract Kilpatrick." He loped off to the shadows.

"You got it," Kareem whispered.

Getting on his hands and knees, Kareem searched the ground for pebbles. He came up with a handful of gravel, aimed it directly at the pane, and flung with all his might. He stayed long enough to press his nose against the glass and see Kilpatrick's reaction.

Noah huddled in the neighboring shrubbery. A minute went by, then another. At last the hatched doorway opened. A dim light illuminated the area as Kilpatrick's head emerged. "Who's there? Sh—!" A string of obscenities followed and Noah assumed that Kareem's second attempt had hit Kilpatrick square in the face. "Get in front of me," Kilpatrick shouted at Eden.

Another shape emerged. Eden clad still in her bra and panties. Kilpatrick pushed her in front of him. He wouldn't risk leaving her alone. Noah swallowed bile. He couldn't afford to get emotional. He needed a clear head. Of course he could try jumping the man, but why endanger another life, especially the life of the woman he loved. The shrubbery to the right of him rustled. Aaron Kilpatrick cleared the doorway, shotgun in one hand, Eden's elbow in the other. They shuffled awkwardly toward the sound.

The hatchway gaped open. It was Noah's only chance. If he could get inside, he might overpower Kilpatrick. The bushes across the way rustled. He heard Kilpatrick's muffled oath as he tugged his captive along. They disappeared into the darkness. Now or never.

In answer to Noah's prayer, the shrubbery shook again.

"Get out where I can see you," Kilpatrick threatened, footsteps thudding in the direction of the sound. "If you don't, I'll blow her head off." After several minutes passed and no one appeared he started back toward the house.

On tiptoe, Noah approached the open doorway. He hunkered down behind a festering garbage can. His hand covered his nose as he peeked over the lid to see Kilpatrick dragging Eden.

Seizing the opportunity, Noah raced for the hatchway. He hurled himself inside, tripped, and tumbled down a flight of stairs. He checked himself. No broken bones. The commotion had not gone unnoticed. He heard Kilpatrick's vile threats. "You're a dead man when I find you," then the sound of running footsteps. Noah pushed through the apartment's open door.

Leaping over stacks of papers, he looked around for a place to hide. Closet. Bathroom. Somewhere not out in the open. Too late. Two sets of footsteps clamored down the stairs. Noah scooted down behind the kitchen counter and peered around the corner.

Aaron Kilpatrick's eyes were wild. He looked like a man gone berserk. The gun wavered erratically. Eden's shoulders shook as she sobbed silently. One bra strap had popped and the bra hung at an odd angle.

"Get out where I can see you," Kilpatrick yelled, firing twice at the ceiling.

Eden screamed. Simultaneously, another set of footsteps clattered down the stairwell. Kilpatrick swung around to take on the intruder. Noah leapt from his hiding place, tackling Kilpatrick. He rode him until the man's knees buckled. Together they tumbled to the floor. The shotgun fell inches away.

As Noah scuffled with the man, Kareem Warner, gun drawn, loomed above them. He aimed the muzzle at the fallen Kilpatrick's head. "Don't even try it."

The howl of sirens pierced the night. Kareem's eyes left Kilpatrick's momentarily. He smiled. "Help's here."

A shot rang through the apartment, then a gurgling sound. Kilpatrick's finger was still on the trigger of his shotgun. Eden screamed. Noah raced toward her, gathering her in his arms.

Policemen poured through the doorway, guns drawn. Neighbors followed. For a brief few seconds Kilpatrick writhed in a pool of his own blood.

"Drop the gun. Put your hands in the air. Don't anyone move," the first cop to arrive shouted.

Twenty-two

Eden felt the trembling begin somewhere behind her kneecaps and work its way upward. Delayed reaction, she decided. She looked down at the still figure of Kilpatrick lying in a pool of his own blood. Her teeth chattered as it finally sunk in. The man had taken his own life. The nightmare was over.

"You okay, miss?" A cop placed his jacket around her shoulders and led her to a rickety chair.

Eden tried to catch Noah's eye, but the cops had him up against the wall. "Leave him alone!" she shouted, pointing a finger at the still figure stretched out on the floor. "That man attacked me and tried to kill us."

Her words got the cops' attention and although their guns remained drawn, they'd stopped patting both men down.

"Show me some ID?" the beefier of the two said.

Noah was the first to produce his.

"You're Noah Robbins?" Surprise registered in the voice of the heavy cop. He assessed Noah's filthy sweat suit and perspiring face and shook his head. He holstered his gun. *The* Noah Robbins?"

"I am."

"Who's he?" The cop gestured to the man beside Noah.

"Here's my proof, man." The stranger dug into his jeans pocket, producing a laminated square.

The skinnier of the two cops palmed it, reading aloud. "Kareem Warner, Angel? What the hell kind of ID is this?" Then recognizing the group, "You're with the Angels?" Putting away his gun, his voice dripped sarcasm, "Self-appointed vigilante is hardly a real job."

Outside a siren wailed.

"Ambulance is here," another cop shouted, bouncing downstairs. A flurry of movement followed as paramedics carrying a gurney raced in.

Eden took a step toward Noah. He held his arms open. Forgetting about the medics and the unresponsive man on the floor, she raced toward him. No mistaking what she saw reflected in those eyes. Love. Pure and simple.

"Baby, I was so scared. If anything had happened to you—" his voice broke as he gathered her even closer.

"Sssh! Don't say it." She wrapped her arms around his waist, found a haven on his chest and said, "I owe you my life."

"Honey, my life would not be worth living without you."

It was a heavy-duty confession. She believed him. He'd put his life on the line for her, came through when it really mattered. "I love you," she whispered. It was true. She did love him; an indisputable fact.

One of the cops cleared his throat, and reality returned. Eden focused on the paramedics who'd given up their attempts at resuscitation. They were loading Kilpatrick's body onto the stretcher, covering him with a sheet. She averted her eyes and pressed her face into Noah's sweatshirt.

"We'll need to take you down to the station," the same kind cop who'd offered her his jacket said.

"What about Noah—and his friend?"

"Kareem," Noah supplied.

"They'll be coming with us."

Stepping away from Noah, she wrapped the oversize cop's jacket around her body, then snuggled back into the crook of his arm. "I was petrified," she said. "I thought that monster would kill you."

"You guys can finish your discussion down at the station." The portly cop nudged them gently. "Believe me, you'll be there long enough."

A day later, Eden sat on a raised dais, Noah at her side. To the right of her was Phil Feiner, Pelican's public relations man. He fielded the more challenging comments and answered questions with questions. Under the table, Noah's hand sought Eden's, squeezing gently. She stared out at the sea of faces, ignoring her queasy stomach and flashing a confident smile. The newspapers had had a field day so far, painting Pelican as a fly-by-night carrier with substandard safety and security practices. Pelican Air, in a futile attempt at damage control, had been forced to call this press conference.

Eden faced reporters, a microphone thrust under her nose. She hated being placed in the spotlight. Even worse was hearing the whole sordid story hashed and rehashed. The irony of it was despite Kilpatrick's role, the press hadn't vilified him. They'd portrayed him as some kind of martyr.

In its inimitable way, the media had painted a picture of a lost young man who'd turned to drugs for solace. Kilpatrick's extremist leanings had been explained as a cry for help. And the airline had been the one placed on trial; management taking a beating. After all, they'd been the ones to terminate a poor ramp agent desperately in need of a job. An emotionally unstable man had been turned out on the street without benefit of counseling. No wonder the poor guy flipped out. Pelican Air had been labeled irresponsible; a carrier with little regard for FAA regulations or the safety of passengers.

"Ms. Sommers?"

Eden's attention returned to the press conference. She tuned in just as Phil Feiner adroitly sidestepped a question.

"Ms. Sommers you were engaged to a pilot who went down in the crash," a pushy reporter in the third row shouted.

Catching Phil's subtle nod, Eden responded. "I was."

"That prompted you to conduct your own investigation?"

Eden deferred the question to Phil.

"I wouldn't exactly call it Ms. Sommers' investigation," Phil said, "Let's just say that she had a vested interest in uncovering the truth. Some good has come out of this crash though. As a result of what we've uncovered, Pelican's made several changes—"

"Like getting a new president and chief pilot," the same bulldog of a journalist muttered making the entire room titter.

"Yes, we admit there've been changes in senior management . . ."

"Your president and chief pilot were fired."

Phil shook his head. "Speculation on everyone's part. Vernon Bond, our president, resigned to pursue other opportunities, and our chief pilot, Jack Windsor, retired."

"Windsor's decision have anything to do with his relationship with Kilpatrick?" a rotund reporter with a lopsided toupee shouted the question from the middle of the room.

"I'm not sure where you're heading."

"Must be embarrassing for the man. Your own nephew

steals a company car and plants a bomb that kills a bunch of people."

"What about the breach in security?" Another reporter shouted. "Does this mean any Joe Shmoe employee can hand an item to a flight attendant? What about screening procedures?"

"I thought the FAA required all passengers' bags and cargo be scanned?"

"What's to guarantee the same thing wouldn't happen again? That you wouldn't hire another unstable employee who sneaks an explosive aboard," someone else shouted. "Do you do background checks on these people?"

"Ms. Sommers is it true that an anonymous person sent you the cargo manifest, providing a major clue?"

"That's true. We never did find out who," Eden managed to get in. "Noah and I are grateful to the person who sent it."

"Your passengers are canceling like crazy," the bulldog interjected. "Your last flight went out practically empty. At this rate your airline's about to go out of business. Ms. Sommers what will you do if that happens?"

The press conference had rapidly grown out of control. Reporters shouted question after question, not waiting for answers. A diminutive young woman stood. Her voice like a bass drum caused everyone to sit up and listen. "Ms. Sommers, is it true that you and Mr. Robbins are involved?"

Sensing Eden's discomfort, Noah again sought her hand under the table. "Depends on what you mean by involved," he quipped.

Phil came to their rescue; fingers splayed like a traffic cop. "Ladies and gentlemen stick to business or there will be no further comments."

The media continued shouting questions as if he hadn't spoken.

* * *

Back in her apartment, Eden flopped onto the divan. "Whoosh! What a day." She made space for Noah as he slid onto the seat and positioned her head in his lap.

"You did wonderful sweetheart. Handled those questions like a pro."

"Couldn't have done it without you."

He smoothed her hair, then bent over to brush her lips. "Does that mean I'm finally forgiven?"

"You know it." She returned his kiss, winding her arms around his neck, pulling him down on top of her. Over the last few days, their relationship had undergone a subtle change. In her mind he'd proven himself; put his life on the line for her. Since then, he'd been there every step of the way. How could she forget all he'd risked coming to her rescue?

"I love you, baby," he said nuzzling her neck.

"Then show me." She gathered him closer.

"Later. Right now there are a few things we need to get straight."

Eden sighed. "Uh! Uh! Sounds serious." She pushed into a sitting position, bringing him up with her.

Noah draped an arm around her shoulders; the tips of his fingers drawing circles on her upper arm. His face was serious. "Sweetie, what are we going to do about us?"

She could tell by his voice that a flippant response wasn't going to cut it. He meant business. She'd need to choose her words carefully because whatever she said might or might not destroy their new closeness. "What is it you'd like to do about us?

"I've made no secret of the fact that I love you. And you've admitted to feeling the same way. I'm thirty-five years old. I want marriage, a family."

This from a man who'd said he'd been badly burned and didn't trust women. Who'd told her that he'd sworn off travel-industry types, dismissing them as shallow and flighty. Though her stomach fluttered, she managed a tiny smile. "Is this a proposal?" *And what if it was? Geography alone created a problem. Her job was here, provided the airline survived this scandal.*

Noah's hand reached into his pocket withdrawing a little black box. She knew her eyes must be popping right out of her head. He snapped the cover open and she gasped with delight. Sapphire and diamonds. Favorites. No end to his surprises.

"It is, if you'll have me?" he said, holding out the box.

She knew she must look like an idiot with her mouth hanging open. She loved the man, unequivocally, totally, with every ounce of her being. Geography was a straw man's argument. She'd always considered those in commuter marriages crazy, but this was different. Taking the shuttle back and forth from New York to DC would be a piece of cake. In many ways more convenient than a bus. With her travel benefits it would cost nothing and she'd have him in her life forever.

"If you're worried about how we'd work out the logistics, things like your job," Noah said, tuning into what she was thinking, "consider commuting, or better yet, one of my buddies manages a flight academy, they're looking for someone to develop and present courses on managing the fear of flying. You'd be the perfect presenter."

"Oh, Noah. You've thought of everything."

"Wait," he said, placing a finger on her lips then getting down on his knee. Kahlua chose that moment to stalk the room, getting in between them, rubbing her head against Noah's legs, and purring as if to say, *"Come on girl, say yes."* Eden's attention shifted to the man declaring his love. One look at Noah's face, the sincerity reflecting in his eyes, and she needed no further convincing. "Eden Sommers will you marry me?"

"Yes! Oh, yes!"

She hurled herself into his arms, almost sending him toppling. Noah steadied her long enough to slip the ring on her finger, then scooped her up.

His kisses sent her whirring into orbit. With purposeful strides, he pushed the divider aside and entered the sleeping area. "Later's arrived," he whispered, easing her onto the bed and settling himself on top of her. His fingers stroked the sides of her face, moved downward, and fumbled with the buttons on her shirt. She moved against him, positioning his hands to caress her breasts, to tease the nipples through the lace. Eden cupped his buttocks, pulled him closer, enjoying his strength, the long silky length of him.

"Oh Noah," she said, her warm breath caressing his face. "I want you so badly it hurts."

"You've got me, baby. Forever and ever."

Later, she lay in the hollow of his arms dozing. She dreamed she was on a plane heading for an unknown destination. Around her passengers, dressed in tropical garb, laughed and talked. Champagne flowed. She settled back in her seat enjoying the festive atmosphere. Her head lay on Noah's shoulder and the tips of his warm fingers wove their way through her hair. Sweet kisses covered her eyelids and face. A soft hand caressed her breasts, probing her into wakefulness. "Oh, Noah," she whispered, coming out of the dream. "I love you."

"Not half as much as I love you."

They would debate that statement a lifetime.

Marcia King-Gamble was born on the island of St. Vincent in the West Indies. At age fifteen she relocated to the United States and has since lived in New York, New Jersey and Seattle. Currently she resides in Florida. Marcia is a graduate of Elmira College and holds a Bachelor's degree in psychology and theater. Marcia is also an executive with a major cruise line. Her specialty is quality assurance and guest services.

When she is not working, writing or globetrotting, Marcia serves on the executive board of the Society of Consumer Affairs Professionals in Business. She is married and has a menagerie of animals. Despite her many commitments she still makes time for step aerobics and fund raising. Marcia's third novel is scheduled for release in July of 1999.

Dear Reader:

To those of you who enjoyed *Remembrance*, here's hoping that *Eden's Dream* will capture a special place in your heart.

Noah and Eden were characters that grew and developed as my story unfolded. I came to care for them as much as I would my very dear friends. And I must admit that I got separation pains when their story concluded. I hope that you will feel the same way.

You've been a great support and I thank you for the wonderful and uplifting E-mails you've sent. Please keep those E-mails and letters coming. Feel free to write me at P.O. Box 25143, Tamarac, FL. 33320. Include a self-addressed stamped envelope to ensure a reply.

My next (untitled) release is scheduled for July of 1999.

Warm Regards

Marcia King-Gamble

ENJOY THESE ARABESQUE FAVORITES!

FOREVER AFTER   (0-7860-0211-5, $4.99)
by Bette Ford

BODY AND SOUL   (0-7860-0160-7, $4.99)
by Felicia Mason

BETWEEN THE LINES   (0-7860-0267-0, $4.99)
by Angela Benson

COMING IN DECEMBER.

FOOLISH HEART, by Felicia Mason   (0-7860-0593-9, $4.99/$6.50)
CEO Coleman Heart III inherited his family's chain of department stores and focused only on saving it from bankruptcy. Business consultant Sonja Pride became the only person he felt he could trust. But Sonja had a debt to pay the Heart family, and being close to Coleman seemed the perfect way to make them pay. Until she found out he was a caring, honorable man to whom she could give away her heart.

DARK INTERLUDE, by Dianne Mayhew   (0-7860-0594-7, $4.99/$6.50)
Sissi Adams and Percy Duvall had a relationship based on trust. But when Sissi admitted that she didn't want children, Percy was devastated. An____ when they discovered that Sissi was pregnant and that she miscarri____ Percy broke off the relationship believing she aborted their child. ____ later, Sissi is unhappily engaged to another, unable to forget he____ love. She places Percy on the guest list of a celebration for her up____ wedding for one last chance to see if they were made for each___

SECRETS, by Marilyn Tyner   (0-7860-0595-5, $____
Samantha Desmond raised her young stepsister, Jessica. To____ from calculating relatives, Samantha pretends Jessica is her____ relocates. When she meets pediatrician Alex Mackenzi____ attraction between them to keep him from getting to____ finds out the truth about Jessica and his trust in Sa____ They soon learn that neither can do without each o____

OUT OF THE BLUE, by Janice Sims   (0-786____
On a research trip to frigid Russian waters in p____ marine biologist Gaea Maxwell doesn't expect t____ Micah Cavanaugh—a man capable of thawin____ was asked to recruit Gaea for a teaching pos____ didn't expect her to be a beautiful, charn____ position and returns home to Key West____ disappointed. He follows her to Florida,____ runs as deep as the ocean.